The Fire by Night

The Fire by Night

Teresa
Messineo

wm

WILLIAM MORROW
An Imprint of HarperCollins*Publishers*

THE FIRE BY NIGHT. Copyright © 2017 by Teresa Messineo. All rights reserved. Printed in the United States of America. No part of this book may be used or reproduced in any manner whatsoever without written permission except in the case of brief quotations embodied in critical articles and reviews. For information address HarperCollins Publishers, 195 Broadway, New York, NY 10007.

HarperCollins books may be purchased for educational, business, or sales promotional use. For information please e-mail the Special Markets Department at SPsales@harpercollins.com.

FIRST EDITION

Designed by Fritz Metsch

Library of Congress Cataloging-in-Publication Data has been applied for.

ISBN 978-0-06-245910-7 (hardcover)
ISBN 978-0-06-266209-5 (international edition)

17 18 19 20 21   OV/RRD   10 9 8 7 6 5 4 3 2 1

To Sister Jonathan Moyles, SCC,
for giving me a second chance

and her fac

The Lord was going before them in a pillar of cloud by day to lead them on the way, and in a pillar of fire by night to give them light, that they might travel by day and by night.

—EXODUS

The Fire by Night

War

Jo McMahon

Spring 1945, The Western Front

The main problem was her hands. They were raw and cracked and bleeding, and she couldn't get them to heal. A shell exploded outside the tent—somebody screamed and somebody laughed and someone else just said "fuck." Jo steadied the rickety supply rack in front of her, pressing her body against the shifting white boxes, pushing the brown glass bottles back into place with her thigh. The generator made a grinding noise as the lights flickered, went out, came back on. Her hands felt along the highest shelf, searching for a stray box of penicillin someone might have left behind in the initial rush to pack up, when the order to pull out had first come down. Her hands moved deftly, knowing exactly what they were searching for, by touch, and she found herself looking at them abstractedly, as if they were someone else's entirely, hands belonging to a brave and noble heroine in a novel or movie; a woman whose hands might be ugly, but whose face would be lit by an ethereal light; a person she could feel sorry for and admire at the same time; someone she could leave in the theater or shut up in a book and never have to think of again. She would have to do something about her hands.

It was the surgeries that did it, really. Washing up in the freezing water basin, the caustic soap eating into open fissures; the thick brown gloves ripping off what was left of her knuckles when she tore them off, hurriedly, in between patients. But there was nothing for it, no way around it that she could see; she just couldn't figure this one out. Her aching fingers closed upon the elusive box, and she wheeled around just as a second explosion went off, this time on her bad side, where her eardrum had been punctured when the *Newfoundland* went down. She lost her footing, hitting the cold ground of the tent hard. She stuffed the medicine into the pocket of her six-fly pants—men's pants, with their buttons on the wrong side— then stopped for a moment to tie her shoe, thinking boots would have been nice for the nurses, but still no match for the mud as this, the coldest European winter on record, slowly thawed into an increasingly impassable mess. Two more shells went off, not as close as the last, but still, she noted absently, much too close—closer even than Anzio, and there the shells had been right on top of them it seemed, the shrapnel flying through the ineffectual canvas of the medical tents, killing surgeons where they stood, the orderlies removing their warm bodies and popping helmets onto the heads of the remaining doctors and nurses who carried on where they had left off.

Here, on this frigid night, the lines would have changed again, too quickly; they would be right up against the fighting, the enemy pushing through the center unexpectedly, perhaps creating a new front, one they were near, or at, or even in front of. They were never supposed to be this close to the action, that's what they had been told during training—yet here they were, again. Jo remembered the time their truck had been commandeered and another promised to pick them up. And how the nurses had waited patiently beside that little chicken coop in southern Italy, resting their tired backs against its sun-drenched, whitewashed warmth—until hours later, after the hens had reluctantly gone in to roost, the girls had seen the first U.S. scouts crawling cautiously toward them through the weeds. The men had asked what they were doing there: if they, the scouts, were the very front of the front line, what the hell were the nurses? Or again, that time they had been in Tunisia, waiting for a truck to move out the last of the wounded, watching the women and children run along the dirt road or perch precariously on their camels forced into an unwilling trot. The American MPs, bringing up the rear on their motorcycles, had yelled at the girls, demanding if they knew there were only ten miles between them and the German tanks and not a blessed thing in between. But they could not leave their men.

"How much we got left?" someone yelled outside in the rain, slamming the door of an idling truck. "How long can it last?" *Longer than I can last,* Jo thought wearily. *Longer than any of us can last.* The propaganda leaflets dropped by the Germans that the boys picked up showed exhausted American POWs, carefully carving tally marks into cell walls, keeping track of the date—1955. Another ten years. Jo smiled wryly at the Axis cartoonist's optimism. She'd be lucky to make it another ten months. She was just shy of her twenty-sixth birthday, and already her hair was streaked with iron gray and she had lost two teeth due to malnutrition. Queenie had told the captain she didn't mind when their molars fell out, but when her girls (Queenie always referred to the nurses in her charge as "her girls," and they were her girls, heart and soul) started losing front teeth too, well, then, even she had to say something about it. And they had gotten a few more C rations after that.

Outside, someone was yelling "retreat!" in a voice too high and too shrill for a man's; he sounded more like a terrified schoolgirl than a soldier. "Fall back, retreat!" he screamed again, as if anyone needed encouragement, as if everyone wasn't already running, already jostling, already scared. *Easy enough for you,* Jo thought listlessly, hearing the engines turning over and the men cursing at each other in their eagerness to pull out, their footsteps sounding loudly in the sucking mud. "Just turn around and run, kid." And as she said it aloud she suddenly felt incredibly seasoned and incredibly jaded and, above all else, incredibly tired. "I've got a whole hospital to move first."

It hadn't always been this way. She hadn't always been this way. There was a time when her hands had been lovely—when all of her had been lovely, all of her had been whole. She had been young then, and had had curves—never enough curves, she had thought then, but good God, compared to the hard angles and bones she was now, she'd been a regular Rita Hayworth. Her skin had been smooth, her flesh firm and full— her tightly coiled chestnut hair with a luster that betrayed her Irish father; a brown streak running through the blue of her left eye where her Italian mother always said she could see herself in her daughter. Giuseppina Fortunata "Jo" McMahon. What a conglomerate she had felt, growing up in Brooklyn, where people identified so fiercely with their ethnicities. To be not fully one or the other but, somehow, both. To pray to both Saint Patrick and Saint Gennaro. To eat both lasagna and corned beef and cabbage. But after nearly four years of field kitchens and alphabet rations, she couldn't think about real food. Not now. She couldn't bear it.

Jo walked into the last standing medical tent, the others having been arduously emptied and packed, dripping wet, onto the trucks that had already left. After hours of loading, now only half a dozen patients remained, their stretchers laid atop sawhorses, waiting to be transported farther back. How she and the other young nurses had memorized the transport chain when they first volunteered for the Army Corps! Front line. Aid man. Collection station. Clearing station. Field hospital. Evacuation hospital. General hospital. Safety. "No female officers to serve closer to the front than field hospital, under any conditions." Jo remembered that this last clause had been underlined in their manuals, that the instructor had emphasized it, as if something like that was indecent, as if it could be guaranteed—as if war wasn't one step re-moved from chaos, as if she, serving in a field hospital, wasn't really at the front line right now. She emptied several tablets from the brown cardboard box into her hand, reading with-out reading for the thousandth time, PENICILLIN G, 250,000 UNITS, CHAS. PFIZER & CO. INC., N.Y., N.Y., remembering a time when she hadn't known the abbreviation for Charles and had wondered why some mother back home would have ever named her baby Chas. She lifted the head of one of the conscious patients—conscious, if delirious—some poor Scot, in a kilt no less, incongruous among all the GIs. "Here, try to swallow, soldier," she said, lifting her canteen to his mouth. He tried to fight her, waving his hands ineffectually and cursing at phantoms standing somewhere behind her in a language all his own. But the typhus was too far gone—not far enough advanced for the dreaded seizures, but far enough for the fever to have sapped him of his strength, of his will, of his right mind. She got the antibiotic down.

"Is there room on the truck for this one?" she asked the orderlies, who were dismantling the field X-ray machine in a corner of the tent. One of the hinges was stuck, and as they put their weight to it the table collapsed suddenly under their combined efforts, breaking off one of its legs. None of them answered her.

"Not on this truck, sweetpea. But we'll get him on the next one for sure."

And there was Queenie.

When Queenie walked into the tent from the cold and the rain and the muck outside, rubbing her frozen hands together, she managed to bring summer and honeysuckle and the smell of home cooking along with her. She was tiny—*petite,* she always corrected—wearing the smallest men's regulation trousers, which she had taken in and taken in again and still had to wear cuffed. Her hair was, as usual, wrapped up in a clean white towel, under which one could imagine it still black and shiny as it once had been, instead of peppered with white. But Hollywood could have made a fortune casting Queenie as the original girl-next-door-buy-war-bonds-today-tie-a-yellow-ribbon-round-her sweetheart. Everyone loved Queenie—men and women alike—for her quick laugh, her moxie, her indomitable spirit. Queenie defied description. On the one hand, she could drink—really drink, which was amazing, given her size—and curse as well as the men, and gamble—she had laughed and laughed when she won a black silk negligee playing poker with some French officers in Algiers. (She had given the beautiful, useless thing to Jo, who, fresh to the war and still imbued with social mores herself, had been embarrassed and speechless and secretly delighted by it all.) But if Queenie had a worldly side, this same nurse had also stood with one doctor through seventy-two hours of surgery—seventy-two hours—when all other medical personnel had been injured or killed. Two hundred litters had been lined up outside the tent, and they got to them all, no coffee break. They had both received the Silver Star, but Queenie always said afterwards that she didn't deserve it. No false modesty—she honestly didn't believe she had done anything special. She was, in her own words, "just doing my job." And that too was Regina Carroll, whose first name had been, by now, all but usurped by her regal moniker. To the boys, she was their kid sister, the girl next door, the first girl they had ever kissed, all rolled into one. The person they were fighting the war for. Even now, with hell raining down on them again, Jo looked at Queenie and knew the war hadn't touched her, not underneath, not really; it hadn't gotten to her like it had gotten to everybody else, like it had gotten to Jo. Queenie didn't have to put up a shell to protect herself, to survive. She was still what they once had been: love and hope for dying boys. What all the girls had set out to become, ages ago, when they had first crossed the Atlantic in those rolling titans, heading for the European theater of war, laughing and singing along the way as if it was going to be the best goddamned lawn party of all time.

One of the litters was half in, half out of an ambulance that had backed all the way up to the tent flap because of the rain. The orderlies paused to get their grip on the slippery wood of the handles just as the patient started flailing his arms, eyes wild, making a noise like a gagged hero in a gangster movie. In a second, Queenie was there, snatching up a wire-cutter that had been hooked to his stretcher just as vomit shot through the man's nostrils, his mouth still tightly shut. The man was choking now, and crying, and panicking; Jo could see the whites of his eyes from across the tent. And Queenie kept smiling and talking to him nonstop.

"Poor baby, hold on there now, soldier, just a minute, sweetheart," all the time deftly cutting the wires the surgeons had so recently clamped into place to set his broken jaw. "There you go now, you can breathe again, it's just the nasty anesthesia makes you so sick. I know, go ahead, baby, take a breath, they'll fix you up again at Evac. Now don't worry about a thing, you're all right now, honey, it won't hurt for more than a second." *God,* Jo thought, *not hurt?* What does it feel like to have your face shattered, then operated on, then "barbwired" shut? But Queenie was true to her word, pulling out a quarter-grain morphine syrette, ignoring its general warning, MAY BE HABIT-FORMING, as well as its less equivocal label, POISON. After injecting the soldier, she pinned the used needle to the man's bloodied collar; somewhere along the way, should he make it, someone would at least know what he had had.

And then she kissed him.

Just before they lifted him into the ambulance (the exhaust fumes were filling the tent, Jo felt sick), Queenie kissed him. The blood and the vomit, the stench of fear and death, and she kissed him.

And every person in that tent, who hadn't even known they were watching, stopped watching, envious of the dying man whose eyes were no longer scared, disgusted with themselves for what they had become, for how little they cared anymore, for how tired they were, for how much they hurt, for how cold and hungry and filthy they felt, inside and out, with a kind of filth no water could wash away. They knew they hadn't held a hand, let alone kissed someone, since they had stopped being humans themselves; their world was now one of survival, an animal world of biting and ripping and tearing and, occasionally, licking each other's wounds. Sure, they might patch and bandage and send men farther back along the chain to be patched and bandaged again, but they, the healers, could no longer heal because they could not think and they could not feel and they could not remember when they had last thought or felt anything other than that they themselves were animals, hunted and trapped and cold.

And Queenie had kissed him.

WHEN THE COMMAND comes to fall back, it takes an infantryman less than ten seconds to simply turn around—and run. But not military nurses, whose only creed, whose one, unbreakable rule, is never to leave their patients. Never. So begins the long task of finishing the surgeries already in progress; stabilizing those just coming into the post-op tent; giving plasma, or whole blood when available; lifting the "heavy orthopedics" with their colossal casts, arms and legs immobilized by a hundred pounds of plaster. The shock patients with their thready pulses; the boys with "battle fatigue," whimpering and taking cover under their cots, thinking themselves still in the field; the deaf, the maimed, and the blind, their heads carefully wrapped and bandaged, their tentative fingers reaching out in front of them, seared and melted together from clawing their way out of burning tanks. All these men had to be moved into an endless convoy of trucks and ambulances that could only hold so many and only go so fast in the muddy ruts of what had once been a road. Jo remembered one time when they had been trying to move out, early on, before any of them knew anything, and she and a group of nurses had sewn together sheets to form an enormous cross to mark the field where the injured lay awaiting transport, smugly thinking the thin fabric would protect their men from strafing. The commanding officer himself had come up to them, livid, screaming at the naive girls for putting up not a red but a *white* cross—the symbol for airfield, and a legitimate military target under the Geneva convention.

There were no more white sheets now.

The sound of the shells exploding outside mingled with thunder and it was all one cacophony of death. There had been a time when the girls would wince, or duck, or even jump into foxholes dug right into the dirt of the field hospital "floor." But there were no safe places left, not anymore, and they walked around numb, oblivious to death hovering above them, packing up the more critical of their supplies—the scalpels, the clamps, the enormous steam sterilizer that would make everything usable when they set up again somewhere. The ambulance was ready to leave, and the doctors already on board were calling for Queenie.

"You can ride up front with me, sweetheart."

"Yeah, on my lap."

"No thank you, doctors," Queenie replied, her voice saccharine. "I'll take my chances with the Germans first. I'll be fine in the back with my boys. Come on, Jo."

Jo grabbed her green canvas musette bag—how could everything she owned fit into something the size of a handbag? But it did. Book. Rosary. Some thumbed-through letters from the Pacific. One faded photograph. Curity diapers. A nightshirt. Graying underwear. An extra T-shirt. Two C rations. The absurd negligee. A pen. Jo put on her helmet, the chinstrap long since burned off from years of using the helmet to heat water in for washing. Queenie was already in the back of the truck, instinctively reaching out a comforting hand without even realizing it, when a grating voice near Jo's ear said, "Not so fast, miss."

It was Grandpa.

None of the girls remembered his real name anymore; if they had ever known it, it was just Grandpa now. The nickname originated when they found out he had served in the medical corps during the Great War; they joked, behind his back of course, that he was old enough to have been a doctor in the Civil War as well.

"You can stay with me, Miss McMahon. We'll get the next truck."

Jo sighed. She hadn't noticed she was the only nurse left in the tent. Of course, she would not—she could not, ever—leave before the last of her patients did, but she would have rather sat through the long wait for the return truck with any of the other surgeons, even the fatherly ones in their forties who bored her kindly with talk of tobacco and fly-fishing back home. Anyone but Grandpa, who rambled on about the Deep South, its nobility and "gracious amenities." *Maybe,* she thought, *he really does remember it from antebellum times after all.*

"I'll stay," Queenie began, but the truck had already shifted into gear, and besides, two patients were holding on to her, looking at her with such intensity that it seemed she was the only thing rooting them to reality, tethering them to a spinning world.

"She'll be perfectly fine where she is, Miss Carroll," Grandpa snapped irritably, her real name sounding like an insult as he grabbed a chart hanging crookedly off of one of the litters.

I'll be perfectly fine, Jo mouthed to Queenie, making a face. And Queenie laughed, her smile lighting up the interior of the cold ambulance already smelling of death, and Jo smiled too and made a little salute. And then the truck was pulling away, Queenie bending over one of the men, her hand gently caressing his forehead; then she was lost to them.

Jo took stock of what was left behind, in terms of supplies yet to be loaded—not much really. The X-ray and all but one of the operating tables had finally been collapsed and carried away, most of the medicines and supplies were already gone, except for one or two surgery kits neatly packed into their boxes, propped up against the center tent pole. One genera-tor, still running, remained, as well as one oil-burning stove, now off and cooling before the journey, some lamps used for surgery, and the less important detritus that always littered the tent floor—disinfectant, bedpans, buckets, soap. Grandpa walked over to a chest marked LINEN and proceeded to speak in his most officious voice.

"Miss McMahon, it is no secret to me that you and your fellow nurses refer to me"—here he spat out the word—"as 'Grandpa,' a term you use to convey my age and none of the honor one asso-ciates with that esteemed position. Well, such being the case—and denying any fatigue on my part—I will oblige you by acting out the part insofar as setting down for a spell."

And with that, he sat down stiffly. Jo noticed for the first time how pale and drawn the man looked, more so than he had in Italy, or Sicily, or North Africa before that. He had always seemed aged to the nurses, who were all just over twenty themselves. But this last push through France, closing in now on Germany itself, had been too much for him. Jo noted that his lips were too white, his brows too closely knit together. He looked like an old man who had just realized, suddenly, and with considerable annoyance, that he was in fact old.

"Yes, doctor," Jo murmured demurely, moving off to check on the remaining patients—and to give the doctor some space.

The tent flap suddenly opened, and a man with startlingly blue eyes pushed his way in.

"You still in here? You need to move out," he said, breathlessly, dripping wet.

"We're almost ready, Captain," Jo replied to the stranger, her eyes resting for a second on his shoulder—not one of their corps.

"Almost isn't good enough, bitch."

Jo felt as if she had been slapped in the face. Nearly four years of war and how many thousands of brutal deaths later, this breach of courtesy still managed to shock Jo, more than the concussions outside that were shaking the tent. Jo and her fellow nurses were used to working side by side with surgeons and doctors who considered them almost as colleagues, allowing them to make independent decisions and perform difficult procedures no nurse would ever be permitted to do stateside. (Jo had done her first spinal tap with shaking hands, but had done one earlier that day without thinking about it at all.) Even the Germans (to give the devil his due) were respectful, if confused, by the women officers, having no such counterparts in their own armies. (Their *Krankenschwesters* held no rank and, with their heavy, traditional dresses, were regarded by the men more as nuns than as nurses.) When American nurses were taken as prisoners of war, enemy officers would awkwardly ask the captured women for their word of honor that they would not attempt escape; then, in lieu of imprisonment, the Germans requested they wait out the rest of the war serving in orphanages or makeshift civilian hospitals.

And this man had just called her a bitch.

Grandpa struggled to his feet as quickly as his aging joints would allow, his mouth open in outrage.

"How—how dare you, sir," he stammered at last.

The captain stepped forward aggressively. "What the hell are these men still doing here? You were supposed to be moved out hours ago. I've only got a goddamned patrol to hold this area, and you're gumming up the works with your ambulances blocking the roads and drawing fire."

Jo recovered from her momentary shock, the thick shell she wove around herself adding yet another layer. She did not know this man, she would never see him again. Their paths were crossing for a second only, and that only by chance; soon she would be back with her medical corps, with the men— the hundreds of men—who needed her. This man, she made up her mind, needed no one. "We're waiting for our truck to return, and then we'll be out of your way, sir." She added the "sir" looking level into his eyes, eyes she noted as remarkably beautiful, almost turquoise in color, but cold and lifeless and blank, as if nothing, not even light, could penetrate them.

"Then you wait in the dark, sweetheart," he said, ripping out the generator cord. Everything went dark; Jo heard him fumbling for a second, and then the motor itself sputtered out, as if in protest. In a flash of lightning Jo could see the silhou- ette of the captain as he passed through the tent flap; then all was darkness. There was an explosion, but much farther away this time, to the south of them, maybe half a mile down the road, followed by two more, much quieter.

"Of all the, the—" Grandpa was still stuttering, incredu- lous. Then, in a lower voice, a voice Jo had never heard him use before, almost a whisper: "You all right?"

"Don't be silly, of course I'm all right," Jo replied glibly, too glibly, feeling her way in the darkness for the nearest stretcher. "Silly," she repeated again. But it hadn't been silly at all.

"I'm sorry, soldier," she addressed the blackness in front of her, still feeling for the stretcher in the dark. All the tent flaps had already been tightly shut to prevent light escaping; the ambulances would have been driving without headlights, as always; both precautions making the captain's behavior seem even more senseless and—*No, I won't think of him anymore, he's gone.* "But we seem to have to make shift in the dark here for a little while." She tried to force cheerfulness into her voice, as Queenie would have done, and failed. "Would you mind telling me which one you are?"

A cockney voice came through the darkness, its edges seeming to curl up in a sympathetic smile. "Jonesy, miss. I'm not as bad off as some of these here other ones. Just the bad leg, if you remember, miss."

Jo smiled. The English patient. A Montgomery, the boys always called them. Now she remembered, broken leg; a heavy cast would be dangling on a wire in front of her somewhere. Whether or not it was just habit, his repetition of "miss" had sounded almost reverential, as if he were trying to make up for what had just happened.

"Can you carry on for a little while here? I'm sorry, our lanterns and flashlights have already been packed up, so it's going to be catch-as-catch-can for a bit." Jo used the English expression for his sake; at least, she hoped it was English. She had read it once in a novel; certainly no one said that back home in Brooklyn.

"Not to worry, miss," came the grinning reply. "I'm not going anywhere."

Jo smiled automatically in the dark, moving now with more assurance from one cot to the next, better gauging the distance between them. The Scot was still cursing; at least he was conscious. There were two post-op patients next to him whose anesthesia hadn't worn off yet; she fumbled for their wrists, taking their vital signs as best she could, guessing without her watch—at least a stethoscope was still hanging around her neck. She bumped into Grandpa crossing the tent. "Excuse me, miss," he said gently, all traces of his usual brusqueness gone from his voice. She played blindman's bluff until she found the last two stretchers. One man was asleep, but breathing raspily and much too fast, his chest sounding like crackling tin foil when she listened to it. The last man was conscious, but groaning, his forehead hot and wet, he nearly screamed when she palpated his abdomen. So they had been right in their initial diagnosis: presenting appendicitis. *Good God, right now.* She reassured him as best she could, but he didn't seem to be listening; it was hard to tell in the inky blackness—his moans waxing and waning without a seeming connection to her words, bobbing, as he was, on a sea of pain. She made her way over to Grandpa, who was trying to take the pulse of one of the unconscious patients.

"This is a ludicrous situation, Miss McMahon," he began, pausing to count as he found another wrist in the dark, lost count, and gave up. "These patients, with the exception of that Scotsman, whom I don't like the look—I mean, the sound—of in the least, appear stable, if in various degrees of discomfort. Rather than knock our heads together walking around in the dark, may I suggest you stay by his bedside and I'll rotate between these two and that major over there—yes, he's a major, they were supposed to move him out first—with the overripe appendix."

It was a plan at least. Something to do until the truck came back, whenever that would be. Jo sidled over to her patient;

he was easy to find. She wondered vaguely if they were really Scottish curse words he was uttering, or the by-product of his fever, or a combination of both. She sat down next to him on the packed ground. And then she thought of Gianni.

She had tried to stop thinking of him; there had been a time when she had tried to forget him altogether, to banish him from her thoughts each time he struggled to resurface, his body disfigured and floating, the dark blood spreading from his open wounds in all directions in the cold water of her consciousness. But she had lost the power to fight her brother anymore. Sometimes, when the pace of war made her unable to function except by memory or rote, there would be a reprieve; he would still be there, but in the back of her mind, hiding in a dark corner of the tent, lying on the last stretcher in the ambulance. But during the few hours of sleep allotted her, or now, with an enforced period of inactivity thrust upon her, Gianni in all his horror, in all his glory, came flooding back. She loved him, and she hated him for haunting her, and wanted him to leave her alone, and felt she would die if he ever did.

"What were you thinking, Josie?"

She could see him now, looking down on her again, his dark olive skin, his even darker eyes, eyes that were so angry with her, eyes that would love her and pain her and punish her forever.

"What were you thinking?"

He had grabbed her arms rudely and held her in front of him, shaking her, shaking himself. He had to be brave now, and he couldn't be brave, not with her doing this terrible thing, not with her leaving too.

"I was drafted, that can't be helped. But Mama and Papa will be all alone when you leave. How could you sign up?" Again, that reproach: "What were you thinking?"

She had stammered something about the war and about duty; about how they were calling for nurses, thousands of nurses, an army of nurses to fill the ranks; how the other girls were going, how it was the right thing to do. In her dreams (waking and sleeping), her words changed, got mumbled, turned around, twisted. It didn't matter—Gianni hadn't heard them then, he didn't hear them now.

Then he was crying. She had never seen him cry, not ever, not even when he broke his wrist in the park—where they weren't supposed to be playing in the rich kids' neighborhood—and he had turned white from the pain and wanted to scream but hadn't because of his scared baby sister looking up at him with her wide, blue eyes, one streaked with brown.

"It's not just Mama and Papa," Gianni had begun, but couldn't finish. He had stopped shaking her now and was holding her close, sobbing, wracking sobs, worse than his anger had been; this was good-bye. They were, to each other, all they had ever had. Their parents (a loveless arranged marriage) had grown prematurely old from lives spent slaving away in navy yards and sweatshops; it had been the nuns at Saint Cecelia's who raised the two immigrant waifs. But for affection, for compassion, for protection in a strange new world, Gianni and "Josie" (his pet name for her—to everyone else she would be plain "Jo") had only ever had each other; two people, one mind, always in agreement, always together; now, suddenly, about to be torn apart.

In her dreams he dies then. He dies in her arms, their parents coming into the small apartment looking older than ever, glancing up tiredly, mumbling that they would like to come to the funeral but have to work in the morning, an extra shift, what can we do, if we don't, we'll lose our jobs. It is a nightmare of course. But it is a dream too, because he dies there—not later, not on that carrier, not with the hundreds of other boys screaming and choking and slipping on the decks wet with blood and water and gasoline as the planes roar overhead and the explosions go off and they're hurled into the sea and he's dead before he hits the water; sinking, crushed by the incredible weight, his mouth filling with seawater, drowning out the last word he would never get to say, the last word he was saying to her now, the same word he always said to her.

"Josie."

JO STARTED AWAKE. Not that she had been asleep, but she hadn't been there, in that tent, sitting in the cold and the dark. The Scot was trying to get out of bed, asking for his shoes in English; then it was a jumble of words again, nonsense in any language. She got up and pushed him back onto the cot. "Pushed" is too strong a verb; he was so weak, she held two fingers in place on his chest; he moaned, delirious, and fell back.

Gianni was dead, and her parents now too—they had died while she was overseas. What did it matter anymore? Everywhere was death, and where it wasn't yet, it was coming. She noticed the bombing had stopped outside and switched to gunfire. The captain hadn't come back. He would have his work cut out for him, defending this useless patch of France—or was it Germany?—with only twenty to a platoon. The truck was taking forever too. Had it been an hour yet? Two? Time was uncertain for her—her reveries sometimes lasted mere seconds, and at other times an entire night's sleep would be sacrificed to watching Gianni die again and again. The truck might not be back for hours now, even if the roads weren't taken out, even if they did find a way around the lowlands and the mud and the

Germans. She tried looking at her wristwatch, angling it to pick up even the faintest glimmer of light, but it was useless; the darkness engulfed them completely. The tent was wrapped in its own envelope of blackness and rain, and there wasn't even lightning anymore to split the sky.

After a long while, it grew quiet. For some time the gunfire had come from farther and farther away, until Jo thought it had either stopped entirely or was continuing on in some ravine or valley too deep or far away for the sound to carry. The Scot seemed to be praying, just by the cadence of his speech alone. There was a petition of some kind, a labored pause for breath, a response. None of it made sense to Jo; maybe God could unravel it in heaven. It seemed important to him, though, whatever it was. She tried to imagine what it could be. A litany? A rosary? Something embedded and a part of this man, surely, for it to rise to the surface like this when all other senses had left him. As his voice rose and fell with the desperate intercessions, she felt for her musette bag, took out her rosary, and held the weathered beads in her hands, pressing them hard between her fingers until they hurt, the pain clearing her mind for a second. But no prayer rose to her lips—at least, not the Our Fathers and Hail Marys she had anticipated, the prayers she had used to plead with God when the telegram had first come, when she had learned Gianni was killed in action, when her own life had ended but, cruelly, her body had been forced to keep going through the motions of being alive. *And lead us not into temptation, but deliver us from evil.* From evil. She was surrounded by evil, it was everywhere. There was evil in Germany just ahead of them, and there was evil in Japan, half a world away. There was evil in the bottom of the sea where dark things fed on the bodies of the lost, and there was evil in the mountains around them where the traitors and the deserters and the lovers had fled.

But, now, there was evil, too, right among them; the captain tonight had seemed evil—but maybe she was still naive, for all her experience, maybe this was the real world now, the world they were fighting to save. Maybe this would be as good as it ever got, even if the Axis powers were ultimately defeated; maybe the Allies had become little better than the thing they had set out to destroy. After all, what had just happened in Dresden? Even with their mail and radio so closely censored, they knew something obscene had happened there, something wicked and wrong, something that was not them—or not them as they still imagined themselves to be. What had happened in Dresden was the kind of thing the "other side" did, not them, not the upholders of justice and freedom, not the liberators, not the good side.

But was she good anymore? Was anyone good? This was hell, with no chance of heaven. She saw herself again as a little girl, her voluptuous hair severely restrained by tight braids, her secondhand school uniform fitting too tightly under her arms. She was reciting her catechism answers for Sister Jonathan, the nun's parted white hair peeking out from under her wimple. "War is the punishment for sin, Sister," she had said from memory, along with a hundred other pat answers. Punishment for sin. What colossal sin had some fool committed for this to be its outcome? Or was this the fault of all of them collectively? Was this everyone's sin, everyone's hatefulness, all the small, petty, stupid crimes piled up, multiplied a million million times over—lust and envy and greed and betrayal, pressed down, running over? Was this the whole world crying out, proclaiming its suicide creed of hate, vengeance, murder, power, death? And then their unholy prayer finally being answered with firebombs raining down from the sky.

The wind picked up outside, buffeting the tent. Jo was deathly cold; if the truck didn't come soon, she would have to start the oil stove again, and the orderlies would curse when they had to load it onto the truck, still hot. The Scot was crying, not like a man, but like an exhausted toddler put into his crib to cry himself out, pitiable and whimpering and small. The major shouted, but then cut off his yell midscream; he must have bitten his hand to stop himself. Grandpa was shushing his groggy patients, who were asking where they were, what had happened, where was Bobby, Joey, Ted. The rain was pelting the side of the tent, running in under the canvas and into Jo's shoes. It seemed like forever until they heard noises outside—a faint rustling over the wind at first, then the unmistakable sound of men surrounding the tent, coming closer. Jo tried and failed to make out whether their muted words were in English or German. She wondered what would happen to them all if they were taken prisoner this far into the war. The Geneva convention was still in place, on paper; she and Grandpa, as noncombatants, were protected. But food, the first and most powerful of man's weapons when withheld, was scarce; in a prison camp at the end of winter, there would be hardly anything left. Jo did not relish the thought of dying that way, separated from her work, from her dying countrymen, from her dying cause.

The tent flap shot open, revealing a figure as he entered, his rifle level with the flashlight he now switched on. For a moment, everyone was blinded as the piercing light shone on them. Just as quickly, it was shut off, and the figure darted to the far end of the tent, opening the flap there. After what seemed like an eternity, they could feel the phantom relax and hear him walk back to the center of the tent, turning on a flashlight and standing it, end up, on the cool iron of the stove-top. It was the American captain.

He looked at Jo, the doctor, and the six men in turn, rubbing his stubbled chin in thought as if he were about to bid on them at auction. As her eyes adjusted to the light, Jo looked from litter to litter, noting instinctively where a line had to be removed, a cast adjusted. One of the post-op patients looked straight at the light with his dilated pupils, dazed yet unable to turn away. Still the captain was silent; he seemed uncertain how to begin.

"Here's the thing," he started, then fell silent again.

"Captain Clark," one of his men called hoarsely through the tent flap, walking up and hastily exchanging whispers with him. When the soldier left, the captain began again.

"Okay, well, there's nothing for it. Here goes. The fighting has moved off to the south of us for the time being. There's no telling how long that will last, and at any moment it could shift back this way. But for now, for the next couple of hours anyway, possibly days, you should be okay."

To Jo, the captain's manner seemed inconsistent with the (relatively) good news he was bringing them: he kept looking at the floor, then at the tent flap, but never at her or Grandpa directly. He turned almost angrily when one of the patients cried out in pain, lifted his hand as if to say something, shook his head hastily, and turned away.

"When might we be moving out?" Grandpa ventured, uncertain if the captain might again disappear into the night.

"What?" came the puzzled reply of a man thinking along

entirely different lines, jolted back into the here and now against his will. "Oh, move out. No, no. You're not. I mean, you can't. The road's blocked. Gone, really."

The captain started pacing back and forth, looking at the patients as if, by sheer willpower, he could somehow get them off of their stretchers, off of his hands.

"I can't have you stay here," he said, almost to himself. "Any one of these men calls out, in their sleep even, and the game's up. The Jerries could be anywhere, we could be surrounded right now and not know it."

He stopped pacing.

"But you said the road was blocked?" Grandpa asked. "For how long? I mean, how long until they clear it?"

"They? There—there is no 'they,' pops," the captain stammered. "I'm it. I mean, we're in a fucking big hole right now." He took off his helmet and ran his hand through his fair hair, his voice rising despite himself. "I mean, somehow they just fucking slammed right through the middle of our guys, I guess. I don't get it. Hell, I hope we're holding on to it somewhere, at the edges maybe, but not here—the line's completely gone. No one's supposed to be here, I mean, not us, not anymore. There will be no 'they' coming—unless it's the Germans. And if *they're* coming . . ." His voice trailed off as he replaced his helmet slowly.

Jo tried to think of what Queenie would do. She wouldn't have liked this rough soldier any more than Jo did, but Queenie could be so good at saying the right thing at the right time. Queenie could have bucked him up—bucked them all up—with some cock-and-bull about how she was sure the enemy would pass to their south completely, or if not, how she was confident they could manage nicely right where they were, with her and the doctor taking care of the wounded while the brave, outmanned captain protected them all.

She looked at the captain, his eyes now covered with his free hand, lost in thought, his rifle pointing impotently toward the ground. She tried to feel inside like Queenie would have felt, tried to cue the glorious background music of her mind the way she used to be able to do. Jo could be indomitable too. She could whip herself up into becoming indomitable, precisely because people like Queenie existed and would always exist in the United States of America and anywhere else in the world she sent her citizens to defend freedom. She would prove that right was right—*despite Dresden, don't even think of Dresden, Dresden couldn't really have happened*—and justice would reign. Jo might not live to see it herself, but this war was almost ended. And in the end, goodness would prevail.

Although they ached, Jo drew back her tired shoulders and painfully straightened her spine, coming to attention, coming to life, for the first time in a long time. The captain shook himself all over like a terrier, as if he had just made up his mind about something, and turned toward the flap.

"Captain," Grandpa asked in passing, turning back toward one of the men on the cots. "What blocked the road?"

"Hmm?" The captain seemed genuinely confused for a moment, as if he had already explained a crucial point that had not been comprehended. "Oh, didn't I tell you? The medical convoy. They got strafed. We got there all right, in the end, but everyone was dead."

"The *men* were all dead," Jo corrected him, smiling nervously, walking toward him now, her stomach dropping, picturing the burning ambulances, upside down, piled up on the side of the obliterated road. But in her mind's eye, the nurses were still racing from fallen soldier to fallen soldier like they always had, like they always would, Queenie at their lead, her face covered in soot, her towel come loose and her dark hair messy around her face in the whipping wind, looking wild and beautiful and radiant in the red of the fires burning about her, calling out for the girls to rally round her and smiling. "All the patients were lost. The drivers."

The captain looked at Jo as if she were a little girl, a very stupid and tiresome girl who asked senseless questions of a man in a hurry. In his vacant eyes was something that could have been mistaken for pity but was in fact a most profound sense of irritation. Only with great effort did he suppress the second word of his intended sentence; simply repeating, instead, the single word, "Everyone." Then he pushed aside the tent flap and stepped out into the night.

2

Kay Elliott

May 1942, Malinta Tunnel, Corregidor

Kay was running, she had always been running, she
was running now. What she was running toward was
death—dark, suffocating death with no air and no light and no
hope—but the thing she was running from was worse. Down
the hill she ran, chest pounding, her fitted skirt impeding her
flight, limiting her strides, digging into her thighs with each
step; she had never gone so fast, she had to go faster, she could
never go fast enough. The rough grass and vines lashed angrily
at her bare legs as she sped by; they were crisscrossed with
blood. Behind her a monkey—or a man—started screaming.
An enormous explosion went off in the jungle, then another,
its heat searing the back of her neck where it was exposed between collar and victory curls that were somehow, ridiculously,
still pinned in place. Sweat poured down her face, the sunlight
catching on her wet eyelashes, distorting her vision. A terri-
fying noise was pounding in her ears, a sickening sound she
could hear above the monkey's cruel laughter and the ammunition dumps igniting behind her, the sound of someone gasping for breath and crying and gasping again. Her neck aching
from her crazy pulse, she realized the noise was coming from

herself. The monkeys swung from vine to vine above her, in
front of her, mocking her—or were they scared too, escaping
from the holocaust of their home? Another blast came, stronger than the last one, knocking her into the air like a long-
jumper, legs turning in empty space—and then the jungle
came crashing down in a myriad of small colored blocks. Black
snakes floated up into the sky with her, dancing; trees burst
into a million splinters of glass that hung suspended in the air.
When she tried to scream she found there was no air left in her
lungs. She was dead.

And then she woke up. When she opened her eyes it was
hard to tell that she was alive, that the utter darkness she found
herself in was any different from complete annihilation. She sat
up, her forehead painfully grazing the curve of the tunnel wall
where it sloped down near her top bunk—and then, with a
despair greater than Persephone's, she realized she was still in
Hades. Only here they called it Malinta. She hated Malinta
with a hatred more powerful and suffocating than the air it
forced her to breathe. Malinta. *Linta*—Tagalog for "leeches."
Ma—"full of." She would have preferred the long corridors of
this tunnel be filled with those bloodsucking parasites instead
of the horrors that really awaited her; would rather they sap
the life out of her than have the stench and the filth and the
slow inevitability of death do it instead.

Somewhere far above her she could hear a rumble as the
vast mountain shook, its reverberations finally reaching her in
its necrotic bowels. Carved deep into the solid rock, their im-
penetrable stronghold, their unassailable fortress, was about to
fall. They had surrendered to the Japanese twenty-four hours
ago. It was over—why did they keep bombing, bombing,
and bombing them, as they had for weeks now? Death surely

awaited them outside—rape first, maybe, for the women, followed by starvation; if they were lucky, maybe a quick bullet
to the head, instead—but she felt it would almost be worth it
if she could take just one breath of fresh air first.

The smell of the tunnel was insufferable. Since April they
had been trapped down here like rats—she had thought at
first, with her claustrophobia, that she wouldn't last the first
night, that the air would give out. She had survived, but still,
the air was largely the same as when they had first sealed
themselves up in this living tomb. The stench from the lateral
where they had butchered the starved mules; the accumulated
diesel fumes from the ambulances that sped down the halls;
the stink of urine and vomit and rot rising off of a thousand
hospital beds—that was the air they breathed in, choked on,
expelled gagging, breathed in again. This was the air they
slept in, ate in, tried to think in, the air they cried in and spat
out, sick, their mouths tasting like metal. And no matter how
foul and putrid and used up the air became, their bodies forced
them to breathe it in again, against their will. She remembered how their head surgeon—she had liked him, really liked
him, a decent fellow from New England, all Adam's apple and
freckles, with a young wife back home and their first baby on
the way—had gone stir-crazy suddenly one day, escaped from
their grasp, and, ignoring their cries to stop, opened the door
to the tunnel and stepped outside—only to be shot instantly.

After that, the Japanese had allowed nurses and officers
"twenty minutes outside each day." At first, they couldn't believe it; the very thought of feeling the Pacific breezes again,
of feeling the sun on their faces, even for a short time, filled
them with hope . . . but then there was the horror of what they
saw. Not just the bloated body of their fellow surgeon but the

hundreds of other dead and decaying bodies, flies rising off of them in swarms, rodents feasting on their sunburned flesh, an endless carpet of carnage along the road leading up to Malinta. Military dead sprawled alongside civilian men, women, and children, the refugees who had fled to the Americans, to the last safe place, but had arrived after the great door had been shut. All had been bombed mercilessly by their aggressors, and now their rotting bodies filled the air with a reek worse than the tunnel's filthiest recesses. Kay had seen the black, rotted face of a baby looking up at her with missing eyes, still strapped to its dead mother in an incongruously beautiful orange wrap. Kay had thrown up, cursing the Japanese for their brutality, cursing herself for still being alive. This, then, was the generosity of the Japanese; this was the demoralizing purpose of their twenty minutes of freedom. When the Japanese refused the Americans' request to bury the dead—stating that anyone attempting it would soon join their ranks—the great gate was closed and barred. Kay never ventured outside again. She would rather die.

She was about to get her wish.

Kay didn't need to dress after climbing down from her bunk; she was already dressed in the same nurse's uniform she had put on (she shook her head at the very thought) back in 1941. Another explosion went off somewhere above them; the compression sucking her skirt around her legs, the change in pressure playing with her ears; she had to swivel her jaw to clear them. She walked toward the hospital laterals, where hundreds upon hundreds of cots were filled with wounded soldiers, lined up and growing smaller in the lamplight like some gruesome study in perspective. On her way she passed two ensigns fumbling with their telegraph equipment in the heat and glare of a huge standing lamp, adjusting knobs and tugging on wires. Kay, who had worked in a telegraph office summers back home in Mount Carmel, could make out, "They are coming stop say good-bye for me stop."

Stop. She felt the thought that her life was about to stop, that the world outside of Malinta could somehow be even more "nasty, brutish, and short" than her existence within it, should have filled her with terror, but it didn't. *Something must be wrong with me,* she thought sluggishly, then shrugged. There was so much wrong with her that it was best it would all be ending soon; she was—life was—beyond redemption.

Her patients, the ones who had still been alive that morning when she got there—she had had to call in the orderlies to remove the corpses stuck to the cots with their own blood—were scared; word of the surrender had reached them. They pulled off rings, stuffing them into her hands, giving her explicit instructions. *Give this to Pamela Murphy, Reading, Pennsylvania . . . to Eloise Drew, Rapid City, South Dakota . . . Tell her to sell the farm . . . to marry again . . . to name him Hank . . . to remember me . . . to forget me . . . Tell her that I love her.* Kay nodded soothingly as they spoke, the countless names and places, the frenzied list of last wishes passing through her consciousness unheard. What did these men think would happen to their nurses? That the Japanese would send them home, unscathed, laden like pawnshops with their silver scapular medals, gold watches, and a hundred class rings?

She never knew how she made it through that day. How she found the last bit of compassion and humanity she thought had been driven out of her—found it and passed it along to these men. But she did. Perhaps it was because she and the other nurses, no matter how harrowing their own fate might soon be at the hands of the enemy, knew with a cold certainty that this was the last day on earth for these men. The Japanese did not take injured prisoners of war, prisoners who could not stand and walk and march. So Kay and the other nurses promised a thousand empty promises, with a thousand empty smiles—that she would go to Jersey City after the war, that she would comfort a grieving mother, that she would look up an old friend, an uncle, a sister, a lover. She would tell a brother he was forgiven, and admit to Rosie that the baby was his after all. That the money was hidden behind *Lucia di Lammermoor* in the study . . . that the will was in the pantry, buried in the flour . . . that the key to the safe was in the old hollow oak, the one in the middle of the lower pasture, right next to the stream. She promised a thousand, senseless, useless things she would never do and could never remember, promised them on her word of honor; she heard without hearing the flotsam of a thousand, unfinished lives, the things they had not said and had not done and now would never say or do. She tirelessly changed bandages as if it mattered, as if there would even be time for them to soak through again, to begin to harbor infection. She gave out the remaining doses of medicine, of sulfa, of whatever they had left—this was mortuary care, not nursing. She gave everything out, everything but the tiny glass vials of morphine.

These she took. She and the other nurses, at the end of their graveyard shift, took all they could and, in the dreary light of their dormitory lateral, pinned them up in their victory rolls. The vials were small, transparent, fragile; carefully, they helped each other secure them inside their blond, black, auburn curls. "Make 'em good and tight, girls," they told each other grimly, just as their head nurse had told them last year, jokingly, "Eat up your biscuits, girls, for when the Japs take you prisoner." They had laughed at that impossibility and passed up the buttery rolls, already full from their lavish meals, supplemented by the never-ending supply of tropical fish and fruits and fatty nuts. They'd been worried about fitting into their evening dresses for the embassy gala, the officers' dance, the nurses' ball. Kay thought of the biscuits now and tears rolled down her sallow cheeks.

"But it's wrong," Rosaria said timidly. She was the dark little nurse with sideburns whose Italian accent came out when she was scared. "Killing yourself, she's a sin." And silently, they all agreed—Catholic, Jew, Wasp alike. It was wrong and forbidden and they could never do it—they would be damned forever if they did. Then they thought of the Rape of Nanking, of what had happened to those hundreds, thousands of women and girls, young girls, at the hands of the Japanese—and they fastened in yet another hairpin.

The concussions continued all that night. Funny, Kay thought—now that the surrender had happened, the halls and laterals were much quieter. No more racing around, no jeeps honking raucously as they used to do, swerving to miss the nurses, coming mere inches from the heads of unflinching men lined up along its sides, who slept the sleep of utter exhaustion, which is a kind of death in itself. Tonight was quiet—people were praying, or remembering, or whispering quietly in small groups together, steeling themselves for the morning, which would dawn, like all the others down here, in total blackness.

Kay fingered the empty charts she had taken from the hospital earlier on—she would write a letter on their blank sides in a little bit, write to Jo McMahon, her best friend back home; write a letter she would never get to mail but one that needed to be written nonetheless—to clear her head, to straighten out her tangled thoughts one last time. She couldn't die this way. But there would be plenty of time to write it later—there would be no sleep for any of them tonight.

Kay thought back to when she had been given the chance to leave Malinta. The Japs hadn't yet found the secret submarine dock, and one desperate attempt was going to be made to get people out. Not all of them, surely; but, in the hierarchy that existed, the more "important" of them. The ambassador's friends and family. Allied civilian women, separated from their husbands and fathers. Douglas MacArthur himself. They were to go—along with the nurses—head out to sea and never see Malinta again. Kay had considered leaving—considered what it would be like to eat and drink and wash and sleep again, to live like a human being and not like a worm—but she could not bring herself to do it. Not that she felt any great emotion—or any emotion at all, really—for anyone anymore; she was completely numb. In the end, though, she—along with fifty other nurses—decided to stay behind to tend the wounded, to assist at surgeries, to run lines and remove casts. They would fill in the time until their own deaths with duty. She had realized, suddenly, that being a military nurse was all she had left in the world; and in the end, Kay couldn't separate herself from that.

She wondered where Jo was now. She was sorry that Jo would never get her letter, never hear her apologize for rubbing it in that she, Kay, had gotten the plum assignment in the Pacific. Plum assignment! How mad Jo had been—back in the hospital they worked in in New York—when she had had to stay behind and complete her second year of nursing before qualifying for overseas duty. Kay could still see her friend in her starched, white uniform, stamping her foot in frustration, one gorgeous, glossy curl escaping her cap. "It isn't fair, Kay," Jo had nearly shouted, her doubly sharp Irish-Italian temper getting the best of her, eyes flashing, looking all the more beautiful in her wrath. "It isn't fair you get to go without me."

No, I should have stayed with you, Jo, we were stronger together. You taught me to be strong. We could face anything together.

Kay closed her eyes and could still smell the strong antiseptic, could still feel the cold metal of the shelves as she ran her fingers lightly along them in her mind. She was back in the storeroom of their receiving hospital. It was winter, she remembered, cold down in the basement, too far from the furnaces; she shivered in her pale white stockings. She had come down alone. She and Jo had said they wouldn't; they would stay in pairs, safety in numbers—but the tubing on one of the oxygen tanks had worn out, had crumbled in the matron's hand, and she had told Kay to run and get a replacement, to get it now. Kay had been down there, alone, the lightbulb in the storeroom ceiling buzzing faintly, the filament twisted and glowing, the beaded metal chain still swinging from when she had pulled it. And then she hadn't been alone, he was there, she could smell him, hear him breathing. How had he followed her? She hadn't even known she was coming down here herself, she had run all the way, but he was down there now, between her and the door out of the storeroom closet. The shelves had begun to close in on her, squeezing her tight, she couldn't breathe. She saw his eyes—they seemed red . . . no, black—but she saw them only for a moment; in another instant he was right there, too close for her to focus on him, a dark, hard mass pushing her back against the cement wall, against the hard shelves, she was struggling, *don't, just don't,* but the words couldn't come out because she couldn't breathe. She was fighting him off, his breath hot on her neck, his hands rough as they fumbled with her garter. And just as he reached above him to yank on the cord, to stop the soft buzzing sound, to disperse the last of the light and thrust them both into darkness, there'd been a sound behind him and he had turned and seen Jo, arms akimbo, another nurse at her side, and Jo was saying coolly, saying coldly, "Doctor," just the one word—*doctor.*

He fixed Jo with eyes filled with hatred, filled with nothing at all. "You'll say nothing, nurse, nothing, if you know what's good for you. Remember what happened to the last nurse who spoke up. No one believed her. It's only your lousy word against mine, and you're nothing, you're nobody. If you talk, you'll never work in this city again." He shoved Kay from him as an afterthought, and then in an instant the man had changed, his mask back in place. Suddenly, it was impossible to believe that this dignified man straightening his tie, preparing to ascend into the light of his reputation and his godlike skill, was the brute of a moment before. He walked quickly past the nurses, buttoning his long white coat, his polished shoes making a clicking sound on the painted concrete floor. Kay slid down the rough stone wall, hugging her knees to her chest, and Jo was there, holding her, smoothing her hair and holding her, crying softly and saying, "We'll do something, sweetheart, we'll do something. We've got to think of something."

KAY SHOOK HERSELF. She wouldn't think about that, about what had happened next, about what had bonded them together so closely that even now, half a world apart, they were still part of each other's lives. Jo had been by her side, had gotten her through it; they had both helped each other, been there for each other, but then Kay had left, gone overseas. No, Jo was right, it *wasn't* fair that Kay had gotten to go to the Pacific.

And the letters Kay had sent back—half out of friendship, half just to show off—they weren't fair either, were they? The volcanic beaches, the swaying palms, the beautiful blue of Pearl Harbor. "This is where I'm stationed, Jo," she had scribbled to her friend, biting the pen between thoughts in her excitement. "We only have four-hour shifts because of the heat and, get this, Jo, we don't have to wear any stockings!" That had seemed wicked enough to Kay, and she was running out of room anyway. She didn't have space to write about their bungalows standing storklike over the shimmering, crystal waters; about their servants and private cabins; about the officers at the nightly dances, thrilled at the new infusion of American women—Kay had three suitors for every dance. "Poor Jo, stuck in dreary New York," Kay had sighed, trying to be somber for her friend's sake, failing, then laughing at herself for her incredible luck; at a poor girl from upstate Pennsylvania blossoming into a Cinderella, against a backdrop of paradise no less. Now if only she could decide whether to wear her blue chiffon or organdy to the ball.

There had been a time when that was her biggest problem.

Kay passed one of the nurses, coming off of her shift.

"You okay, Elliott? You're not due on yet."

"Hmm? Yeah, sure. I just need to walk a bit. Can't sleep."

Kay walked aimlessly along those halls she could never

get lost in, halls she knew so well by now that they would always be a part of her—like a cancer, deep-seated and malignant. She wandered around the tunnel built with Baguio gold mining equipment, condemned powdered TNT wrapped in old magazine pages, and a thousand convicts from Bilibid Prison. The U.S. Army Corps of Engineers had constructed the whole nightmarish labyrinth, never imagining for a moment that this wraith of a woman would be flitting around it in the dark, awaiting her own death in the morning; never imagining that a storage bunker they constructed would become the last bastion of freedom against the Nipponese Empire (hell, the Corps had bought the cement for the project from the Japanese themselves).

Kay passed a few clerical staff walking quickly up the corridor, sheaves of paper heaped in their arms marked "FEAF" and "U.S. Air Force Far East." Most of the classified stuff would have been burned by now—this would be the last of it. She passed some men prying open expired cans of sardines, ripping open with difficulty packages of crackers sealed tight against the tropical humidity. "Would you like some, miss?" they offered. "Better us tonight than the Japs tomorrow." She smiled and shook her head, feeling sick and light-headed all of a sudden, and they went back to their last supper. Kay thought of the submarines that had been sunk trying to bring them food—out of the half dozen or more that made the attempt, only one had ever made it through. She had overheard the sailors saying that they'd removed all the torpedoes except the ones already in the tubes and then packed forty to sixty tons of food onboard. Forty to sixty tons. And all those laden submarines, with the exception of one, had been destroyed by the Japanese. She thought of all those inaccessible packages, boxes, cans full of meat, and rice and coffee and chocolate that must have survived, even if the men trying to deliver them had died; food that must have washed up somewhere by now on some remote island, or might still be bobbing, uselessly, in the middle of the Pacific Ocean.

Kay stopped at the open area of the main tunnel that had served as their receiving dock during their first few days in Malinta. In the half-light of the lamps, she could see that the concrete was still stained with blood. The nurses had been overwhelmed, it had been even worse than the panic and chaos of December 7. So many men, so many wounded, seriously wounded. Kay remembered screaming, almost delirious, "Just bring me the live ones," as she bent over corpses still warm and bleeding. And the refugees running by, silent, wide-eyed, pouring into the tunnel before the door was shut, hundreds of them, young, old, babies jogging on the backs of older siblings, pregnant mothers holding toddlers' hands, scuffling along barefoot and blessing their luck at getting past the Japanese, at making it this far. Of course, they could not know what awaited them months later, could not know that the Japanese had not only witnessed their flight to Malinta but facilitated it, opening up their lines, allowing the streams of desperate humanity to pour through, knowing their softhearted enemy would foolishly let refugees into its stronghold, each additional mouth bringing the Americans that much closer to surrender.

Even their mercy was a cruelty.

The receiving dock was empty now, the refugees huddled in a different lateral, praying to their gods, to the god the missionaries had brought them, to any deity that would save them, that would listen, that could hear them buried beneath the great rock that was Corregidor. Kay thought of the first time she had been underground, when her chest had constricted in panic in that unnatural world. Her father had worked the main coal mine for years, for pennies that would somehow raise his family. But to heat their own home, he and Kay's brother had dug out a "bootleg" mineshaft coming off of their uncle's property, burrowing into a lesser vein on the far side of town. One sweltering July day her brother had taken her down into their shaft's chilly interior. At first, it had been alright, in the light of their father's lantern, the coolness seeping into their bones. But as they descended deeper and deeper, Kay lost all sense of proportion and perspective, her ears ringing, a dead weight resting on her chest. "I need to get out, Pete," she had said in a small voice. He didn't take her seriously at first, telling her not to be a girl. But the claustrophobia, the irrational fear—not of the mine collapsing, not of bats or pitfalls or even poisonous gas, no real fear she could put her finger on and contend with, but a fear she could not name and could not stop—grabbed her, possessed her, and she turned and ran blindly. Her brother called for her to wait for him, to wait for the lantern, to quit being a sissy, to stop it already, you'll get hurt. And she—her heart pounding in her throat, words failing her, trying to breathe—scrambled toward the slanting afternoon sunlight, her panic lasting long after the warmth and humidity had touched her face again and frizzed the little blond wisps of her hair. *I need to get out.*

Now, after weeks of being buried alive, she was about to get out. But this time Kay knew there would be no warm Mount Carmel waiting for her when she emerged from the inky blackness, no sleepy Pennsylvania town nestled high in the mountains, no onion-domed or sharply peaked steeple to ring its bells and wake her from her nightmare, no dusty road to lead her to the places she had known and loved all her life.

This was war. And Kay Elliott was about to become its next casualty.

3

Jo McMahon

Spring 1945, The Western Front

J o opened the tent flaps to let in the dawn's early light. The rain had stopped, but the canvas was still wet; as she untied the straps above her, icy cold water ran down her arms. She stood rooted in place, staring at the rough fabric in front of her, not wanting to turn around, unable to face the new day. They all were dead. The captain had said they all were dead. All the patients they had struggled so hard to save; the surgeons with their skilled hands, now motionless; the nurses, lying crushed under the weight of the trucks, the weight of stone and dirt and rubble. Grandpa had collapsed when he heard, put his hand to his heart and collapsed. Jo had revived him, her own world swirling unsteadily in front of her. Although he was now up—up even before Jo on this steel-gray morning, moving silently from patient to patient—Grandpa was not himself. He had asked her twice when the next batch of post-op patients was due, what was keeping the surgeons. In his day, he proclaimed, doctors had known not to dilly-dally around. She had caught him talking about the Battle of the Sambre as if it were happening now.

"But that was the last war, doctor," Jo had said quietly, looking into his tiny eyes hidden behind his glasses.

"Don't you presume to tell me what war I mean, you little—" and then he had caught himself, caught himself in his
own mistake, his mind seeming to clear for a moment. But not
an hour later he had told Jo she had worked long enough, her
shift was over; to go get one of the other nurses to take over
for her, she needed her rest; the other girls were getting lazy.

Now Jo stood stock-still. She could hear the doctor humming a little tune under his breath, hear the snap of canvas
as he walked out of the tent, headed God knew where; hear
the men beginning to shift and moan and complain in their
beds. They would be hungry, cold, needing their bandages,
their bedpans changed; they would need medicine, and some
of them would need surgery, and all of them would need a
miracle to get them out of there alive. Jo was out of miracles.

"Miss," came a shaky voice. "Miss."

Jo swallowed. She could not bring herself to turn around.
The tent would be empty of personnel, and she needed to see
it full and bustling again, with orderlies, surgeons, dentists,
doctors, nurses—above all else the nurses, dozens of nurses
keeping soul and body together by their skill and their sheer
determination. She looked out of the corner of her eye and
saw Gianni standing there, watching her, the back of his
thumb pressed to his lips pensively, impatient. He had been
there all night, hovering just out of reach, not replaying his
last moments for her as he always did but waiting impatiently.
Waiting for her. Queenie and the other nurses had joined him
already but, by a twist of fate, not her, not Josie. He was waiting for Josie.

"Miss." The voice was higher now, in pain.

What did they want from her? Her youth and her beauty
and her health were all gone; her very will to survive had left

her. What did it matter now if the Germans won? Would it be that different? The Germans were cold and starving and dying, just like they were. Their women had lost their babies; their mothers had lost their sons. *Die here or die at home, you are equally alone . . . come to me, come to where you will never be lonely again.*

Jo was shivering. Not from the cool air coming through the small flaps, not from the water that had snaked down her arms and spread out, making dark outlines in the armpits of her faded green shirt. She was shivering all over, her teeth chattering, her hands shaking; she closed her eyes tightly, shutting out the world. She was lost. She had lost everyone in her life. America was losing the war. If she died, it wouldn't make the slightest difference, not to anyone; everyone who would have cared was gone by now. Then, suddenly, she was outside herself, thinking of herself in the third person, seeing herself again as the noble, tragic heroine pushed beyond all endurance. It was easier to think about it that way, so much easier. It didn't hurt anymore because she wasn't a small, lost stranger, just a character in a play who was to be pitied, poor thing. Jo stopped shaking. Breathed deeply. She had made up her mind. She would do it, end her life; she would join him. Gianni smiled and started toward her, with that long, lanky walk of his. Jo's only fleeting regret was that there would be no one left among the living to mourn her. She turned to face her brother.

"Miss." This time, it was more a yelp than anything else. Jo whirled around angrily, a curse on her lips at this final interruption.

"Good God in heaven," she said instead.

What she saw would have been comical anywhere else at any other time. Jonesy had unhooked his leg from the wire above his bed and was half out of his cot and half into his neighbor's. There he was fending off the accursed Scotsman, who had decided, in his delirium, to teach the asthmatic a lesson. He was bringing his bedpan down again and again on the helpless man, who was wheezing audibly, hands upraised against the Scot's fury, silent and relentless. The major in the next bed watched them with glazed eyes, threw up, and rolled over, disinterested. One of the postsurgery patients was staring straight up at the tent ceiling, moving his lips silently in prayer or hallucination; the other, head and eyes bandaged, had tried getting out of bed and fallen over the surgery kits still stacked on the tent floor. Grandpa was nowhere in sight.

"Miss," Jonesy cried out again, frantically.

It might not have been funny; but the utter absurdity of the scene had the effect of cold water splashed on Jo's face. Without thinking, the nurse in her sprang into action, wrestling the Scot back to his cot, helping Jonesy back into his; she had picked up the blind man, and cleaned up the major's mess. She was struggling to lift the enormous cast, heavy and cumbersome, back onto its wire line as Jonesy prattled on in his easy, lilting voice.

"Sorry to bother you, miss, I could see you needed a moment, but there was no holding back that damned—I beg your pardon, miss—that infernal Scot. What he thought he was doing, well, no one knows, poor devil; probably thought he was fighting the Führer himself. But as my mum used to say, where there's life, there's hope. Not very original I used to think at the time, but Lord, since I've seen a bit of this war, I see how right she was. Life's the main thing, really; I mean, you never notice it until some fool's constantly trying to steal it away from you, more's the pity. When my leg got hit, I thought my number was up, I did. But it wasn't. It's not over yet for me, not if I can help it. Now, this war's put us all in a bit of a spot here, and no denying it. I'm not licked yet, mind you." He paused for breath and smiled broadly. "But I'm glad you turned around, just the same, miss. I needed you."

Jo got the cast in place and stepped away from the cot. Hearing Jonesy reduce the entire world war to "a bit of a spot" had made her throat catch, his saying he needed her had decided her. Here, then, were six people who did need her. It wasn't much, perhaps, in the grand scheme of things. They didn't even know her name. But if she weren't there, it would make a difference to these half-dozen men. It would matter to them. If she wanted to honor Queenie and all she had stood for, this was the only way to do it. This could be, small as it was, something for her to live for.

I will not lose these six men, Jo vowed to herself, repeating aloud, "I will not lose them."

"What was that, miss?" Grandpa reentered the tent, dull green cans propped under his arms, his hands laden with assorted boxes and packages. "Here, help me with all this."

"Where have you been?" Jo asked, looking at the supplies— canned meat, crackers, rice, beans.

"Foraging, miss, foraging," Grandpa answered, almost gleefully. "We've got a hospital to run, and I'll be damned if some penny-ante captain's going to keep all the supplies for his own men."

Jo smiled incredulously at the old man. "But how did you get him to give it to you?"

"Easy, miss. They were all hushing and whispering and motioning for me to get down with their guns. Seemed to be hiding from something or other. Well, I didn't put up with their shenanigans for a moment. Told them I had come for rations and would stay there and yell to high heaven until I got some." At this remembrance, the doctor cackled delightedly. "You should have seen how fast they ran to get me food." The doctor managed to remove the tricky wrapping on some ready-to-eat biscuits, crumbs flying everywhere. "Christmas!" he started yelling at the men, prancing in a circle like a satyr. "Eat up, it's Christmas!"

"Doctor," Jo began. If the Germans were anywhere near, noise was the last thing they needed. No wonder the captain had given up his supplies so readily. "*Doctor.*"

"Well, don't eat if you're not hungry, miss," the man said, turning suddenly nasty. He tossed the crackers to the ground. "The next shift will appreciate them, even if you don't. Miss McMahon, prepare the major for surgery. That appendix has got to come out."

For the first time in the war, Jo was truly scared. Surely, she had felt fear before—with their first amphibious landing— not Normandy, no, by Normandy they had known better. But in North Africa—she had felt fear there as they landed the nurses along with the infantrymen, the smaller girls sinking under the packs that weighed as much as they did, the men going down after them, hauling them back up to the surface. Then the insanity of the beach; the nurses indistinguishable in their men's uniforms, awkward and clumsy, struggling out of the breakers like drenched cats. Jo remembered bullets flying, someone yelling *Get down,* an explosion of gunfire, someone body-slamming her, pinning her to the sand, saving her life. Laying there forever in the salt and the blood, crushed by his weight, waiting for the shooting to let up. Deciding to run for the trees, thanking the soldier for protecting her, only to realize he had been dead since he fell. And for the next two days, waiting idly for the first wave of casualties to arrive, hidden in the filthy, lice-infested villa they were to use as a hospital, she had felt fear again, her first real fears of the war. So, yes, she had felt fear in North Africa, but her heart and mind had still been her own. Gianni had still lived, somewhere, on his carrier at sea; the nurses had still sung as their trucks rumbled through the scruff-lands and deserts with their headlights off. She had felt fear then, but that fear had always been outside of her, the fear of what others might do to her or to the other nurses or to their men. She had never felt a fear of what harm they might inflict upon themselves. Not like now. She was scared, and she did not know what to say to Grandpa now.

If the major's appendix was not taken out soon, he would die, that was certain. His fever was no better, his abdomen rigid and painful to the touch; he wouldn't even let her check him anymore, grabbing her wrists defensively if she tried to turn down his blanket. But Grandpa was in no condition to operate, snapped back as he was into some different time, angry one minute, giddy the next. The man was not fit to per-form surgery. But her patient—one of the patients she had so recently sworn not to lose—would die if he didn't.

"Yes, doctor," Jo mumbled, stalling for time. "Let me just check on the other patients first. Let me get them settled." *Give me a second here to get my thoughts together. I have to think of something.* She walked over to the bandaged man, sitting down beside him.

"I'm sorry, soldier, I haven't had a moment, this must all be so confusing for you," she began. *Confusing for him?* She herself didn't know which way was up. "We'll be—we'll be busy with surgery for a little while here. Is there anything I can do for you before then?"

The man reached out his maimed hand, feeling along her arm, taking her hand in his. What could she possibly give this faceless person, disfigured and blind for life most likely? Even if she had had an entire general hospital at her disposal, nobody could do anything for him.

"Yes, miss," came the quiet reply. "I've been lying here, thinking there is one thing . . ." Jo drew back within herself. *No. Don't ask me to kiss you. To take off your bandages and kiss the twisted blobs of flesh. Even on her best day, Queenie couldn't do that. Please God, not that—*

"I was wondering," he continued shyly, almost apologetically. "Could you tell me where I am?"

Jo's racing mind was stunned into silence. The man went on, slowly, deliberately.

"I can't see anything, you know. I realize I might never see anything again. But the worst part is feeling helpless, not knowing what's around me, where I am. And it would help me feel less useless too, miss. I'm not that badly off—I mean, the rest of me. Sounds like you've got your hands full here. I'm not much use now. But I'd like to at least know where I stand." Here the bandages tightened slightly, as if he were smiling underneath them. "Literally."

Jo was taken aback by the simplicity of his request, the last thing in the world she would have thought mattered amid all this chaos. "You're in a field hospital, soldier—what's your name?"

"James, miss."

"James. You're in a field hospital, James, or, really, just the tiniest piece of it—what's left of it. There used to be other tents, but—anyway. The closest tent flap is about fifteen feet from your bunk, this way." She turned his body toward it. "There is a bunk on either side of you, and three across the way. The man next to you has—well, he's seeing things right now, it's not his fault, just the fever. We'll try to keep tabs on him, but he isn't all that strong, so if he does bother you, just hold him off until I can get to you, all right? The patient to your right is pretty badly off, a paratrooper injury. I need to check on him next, but he shouldn't worry you at all. Across the way are three men—the one we are about to operate on, just an appendectomy (*"just,"* Jo thought—*good God*), one's having a little trouble breathing, and the last has a broken leg. He's a Tommy, but he's a real okay guy. It's just the one doctor and myself now, I don't know if you heard—" her voice trailed off.

"Yes, miss, I couldn't help overhearing. I'm sorry."

Jo continued quickly. "And the Germans seem to have really made some inroads around here lately, so we're trying to be as quiet as possible until the roads are—well, until we can move everybody out. By the way, I'm sure you can feel it, but the stove is directly in front of your cot, near the tent pole. Try to avoid it, James."

"Yes, miss, I have enough burns already."

She squeezed his hand. How could he joke? The world was ending and he was cracking jokes. For some reason she was so proud of him, irrationally proud, as if he were a little boy who had just gotten through a difficult recitation with no mistakes. She squeezed his hand again, unthinkingly, as she rose from his bed, not seeing him wince under his bandages, his own gratitude and affection for his nurse mingled with the agony of his raw hand.

"Hello, soldier," Jo began again, sitting down casually at

the foot of the next man's bed. Then, rereading his chart, she stood up quickly. "I'm sorry. Father." She hadn't noticed the prefix before, couldn't believe this boy in front of her could be a military chaplain. But there was the information taken down before surgery—chaplain, Catholic, date of birth, June 4, 1920. She looked again at his round, farm boy's face sprinkled with freckles, at his small, upturned nose. She imagined that in peacetime his short-cropped hair would have still run to curls, his cheeks rosy year-round, as if kissed by the sun. She curbed the desire to call him "son," repeating instead, "Father." Then, "Is there anything I can do for you?"

She had already changed his bandages in the light of the captain's forgotten flashlight. She remembered his massive abdominal injuries, looking like he had been shredded, slashed by a dozen knives. They had patched him up the best they could, hoping Evac would be able to do more for him later on, loaded him up with penicillin. There was a good chance he would make it, physically. But now he lay there straight and silent, his hands folded neatly over his chest as if he were already laid out for burial, staring straight up but not at Jo—he hadn't even turned his head when she spoke. She looked into his eyes—pupils regular, equal, round; they had reacted normally to the light of the flashlight when she had checked him earlier. Not his brain, then, but something more, something deeper, was damaged. He probably would have called it his soul. She placed a hand on his, and, almost imperceptibly, his body stiffened.

As she crossed the tent, Jo avoided even looking at the major, who was twisted under his blanket, moaning. She sat down, instead, with her back to him, on his bunkmate's bed and listened to his lungs.

"How did you ever get into this war?" she asked him bluntly.

"I lied," came the equally pointed response.

"I see. You must have always had this asthma, even as a little boy?"

"Oh, yes, miss. Used to scare my mother something fierce." Here he had to pause to breathe, fast, little breaths, the oxygen never reaching his constricted blood vessels; breathing in and breathing out virtually nothing. "I was air raid warden, but that just didn't seem good enough. Not for me. Not for my girl either. I mean, people started to talk, why wasn't I doing my duty—"

"But that's ridiculous. You can't serve if you can't even breathe."

"That's what I found out, miss." His blue lips curved wryly. "I could fudge my way good enough when I was well. But ever since I caught this—"

He couldn't continue, his chest rising and falling rapidly, looking for all the world like a fish out of water, drowning in a sea full of air he could not use.

"That's enough for now—William?" she asked, checking his chart.

"Bill, if you don't mind, miss. Billy, if you could manage it."

"I'll see what I can do. All right, I have a couple of things I have to take care of first—but first chance I get, I'll be over with some hot water. Growing up, I used to babysit these two awful twins next apartment over. They got croup regular, so there's not much I can't do with a towel and some steam."

Billy tried to smile, his dark lips looking ghastly in his pale face. Jo patted his foot under the blanket and moved on.

"You still okay, Jonesy?" Jo asked.

"Yes, miss. Is there anything I can do for you?" He looked up expectantly, like a spaniel.

"God bless you, Jonesy, yes. Here," she said, picking up the fruits of Grandpa's labors, strewn over the floor, "I don't know when we'll get more food, so this has got to last; but could you see about opening one or two things? Anyone in here who can eat should get a little something. You too, Jonesy."

"Oh, I ate two days ago, miss," he replied, grinning, happily sorting out the various cans and boxes on his blanket. Jo tried to think of a time when a rejoinder like that might have been taken as a joke, and failed.

Jo needed more time to stall. Unless she was ready to risk the major's life, that only left one patient. She picked up his chart and read aloud over the now-inert figure of the Scot: "David MacPherson. Well, you've been a regular pain in the ass, David, and that's a fact."

"Not as much as you," came his immediate reply.

"David?" she asked, astonished, sitting down next to him and pulling back his eyelids. "Can you hear me?"

"Not as much as you, Bumpy. You're ever so much heavier. Get off and give me a turn."

Jo sighed. No, the penicillin couldn't have acted that quickly, even at the high dose she had been giving him through the night. There were only four more tablets in the box she still carried around in her trousers—would it be enough? Another box might have done it, but there simply wasn't any more; penicillin had been the first thing they packed up. And post-surgery, what would the major do without it, even if he did survive the appendectomy? She thought of how their lives had changed since 1943, when Washington started sending over the miracle drug. At first they hadn't known what it could do, treating it as interchangeable with sulfa, as something to help out, to cut down on infection. And then, before they knew it, they were using it for everything—gunshot wounds, infectious disease, postsurgery, VD—and miraculously, their mortality rate plummeted to 4 percent. Four. That meant, if they managed to pull a boy off of the field, he had a 96 percent chance of surviving. Incredible. Jo shook her head, fingering the battered cardboard box with something bordering on awe. If they somehow ever managed to win this war, it would be in large part due to the tiny pills rattling around inside the box—the "secret weapon" the Germans wanted so badly but had, as of yet, been unable to reproduce.

"Come along, David, let's do this again." She cradled his head in her arm, lifting her canteen to his mouth. "No, Kit, tell Bumpy it's his turn." At least she could make out his words today, if not his meaning; his blue eyes were open now, staring through rather than at her face as she looked down on him. "All right, all right, David, I will, but only if you take this."

"No, I don't want to take it. Make Bumpy take it."

"I will, he'll take it next, I promise. Just open up."

"That was nasty, I don't like it."

"It wasn't nasty, David," she said, replacing his head gently, as he swallowed. "It might have just saved your life."

Jo was used to treating dozens, even hundreds of men on one shift, and practice had made her too efficient. Long before she was ready, the five patients' needs had been taken care of and Jonesy had handed around some meager rations. There was nothing left but her surgery patient. Every inch of her—her training, her common sense—cried out in protest that she could not put her patient at risk like this. Yet avoiding one risk would only bring on another, even greater one. She would have to try to talk to Grandpa, to gauge how severe his mental shock was, to see if there was any chance of the surgery succeeding.

At one corner of the tent, the nurses had set up three sheets—"three sheets to the wind," Queenie had always quipped, grinning wickedly. One was clamped to the ceiling of the tent—just like the sheets that used to hang over each operating table—and the other two were hanging down at right angles, making a little enclosure—the "nurses' office," they used to call it, though it looked more like a changing room in a thrift store. Here they could talk briefly, away from the patients and doctors, discuss their schedules, give advice on difficult cases. More practically, in a world with no privacy, here was a place they could duck into for a moment—to curse under their breath, say a quiet prayer, adjust a falling brassiere strap—before walking back out, ready for whatever faced them. Now Grandpa sat in their inner sanctum, on the huge packing cases Jo had slept on fitfully the night before. He was kicking his heels against the green metal boxes like a boy at a soda shop counter. Jo tried to swallow and stood in front of him, unsure of how to begin.

"Is the major ready for surgery, miss?"

"Doctor," Jo hesitated. "I know you'll forgive me for saying this, but I'm not sure you're up for this surgery."

In fact, Jo was not at all sure he would forgive her for that outrage. After all, how could she, a lieutenant ("with only *relative* rank, miss—I'll be damned if I call any woman 'Lieutenant' "), dare question him, a doctor? But to her amazement, he stopped kicking his heels, raised his eyes to hers, and smiled, chuckling good-naturedly.

"Now, maybe you're right, miss, after all. I don't know when I've been so tired . . . just plum tuckered out." Then he seemed to brighten up a little.

"Have you ever been to Savannah, miss? No? Well, that's

a great pity, a great pity indeed. I'm from Tybee Island, to be exact, miss, spared by the Yankees along with Savannah. It's what they call a barrier island—Tybee means 'salt' in the Euchee tongue of the ancient Indians. It's a wonderful place, miss. I've been thinking of it a great deal today."

Jo searched the old man's face for signs of mental instability, but he seemed more lucid than he had been since he had received his initial shock. As if reading her thoughts, he smiled—a benign, paternal smile.

"No, miss. I know where I am. I'm here with you, in hell. I'm not on those beaches of my youth, watching dolphins leap out of the water or those old pelicans dive into the sea. I'm not a small boy swimming with sea turtles or running along the sand to Fort Screven and catching it from my mammy because I was late coming in. Did you know the rifled cannon was first shot from Tybee Island on April 11, 1862? Fired from the island to Fort Pulaski, which surrendered in thirty hours—thirty hours, miss, imagine that—making all such brick fortifications obsolete after that."

The old man's eyes shone at the military accomplishment, as if it had just happened, as if it mattered. He took hold of Jo's hand, gently covering her scarred fingers with his wrinkled ones, tapping the back of her hand reassuringly. "Now, don't bother your head none over me, miss. I reckon I got one more surgery left in me someplace. Go on now and get the patient ready. It's just like my mammy always said."

The doctor stopped speaking, smiling warmly at the recollection.

"What did she say, doctor?"

"Hmm? Oh, my mammy? She was a woman all right, let me tell you. Well, it was a rhyme, a special favorite of hers, let's see if I can recite it for you. It began, *W'en you gits up frum de table* . . . Give me a minute here, Lieutenant, it'll come to me."

Jo walked out of the small enclosure; it had been closer in there than she had thought. It was much cooler outside in the tent; she felt like she used to feel when she had been a little girl playing under her sheets, using up all of the air until it was too hot and stuffy for her to stand it any longer, then throwing off the sheets and blankets and taking in great gulps of fresh air, relieved. She walked toward the major, who was resting fitfully on his cot. Maybe he could actually survive the surgery. Maybe Grandpa could help him. Maybe she wouldn't lose him after all.

From behind the sheets she could hear the doctor fumbling over the lines of the old nursery rhyme.

"*W'en you gits up frum de table, don't cha nevuh knock ovur de table* . . . no, that doesn't make sense. *Don't cha nevuh knock ovur de chair* . . . yes, that's more like it. How did the rest go? *W'en you gits up frum de table, don't cha nevuh knock ovur de chair* . . . oh, hello, Miss Carroll, it's about time you showed up for your shift."

Jo stiffened, dropping the surgery kit she had just hoisted off the ground. She wheeled around to face the enclosure, shaking violently. Time seemed to stand still. Everything stood out in sharp relief—the signpost that used to hang outside the tent, now carelessly discarded in a corner, CLEAR WEAPONS BEFORE ENTERING; the sound of Jonesy's fingernails as he scratched hopelessly at his cast; the ringing in her ears, the thudding of her own heart in her chest. She took a wobbly step forward.

"*W'en you gits up frum de table, don't cha nevuh knock ovur de chair, kase ef you do, just as sho's yo' bawn* . . . sure as you're born *what*, confound it?"

"*Lieutenant,*" she thought suddenly, her legs starting to buckle. *He called me "Lieutenant."* "Grandpa," she called out, her voice sounding foreign to her own ears, as if coming from someone else and from a long way off; her feet refusing to move; her chest tightening in panic. "Grandpa."

Jonesy stopped scratching and looked up at her, alarmed.

"*Kase ef you do just as sho's yo' bawn, you won' git marrit dis year,*" Grandpa's manic voice ended, triumphantly. Then, as if she knew it was going to happen, as if it was a scene from a third-rate play coming from offstage, a gun went off, blood splattering in stark relief over the whiteness of the hanging sheets. At the sound, her legs suddenly were under her control again, and she ran in to see the old man, dark blood oozing like molasses from his temple, the pistol still gripped in his weathered hand, the words of his mammy's nursery rhyme still dancing crazily in her head.

4

Kay Elliott

May 1942, Malinta Tunnel, Corregidor

Dear Jo,
You will never read this letter, but I have to write it.
Addressing it to you helps me pretend, for a few more hours
anyway, that you can hear me. That what has happened to
me—that what will happen to me shortly—matters. Because,
of course, it doesn't. Not to you, and not to anyone, anymore.
Not even to me. But it helps me pretend, like I said. And I
can't die this way, without even being able to think. I need to
see, on paper anyway, the tangle of my life pulled out straight,
for one second even, before the whole thing recoils, the knot's
cut, and I die. Dear Jo, thank God you didn't come here.

Kay squinted in the half-light to see what she had written.
The generators had been straining all night, surging, growing
dim; suddenly, they went out altogether and Kay noted that
the complaints and curses that usually accompanied the blackouts were absent. It was already like a tomb.

She couldn't see to write any longer, but Kay's mind wandered back to last year, to when she first arrived. She could see
herself walking down the gangplank, dazzled by the vibrant

blue of Pearl Harbor, the sun sparkling on the water; she could feel the heat sinking into her bones once more—but, beneath all that intensity, there had been a kind of peace. She knew it sounded like a dime novel when she wrote home about it, but the breeze really did kiss her face, it was so soft and wet and muted, the water seemed to lap playfully at her toes. She had been young and she had been beautiful and she had run along the beaches singing and screaming for sheer joy. What the hell had she been thinking? Death was just around the corner. But no one had known that then.

The hospital where she was assigned was so different from the one she had worked at with Jo. In New York, there had been steam heat hissing angrily against sealed gray windows, the slushy coldness of an October rain trying to get inside. Here, it was piercing hot sun sneaking through chinks in wooden shutters. Enormous fans spinning lazily overhead, so slowly you could watch the blades go round. Bare legs, and short work shifts for the girls because of the temperature. Some of the nurses had slept during the heat of the day, but not Kay. She was down at the water every chance she got, burning her white skin brown, swimming in a jungle teeming with life, nothing like the cold, dead quarries back home. Swaying kelp, Moorish Idol fish, huge manta rays, and the thousands of oysters that gave the harbor its name. It was on the beach that she had first met him.

Kay could think about Aaron now. Now that she was about to die. That was the only way she could stand it. She knew that Jo would never really read her letter, that no one would ever really read it, so that made it okay, too, to give him life again, to make him real once more. She couldn't die without thinking of him one last time. So she let herself drift back, allowing herself to remember part of the story, just the tiniest part. The part where they met on the beach, in the sand and the sun.

Kay had written to Jo then, on a postcard with a hula dancer on the front. She had started it, "Jo, I've met a man," but never got past that line because he had walked into the room just then and scooped her up in his arms and carried her into the bedroom of the bungalow they were sharing, the waves crashing against its long stork legs standing high above the water, making a sound that was even louder than they were.

Jo, I've met a man. And what a man. Every day after they had first met, he would be waiting for her after her shift, out there on the dusty, sunbathed street. He was so unlike the other officers she worked with and laughed with and danced with each night. Aaron was like his fellow officers in appearance only—handsome in his daytime khakis, irresistible in his white dinner jacket—but he lacked their sophistication, the witty repartee the nurses had gotten used to, debutantes as they were on that glittering isle of embassy balls and formal dinners. Aaron had wanted her. He hadn't wanted to take her out on long drives along the coast. He hadn't wanted the thrill of the chase. He had wanted Kay, desperately, with a passion she couldn't comprehend at first. Standing outside the hospital and staring at her as she slowly descended those huge, stone stairs after her shift, his face lighting up like he had seen a vision. Handing her the tropical flower he was holding, his huge hand brushing her tiny one almost reverently, the electricity palpably passing through his fingers into hers. *I want you, Kay,* he would say. Just that. Simply that.

But she had not been ready to be caught. She had always joked with Jo about not settling too soon. *Play the field a little first,* they had laughed, *see what's out there.* And what a field it was. The men were wild about the new nurses—every night another party, another dance, some new form of excitement, of dalliance. It went to their heads. The wit and the banter. The allure of dark, foreign men with their suave accents, kissing the girls' suntanned hands. The flashy American officers with their smiles and their ready drinks. The venerable ambassador and his glittering circle of exotic friends. Kay was a small-town girl, but no one had known that. To them she was a sophisticated American, a belle even, desirable and desired by a room with ten men to every girl. But just when she was caught up in all that, swollen by flattery, she caught sight of Aaron on the far side of the room, just gazing at her, longingly, hungrily. Her heart stopped at that naked desire, the pain in his eyes at not having her. The lights had dimmed and the tinkle of crystal and the murmur of the guests had faded away. Then there had been only the two of them, running down to the water in the deepening twilight, Kay losing her heels in the sand, wading up to their waists in the rolling waves, kissing each other madly, her wet ball gown clinging to her body, the weight of it pulling her down, Aaron's strong arms holding her, pulling her up toward his waiting mouth. They were in love.

Marry me, Kay, he had said in November, before she had been there a month. He was a captain, he had some money put away, he would inherit his family's vineyards in California or something. Who cared what he was saying? Kay realized she could live a thousand years and never find a man who would want her that much. His wanting awoke something inside her, something she hadn't even known was there. She tackled him and said yes, and their joy exploded, and he was fending her off with one arm the whole time he was trying to get the chaplain on the phone—*There was the rumor of war, sir, could we marry right away, without the exemption? Yes, sir, I'll hold.*

So they were married. She had begun to write Jo about it, but he had picked her up and carried her away, and then later there was no time to write because their world had ended and Pearl Harbor itself was burning.

Dear Jo, thank God you didn't come here.

The lights flickered on for a second before going out again, and Kay reread that line. She felt as if she had to think of everything, remember everything, regret everything, one last time.

She regretted every moment. Every moment she had spent dancing with other men, all the nonsense she had said, the foolish, empty, stupid talk. All the jokes she had laughed at. Every time she had turned her cheek at the last second to tease some would-be suitor and thwart his kiss. She regretted every party and every dance and every dinner when she wasn't with Aaron. She regretted that she didn't sleep with him the second they both knew they wanted each other; she regretted not going to him that very first day, giving herself to him completely, running down those stairs, and throwing herself into his arms. What had she been waiting for? She had never loved like that before—no one had, no one ever could love like that again, she had been a fool to wait even a few days. But how could they have known that a few days would be all that was left to anyone?

She allowed herself to remember Aaron, some parts of his whole. His deadly earnest, his face when he wanted her, his face when he had her; his sudden high spirits, when he'd be giddy as a schoolboy; his laughing and laughing and trying not to laugh as he waited on hold for the Protestant minister to come back to the phone, slapping her backside and telling her to behave. Those parts she let herself recall.

Then there were other things, even now, even with death staring her in the face, that she could not, would not bring back.

Then there were also things she would have chosen to forget because, without their even knowing it, they had been the precursors of doom. Like that time, newly married, when he had let her shampoo his hair, him sitting up to the armpits in soapy bath water, his knees big and bony in front of him in that tiny tub, holding a scrub brush in one hand like it was a wand, chatting about a war, *It's not a real war, it doesn't matter, it'll never touch us*. It was just the same as when he talked about baseball, or his favorite brand of cigarettes, or anything at all—*Keep talking, darling*.

There was a noise far down the tunnel, voices and then someone yelling. The words were too muffled to make out, but Kay knew what they meant. She was already up to the third sentence when the lights came back on, contracting her pupils, blinding her for a second, but she kept writing, kept writing as long as she could.

I'm running out of time. This is it for us. I don't need to write anymore, Jo, I don't need to tell you where I am or how I got here or where Aaron is now or how the Japanese destroyed our air force in one morning or how we rushed across the airfield at Clark, pulling burning bodies off of the tarmac, or how I wish I was home, how I wish I was already dead and never had to see a Japanese straddled over me, defiling me like some Chinese village girl, and I hope you are alive and safe and that you win this war and that you never come here. Or come here much later, Jo, come with the whole army and stop these men. Because they are brutal and because they are cruel and because I am scared and I didn't think I could even feel fear anymore, but I do. The world is ending for me, Jo. I hear them in the tunnel. They're coming

5

Jo McMahon

Spring 1945, The Western Front

Jo made the first incision. She had already shaved the curly hairs off of Major Donahue's abdomen, painted his bloated belly with iodine. The scalpel was razor-sharp. A bright red line followed neatly in its wake, the blood suspended for a moment in time, not moving; then gravity pulled it down the man's sides in little rivulets, staining the sheets, dripping down noiselessly to the mud floor below.

Jonesy looked sick as he held the ether mask in place, whether from the sight of blood or from the escaping fumes Jo couldn't tell. She was through the epidermis now, hitting the tiny bleeders. Next came a layer of fat; she could feel her scalpel sink through it like butter. Then muscle; then something coarse and fibrous impeded her blade. *Shit, the greater omentum, I've cut it too high.* She had known she was too high, knew she might run into that thick layer of fat and lymph and connective tissue, but it was that or risk cutting the internal iliac artery. *One nick of that and he's done. God knows where it is now.* It would have been adjacent to a healthy appendix, she knew, but with this one so swollen and distended, it could have been pushed anywhere by now. *This is like walking in a minefield,* Jo thought and swallowed, her throat feeling like broken glass.

The tent was quiet now. The captain and his men had left. They had rushed in at the sound of the shot, weapons drawn, and found Jo standing over the dead man, not moving, not speaking. She had no memory of the questions the captain had asked her, she had not heard him order the men to remove the body; she hadn't heard the familiar sound of shovel against dirt and stone and a new grave being dug. She was beyond that now.

She glanced up again at Jonesy, who was turning green, and at James, his head still bandaged, who was holding a surgery lamp in place. *The blind leading the blind,* Jo thought abstractedly, wondering who on earth had asked him to help. She finally decided that, although she had no recollection of it, she must have done it herself.

Jo considered making another incision, lower down, but she had already compromised the muscle and another incision made so close to the first would be difficult to heal—assuming he would ever have time to heal. She widened the existing cut, tugging at the sides to open it further, asking Jonesy for the retractors. When he didn't move, she said impatiently, "The things like scissors that don't cross in the middle—come on." He seemed to wake up, handing her the tools, one by one, with his gloved hand. She pulled back hard and locked them into place, looking inside. She had missed the internal iliac by two full inches, but come dangerously close to the larger, right common. *God, robbing Peter to pay Paul.* But she had missed them both.

Jo thought of the first appendectomy she had observed, back in training in Tennessee. They were about to be deployed, and she hadn't seen one yet, so the head nurse had arranged for her to be driven to the segregated "colored" ward on base. Jo remembered how everyone had stared at her, a white nurse, come down to their end of camp. She remembered the dark faces of the men in their cots; the contrast between the white starched uniforms of the nurses and their ebony skin; the black doctors, the young ones with regulation buzz cuts, the older men with wiry gray hair standing up straight from their heads. She had donned her surgical clothes and stood in a corner of the tiny operating room. She remembered the figures huddled around the patient, indistinguishable from the people she worked with every day except for the dark skin showing above their masks, the rest of their bodies swathed in impeccable surgical white. She hadn't seen much of that surgery, and she certainly hadn't learned enough to perform one now. But Jo still remembered her genuine surprise that there was a whole parallel hospital within a hospital—a world that, except on this one rare occasion, never touched hers and that up until that point Jo had never even known existed. The black soldier on the table that night had made it under those skilled hands, the color of which hadn't mattered in the least to his survival. Jo's white fingers were unsure now, and trembling.

When Jo looked at the appendix, she didn't know what it was at first; it was so large and misshapen and not neatly tucked next to the cecum, as it had been on her anatomy charts in school. Half of it was black and necrotic. She blinked slowly, the bright light from the lamp searing her brain. Her mouth felt dry. She eased the slippery, quivering mass through the opening, feeling along it for its base, for where it connected with the mesoappendix. At any point, the appendix could rupture, spilling its deadly contents into the abdominal cavity;

one nick, one split, and it would all be over. Jonesy was looking away, burying his face in his sleeve, the smell of surgery—
something Jo no longer even noticed—overcoming him. What
James felt beneath his layers of bandages, no one could tell. Jo's
fingers came to the end of the wriggling form, to the vascula-
ture containing the nerves and blood endings that would have
to be ligated first.

"Jonesy," she said, her hands shaking. She was feeling giddy,
though not from the surgery—surely not that anymore, she
had assisted at a hundred worse than this. Missing arms, missing faces; an embedded, undetonated bazooka shell stuck in
someone's leg; GI surgeries with white worms crawling freely
in stomachs and intestines, the doctors only stopping to pluck
out the ones in their way, their hundreds of companions being
sewn back up into parasitic bellies. No, Jo was trembling now
from being so close. She was minutes away from this patient
actually having a chance at survival. And Jonesy wasn't re-
sponding.

"Jonesy, I know this is rough if you're not used to it"—
here Jonesy threw up—"but I need just a little more help. The
thing that looks like a loop, kind of like a clamp with thread,
I need that." Jonesy tried throwing up again, but there wasn't
enough food in his stomach and he just dry-heaved a couple of
times. "And I need it *now,* Jonesy."

Jonesy finally proffered the implement, which Jo snatched
from him quickly. In a moment, she had drawn two tight
loops around the thin neck of the mesoappendix, pulling it
tight, stopping the flow of blood. Then, with one deft stroke
of the scalpel, the appendix was out. She dropped it cursorily
into the basin on the floor, where it exploded, filling the tent
with an odor of death. Jo exhaled. Then she began the repair.

Jo began the careful suturing of the layers of fascia and tissue with a mindlessness borne of exhaustion and shock. The stitches were perfect, beautiful, each exactly the same. As she mechanically finished each layer, Jonesy shook powdered sulfa over everything, at her direction. Her concentration was solely on the work in front of her, and yet, at the same time, she was elsewhere, reliving past events, her gloved fingers stitching and pulling and stitching again.

Thoughts came to her randomly. She couldn't find an apartment. Kay couldn't. That was how they had met. Jo and Kay had just finished their first practical. Jo was walking out when she noticed the quiet girl still sitting at her lab bench.

"Hey, you okay? My name's Jo."

"Oh, hi," the other girl had said demurely, looking uncertainly at the waxed floor and smoothing a strawberry-blond wisp back into place. Then looking up, she suddenly gathered courage. "Actually, no. I thought I had an apartment, it was all set up, but now I don't, and I've been washing up in the lavatory here before class the last two mornings, and I don't know what I'm going to do."

The girl looked surprised at herself. She hadn't meant to say so much.

"And it's Kay, by the way. My name's Kay."

That had been the start of it. At first the savvy New Yorker had just felt sorry for the small-town girl bewildered and lost in a big city. But then—somewhere between apartment hunting and Saturdays at Coney and studying for finals and exchanging family stories—something had clicked. They were such an unlikely pair, thrown together from worlds apart. Jo knew the best place to get a corned beef sandwich and which museums were free when. She explained with infinite patience the labyrinthine subway system, which Kay would never understand. Jo talked back to cat-calling men, shutting them up in two languages. (Kay was amazed by that and a little shocked.) But Kay opened up a new world for Jo too. Here was someone who didn't even remember when her family had come over: "We've just always been Americans, I guess." It was so long ago—"My great-great-great-great-something or other, Jo, I can't recall"—that the names, the date, all was lost to memory. They'd always lived there, Kay told her, snug and high up in the mountains. Walking to church, working the land until the mines opened up, and then working the land from the inside out. Watching the endless seasons change, but never changing themselves. In Jo's mind, Kay was what Jo was but what Jo could never be—American. But the kind of American who almost took that identity for granted. Who walked around with a self-confidence, a self-assurance that Jo couldn't assume no matter how hard she tried. Jo felt that she had to scrap every day to prove she was equal. That she was good enough. That she *was* in fact an American. Jo had always been envious of—had always thought she hated—those Americans who knew only one language and one home and one way of life. But Kay made them vulnerable. Kay made them real.

And then we both joined the Army. What were we thinking. That it'd be fun?

Jo thought of the rough crossing of the Atlantic. With Kay already in the Pacific, what had started out as an adventure for Jo quickly became monotonous, even dangerous; she remembered someone had actually died from seasickness. Waiting impatiently in England. Sailing for North Africa, discovering the mountain of amputated limbs there when they arrived, left by the German forces they were pursuing, not even burned but rotting in the desert sun. The Christmases they had tried to keep, the paper decorations and cutout stars, the one good dress the girls had passed around in shifts when they had thrown a holiday dance. Jo had had to stuff its bodice with tissue paper to fill it out when it had been her turn to wear it. The time when they were struggling across the African plains and both sides had actually called a truce to empty the battlefield of wounded. Like kids playing tag and suddenly calling "time out." The tanks—the German Panzers with their incredible range, the American "popguns," little more than mobile, flammable gas tanks—had stopped their fighting, and medics from both armies had pulled the hundreds of maimed and bleeding men out of harm's way. Then they had started killing each other once more.

She thought of the graves detail, "the worst job in the Army," Queenie had always called it, the job they gave to the "queer" ones, to the gays who got past the filters and the draft boards. They were the janitors of the war, bringing up the straggling rear, collecting the dead the corpsmen left behind. They would pull off one of the twin dogtags to send to Washington that would generate the yellow telegram that would destroy yet another family, leaving the other on the body—when there was a body. When there wasn't, they played a macabre game of eeny-meeny-miny-mo, trying to match torsos with nearby arms and legs, assembling "bodies" made up of a half-dozen men, stuffing them into body bags, erring on the side of sending heroes to their final repose with too few instead of too many limbs. Jo wondered how they could stand the job and its utter hopelessness, how they could do it day in and day out, and not go crazy. Then she thought of the chaplains, of every denomination, who had gotten together and given the men on the detail all their alcohol rations so they could get drunk and forget their world for a while.

She closed.

Her hands had been working all the while and, without even noticing it, she had closed. She glanced up at Jonesy, nodded slightly; he removed the ether mask, the sickeningly sweet residue filling the air. That was all she could do. There was no more penicillin. Jonesy had made a little makeshift wheelchair out of a cart on casters and a broken chair, and he slowly wheeled himself to the tent flap, taking in deep drafts of air. Jo removed her gloves and took the lamp from James. He didn't even need her help now to negotiate his way back to his cot. Jo instinctively wanted to remove the bloodied sheets from under her patient, but decided against it. The major needed to be still, to have time to wake up, or not wake up—either way. But she had done all she could for him.

Everyone else in the tent was asleep. Billy's breathing had improved with the steam tent; David was quiet, if still incoherent when awake; the priest ("Fr. Justus Hook," the chart read) had finally unclasped his hands, but his face in repose looked more like a cadaver's than ever.

Jo walked over to the corner where the doctor had taken his own life and started ripping off the white sheets still spattered with blood, now dried and brown. She grabbed these, along with the accumulated linen of the tent, and headed outside into the chilly daylight. None of the captain's men were in sight; they were on patrol again, looking for the enemy, remaining hidden themselves. She threw the sheets and towels into the boiling cauldron she had heated earlier—an old drum, fueled by scrap wood and discarded packing crates. She threw the towels in with bleach and soap and stirred its heavy weight slowly with a two-by-four, like a witch from a fairy tale.

Jo watched the swirling water tinged with pink and her thoughts left North Africa, sailing for Italy once more aboard the HMS *Newfoundland*, painted white with an enormous red cross visible on it, lit up like a Christmas tree in a world of blackouts to proclaim itself a hospital ship. How very formal and refined the British "sisters" had seemed to the Yankee nurses; how even the name of their branch—the Queen Alexandra Imperial Military Nursing Service—had made them sound like royalty. How easy the sailing had been, at first, with only two patients. Then the heat had started, almost tropical for September. In the open air, with the wind, it had been bearable, but below decks the thermometer had stuck at the top. The nurses sweltered, tossing in the night, unable to sleep.

"Queenie," one of the girls complained, "I can't sleep. This is hotter than Alabama down here. The thermometer read 118 when we came to bed."

"Take your clothes off, sugar."

There had been nervous giggles from some of the girls.

"No, I mean it. It's just us girls down here, and it's dark as pitch anyway."

"Are you naked, Queenie?"

"Of course."

"Jo, how 'bout you?"

Jo had stripped down to her undershorts.

"Just about, Ellie. Now go to sleep. Or not. But quit whining about the heat. It'll be dawn in an hour or so and—"

It was then that the aerial bomb had hit. Below decks, the

girls had not heard the single plane approaching, had not seen
it close in on its illuminated target. The side of the ship was
there one minute, dark and impassable, trapping in the heat
and the air, suffocating the girls; the next moment there was
a smash and a whooshing sound and Jo's eardrum ruptured
and anything that wasn't fastened down was sucked out of the
gaping hole in the hull. There were alarms going off, whistles
sounding, men yelling above them on deck. Everything was
noise and confusion and, above it all, Queenie screaming at her
girls to line up, to get out, to leave no one behind.

"Our clothes!" someone was saying. Smoke began to filter
into the darkness around them. They could hear the men
coughing outside.

"Forget them, they're gone," Queenie snapped, pushing the
girls in front of her toward the door.

"But our clothes!" The girls themselves were coughing now,
the black smoke mixing with the black of the night, the heat
from the spreading fire adding to the heat already engulfing
them.

"My rosary," another voice called shrilly, a girl suddenly
breaking from the column and heading back toward where her
bunk had been.

Jo grabbed her arm, smoke burning her own eyes. "We'll
get you another one in Rome, sweetie. Just get back in line."

The girls were climbing the ladder and staggering out into
the black morning, their modesty conflicting with their in-
stinctual need for air. They stood on the deck, huddled together, arms crossed in front of pale breasts, turning sideways,
toward the bulkhead, toward the stern, staring at the huge
pillar of smoke rising from just behind the bridge, at the fire

snaking its way across the ship. Queenie was the last one out. She was holding her arm at a weird angle and didn't seem to be able to move it.

"Jo, someone needs to go back in there and make sure everybody's out."

There was no other way to check. They couldn't be sure how many girls had actually been down there when the bomb hit. Someone was always heading to the lavatories or getting up for a glass of water. The captain had forbidden it, but several girls had even been desperate enough from the heat that they had slept on the tilting decks, risking being rolled, silently, into a dark sea.

Smoke was visibly coming from the doorway as Jo darted inside. She could hear someone frantically say, "You'll get the Purple Heart for this, Jo," but then she was down there, the water up to her ankles already, ducking under the smoke, feeling behind overturned cots, in corners, calling out for anyone who could hear her. Her throat was raw from yelling, and from the smoke, but she didn't climb out again until she was certain they had all made it. When she emerged, men were running by with buckets and hoses, turning their heads toward the girls, unsure of what they were seeing in the uncertain light of the fires.

"Thank God you're okay, Jo. You're a hero either way," and then Queenie had winced a little in pain, from her arm. "We're abandoning ship, the girls first anyway. They don't think they can stop the fire. Come on, ladies."

Queenie cradled her bad arm and led the way, holding her head up high as if she wasn't buck naked, as if this was something her training had prepared her for. Several of the British nurses met up with them along the way, also heading for the life rafts, disheveled and confused and scared. And then they heard the scream.

It was one of the sisters. The cabin she was in was on fire—its door had been completely smashed in with the impact. There was no way out, and she was sticking her head out of the porthole and screaming. The nurses all stopped in their tracks, horrified; the men who were nearby stopped fighting the fire and yelled orders, trying to get to the door, but it was buried under a ton of twisted steel and cable. They couldn't reach her. The nurse kept screaming. It was the worst sound in the world, the worst thing anyone had ever listened to. The women forgot their own fear, their own nakedness and vulnerability, and stood there, petrified, their bare feet rooted in place, unable to cry or pray or scream themselves but just watch, appalled, mesmerized, unable to look away.

"The door is gone, it's gone, there's no way for us to get in, this window's too small."

There was a man outside her porthole now trying to talk to her, trying to explain why they couldn't get to her, gesturing wildly with his hands and pointing. Standing alongside him was a teenage cabin boy, fourteen at best, eyes wide, mouth open in panic. Then the fire reached her and her scream redoubled and her hair alighted and the cabin boy picked up a two-by-four off the deck and brought it down on the back of her head and he started crying and she was dead.

The cinders were in their eyes now, making the nurses blink, forcing them to shuffle out of the wind. "To the lifeboats," someone ordered gruffly, a potbellied man with thick spectacles he kept taking off and rubbing with his shirtfront and putting back on, not realizing it was his tears that made him unable to see.

The boats were being lowered with the first of the nurses—the British sisters inconsolable, the American women silent, in shock. There was another explosion as the oil tank ignited, shaking the ship. Jo grabbed on to the rigging as the lifeboat she watched being lowered struck the side of the ship sharply. She looked around the deck. She didn't see any of the doctors. No one would ever see them again, bunking, as they had been, beneath the bridge. The nurses waited numbly in line, the first light of dawn revealing their figures to the unsuspecting men. Jo's face burned in spite of herself.

"Here you go, miss," said the sailor standing next to her, taking off his shirt.

All around the deck now, men were taking off their shirts, their pants, handing them to the naked girls, who hurriedly put them on, not daring to even raise their eyes in their tangled mess of rage and shame.

"Thank you," Jo murmured. Her fingers were having trouble with the buttons. Only then did she realize that they had been burnt.

"It's okay, miss. They're sending the Tommys over here to pick you up, and I'd be damned to see a sister of mine picked up—well, like that, miss."

Jo stopped stirring and pulled out the heavy sheets, wringing them with her hands. They were more gray than white as she slung them over the thick rope clothesline they had forgotten to take down in their hurry to evacuate. Then the towels, the washcloths—she scalded her hands scooping out the last of the linen with her makeshift paddle. She was no longer off the coast of Salerno, no longer that young nurse being lowered in a lifeboat in a man's shirt smelling of sweat and tobacco; she could no longer hear the frantic screams of that poor nurse, or the desolate sobs of the child who killed her. Jo was here, in this dirty yard, where the water was running off the sheets, making little channels in the dirt. That sister had died, and Queenie had died, and most of those girls sweltering away on the *Newfoundland* that night had died too, half a mile from where she stood now staring at the dirty wash water, kicking out the last of the fire. She thought vaguely about the major, wondering if he was dead. She tried to rouse herself enough to go in and check, but failed. Instead, she stood looking at the deserted clearing where, so recently, an entire field hospital had stood, on the very edge of a war they were now losing. It seemed wrong that she alone should still be alive—wrong, but not sad. No, nothing was sad anymore. She had shut herself off—or the part of herself that had been lovable, that had been her, she had shut that off. The woman who stood alone now among the damp sheets was not herself. This woman might have cheated death, but had not won life in the process.

"We need to get them the fuck out of here."

"Yeah, but how?"

Two soldiers rounded the medical tent: a young man with veiled eyes and a curling lip, and the captain. They separated upon seeing her, making some hand motion Jo could not decipher. The captain walked toward Jo.

Jo looked at the man again and it should have been with wonder, it should have been with awe; if this had been a war movie—a grand, glorious propaganda movie as only Hollywood could put out—he would have been played by Cagney or Gable or Grant. Here was a brave soldier, a fearless leader, defending an outpost against incredible odds. Jo should have loved him for that alone, but she didn't. He was swagger and bravado and military might, but the lives of her men—to him,

six worthless men, injured now and useless—they meant nothing. People were nothing. Military objectives, taking and holding a position, using and expending manpower, these things
made sense to him, these things were real, but not the men
themselves—they didn't exist for him. And if they didn't exist,
the disheveled, half-crazed nurse who looked after them mattered even less. Jo looked at Captain Clark now as he came up
to her, hands on hips, spitting before he spoke, and realized
how much the movies had conditioned her, had prejudiced her.
She'd believed that all U.S. soldiers in perilous positions would
be just as truthful, upright, clean-mouthed, good, and pure as
they were on-screen. Here was an American, and the odds were
against him, certainly. And yet the man was still a bastard.

"We need you, all of you, all of this"—here he gestured
widely toward the tent—"out of here."

Jo stared at him blankly.

"We need you out of here," he repeated, frowning. "I cannot
hold this position with you saddling me. Damn it all to hell,
you're doing laundry, for Christ's sake."

Jo shook herself a little, as if trying to stay awake.

"We've had typhus in the tent, sir. He was deloused with a
flit can when we got him, but you know how those things can
spread." She added another "sir" as an afterthought, as if she
hadn't realized she had been speaking to anyone beside herself.

"I don't care if there's typhus. They can all die for all I care.
Their being here is endangering my men, and that's my only
priority." Here he looked straight into her glassy eyes. "My *only*
priority."

This man was bothersome, simply bothersome. How could
she have ever thought him evil? His ears were so funny. He
was laughable. That was it. Jo felt like laughing. Laughing and

laughing and never stopping. She started to smile, a provocative smile, not directed at the man in front of her but at
insanity with whom she was flirting. She turned toward the
tent, still grinning. The captain grabbed her arm and spun her
around so she was inches from his face.

"What's your fucking problem?"

"Don't speak that way in front of a lady," Jo said without
thinking. It was her line; that had been her cue. The captain
shook her, hard, until she saw spots and winced from the pain.

"When I see a lady, then I'll watch my tongue."

Jo pulled away from him with the last of her strength, the
pain and her anger snapping her back into reality. She turned
sharply and started toward the tent.

"I didn't dismiss you. Salute, Lieutenant." His eyes narrowed, pronouncing her relative rank like it was a joke, like it
was an insult.

Without turning to face him, Jo said, "When I see an officer, I'll salute him."

"That's insubordination," the captain fumed, struggling to
keep his voice down, throwing his helmet to the ground instead.

Jo walked back to him quickly, her voice hoarse and vicious.
"What are you going to do, Captain? Relieve me of my post?"

With that, she hurried back into the tent, the heavy sheets
still sagging down the line, the smaller towels already snapping in the rising wind.

6

Kay Elliott

Winter, Early 1945, Santo Tomas Internment Camp,
Manila, Philippines

Kay looked down into the courtyard below. Palm trees still lined its perimeter, ornately carved windows still looked out onto a rectangular enclosure once lush with Bermuda grass and gardenia and ylang-ylang. But now the ground was packed earth, worn smooth and hard by the thousands of bare feet traversing it. Hastily constructed shanties sprouted up out of it like mushrooms where once benches had stood, where once university students had studied or debated or laughed at their professors who said life was hard and that ideas had consequences. This was Santo Tomas.

Kay turned wearily from the window. Raucous screeching reached her ears from below—dirty children in underpants were fighting over a game played with sticks. "It is not your turn." "Yes, it is, you went last time." "No, I didn't." "Yes, you did." "I'm going to tell." Her ward was full—her ward was always full—with the young, the old, children, those with dysentery, those with dengue fever, the starving . . . everyone was starving. She had no medicine left, but even if she had, there was no medicine for that. When you thought about it, there were two basic ways to starve to death—wet or dry. Every day, she saw people die from starvation—*beriberi* they called it out here—and yet she couldn't decide which way was worse. Wet beriberi was quickest. You'd pass someone in the courtyard and say hello; he'd look okay one day, and the next he'd be swollen, arms, legs, face, beyond all recognition, and inside fluid would be building up too, engorging his heart, impeding blood flow to his lungs, bringing on a heart attack. He'd grab his chest, or his arm, collapse, and it would all be over. The dry kind was more insidious. You could tell someone was fading—a patient in the ward, the person next to you in chow line. You could see their collarbones sticking out and count their ribs, and then, all of a sudden, they would kind of wither right in front of you, shrivel up into themselves, staggering and falling down in a daze. They'd seem to sleep, but it wasn't sleep. It seemed amazing afterward that there was anything left to bury: they were so brittle the wind should have been able to blow their fragments away like sand. *Dust thou art and to dust thou shalt return.* This was Santo Tomas.

Four thousand civilians, eight university buildings, six hundred makeshift shanties. The nurses shared the second floor of the main building with three hundred women; between them, they had three showers, five washbasins, and five toilets. One of the girls could make herself wake up whenever she wanted, so she would rouse her fellow nurses at five in the morning to get a chance at a shower. Even so, there were half a dozen women under each spigot, each vying for a spot; someone had hung up a sign on a scrap of old paper: IF YOU WANT PRIVACY, CLOSE YOUR EYES. Kay felt in her pocket for the four squares of toilet paper she had been rationed that day, making sure they were still there. It was impossible to make do with only that, she knew, but then she thought of the men, who only got two.

She went from bedside to bedside—or rather, from slung sheet to slung sheet, each holding suspended within it another dying, starving representative of the human race. She applied cool compresses, gave patients dirty water to sip, held their hands, like claws, in her own hand, its bones becoming more pronounced, its blue veins sticking up in greater relief, each day. The nurses kept to their shifts like boys playing soldier, like girls playing house, even though by now they would fall down several times on their way to the wards. Kay knew it was only a matter of time now until one day they would fall and be unable to get back up.

There was a bustle behind her, and several Japanese officers entered the ward. Everyone froze. Literally. It was like playing statues. How that had irked Kay when she first came to this place—to have to bow and kowtow or stand, motionless, for hours at a time before these men while roll was called or inspections were conducted, during the endless announcements and proclamations. Wherever they were, they would have to stop—with one foot on a stair, halfway through a door, standing with their hands in a sink. Stand and not move, not sit or squat, not fall down, no matter how tired they were, no matter how their world swam or spun around them. Because she had seen that gentle missionary beheaded in front of her own weeping children; she had seen that insurance salesman shot in the stomach and left to bleed to death—*all day, good God, how had that taken all day?*—for trying to pick papayas for the pregnant internees. She knew what it was like here. She knew what these men were like. By now, she knew Santo Tomas.

But it seemed that they were in for a shorter interview than normal today; this was not an inspection or confiscation, but interrogation of the chief medical officer.

"These death certificates you signed," the Japanese officer yelled, his English perfect; he had gotten his undergraduate degree in California. "You say, 'Cause of death: starvation.' You cannot write that."

The doctor tried to stand erect in the face of the enemy but only succeeded in slumping just the slightest bit less. Kay could see that he was having trouble focusing on his interrogators, widening and narrowing his eyes, craning his neck forwards and backwards in a vain attempt to see them properly.

"But that's how they died."

"Not so many. You cannot say so many died that way. It is not true."

The doctor blinked again, pushed his glasses farther back on his nose, and swallowed. He looked around at the ward. Even with his distorted vision, he could see the bones—scapula, clavicle, sternum, vertebrae, sacrum—pushing up out of the sagging flesh of his patients' bodies. He made a hopeless gesture with his hands.

"They're starving, sir. They're all starving."

The officer looked for a moment as if he was going to strike the doctor, who was already swaying back and forth unsteadily on his feet.

"It is not starvation. You Americans are just weak. You are homesick. Put down 'homesick' as cause of death from now on."

Kay looked nervously at the doctor. She could not tell what he was thinking, what was going on inside. He smiled the tiniest smile and whispered, almost inaudibly, "Homesick?"

"Yes. You will in future put 'homesick' down as cause of

death." The officer looked meaningfully at Kay, then back at the doctor, who understood the unspoken threat. It was the same as it had been, early on in their internment, when one of the patients had managed to escape. Then the Japanese had come in, grabbed the two patients on either side of the empty bunk, and hung the men all day by their thumbs. After that, a sign had been posted on each floor of the hospital stating that the Japanese would not be so "lenient" should another escape be attempted. That if it happened again, the patient on either side of the escapee's bunk—along with the nurse on that floor—would be shot. No more escapes were attempted after that.

"Homesick, sir," the doctor repeated dully, shaking his head slowly in his defeat, the slight motion nearly making him lose his balance. The Japanese officers left as quickly as they had come. The ward came back to life. Kay moved quickly toward the doctor, easing him down into a chair.

"Did you hear that, Miss Elliott? Homesick."

"Yes, doctor, I heard. We're all homesick."

"But not enough to—not so much that a good meal wouldn't—" He couldn't finish his sentence.

"No, doctor, no."

The doctor sighed, and it sounded like the wind shaking dry aspen leaves in the fall. Kay shivered, recognizing the more insidious form of "homesickness" marking out its next victim.

She looked out the window at the Pacific blue of the sky. That was the only thing that could boast any beauty in a world of filth and ugliness and death. Kay remembered how the sky had looked almost blindingly light as she and the other nurses emerged from the tunnel in Corregidor, handkerchiefs to nose and mouth, stepping over and around dead bodies, looking up, forcing themselves to look up at the sky because they could not look down. When she recalled those first few days after surrender, they seemed like a blur—their fear as the Japanese entered the tunnel, interrupting surgeries, interrogating officers, inspecting the nurses' dormitories in the middle of the night, their guards walking around in nothing more than G-strings. The Americans' confusion and dismay as the Japanese walked confidently to a lateral—identical in appearance to any other—and knocked in its sham plaster wall, confiscating the enormous cases of Red Cross cornmeal, canned meat, vegetables, fruit, fresh water—along with an entire field hospital stocked with precious medicines and supplies—none of which they had known about and all of which could have delayed their surrender, possibly even avoided it, if Allied help had come in time. The nurses' agony at having to leave their seriously wounded patients behind in the tunnel; Kay had broken a crate and made a makeshift frame to put over her sickest patient, draping it with mosquito netting, the tiny invaders already swarming into the opened tunnel, landing on men too ill to brush them away, bringing with them dengue fever and malaria and death nearly as certain as that promised by the Japanese.

Now Kay made her way carefully down the stairs—recently, she had begun to hold on tightly to the banister to steady herself—and walked into the squalor of the courtyard. She remembered a time when outside vendors had been allowed into the encampment, offering food for sale to supplement the meager rations of the camp, bringing with them fruit, vegetables, eggs. But since the nurses had been instructed by their commanding officers to burn all their money and checks before being taken captive, they had had to subsist, at first, on the few ounces of food provided—mush, rotting fish, rice stripped of its thiamine-rich husk. It hadn't been enough. So, through an underground system no longer imaginable only three years later, the civilian executives and CEOs imprisoned along with the girls had obtained credit from their companies and, with it, had issued handwritten IOUs to the American nurses. The nurses' pay—which they would receive upon liberation, should they survive the war and should America still stand as a nation—made them viable financial risks. So the girls had borrowed, borrowed extravagantly, to stay alive—an egg for seventy cents, half a cup of peanuts for a dollar; milk for $75. (Sugar remained unavailable at any price.) But even at those outrageous prices, the food was worth it: one meal, even one part of one meal, could mean the difference between life and death. Kay thought of the two Red Cross comfort kits she had received; they had been divine—the coffee, the meat, the chocolate. They had brought her back to life, made her feel human again, but it hadn't been enough, it could never be enough. She thought of the man who had sold his for $3,000. They had buried him the following month.

She was sure the Japanese were stealing the comfort kits, just as they stole or destroyed their mail, just as she had heard they confiscated the boxes marked SQUIBB and PARKE DAVIS and AMERICAN RED CROSS down at the pier and then offered the precious, donated supplies back for sale to the American doctors and nurses—as if they could afford it, as if they had any money or credit anymore, as if there was any currency in a world of starvation other than food. All of Manila was falling. People broke *into* the internment camp.

They had no way to know what was happening in the outside world. She had received only one letter in all this time, a letter from Jo, a letter Kay had read and reread and thumbed through until the sweat from her fingers had made it grimy and blurred the edges of the cursive characters. She wished Jo was with her, and then she berated herself—of course she didn't wish Jo was here, in this hell. She just meant, *Jo. What we got through together.*

Kay tried not to keep looking back, but when she least expected to—when she least wanted to—she remembered New York, remembered that doctor, that man, a predator, really. Their last year of training, when they met him, he had been so beautiful, so charming at first; she could still see the way his perfect eyebrows cut into the perfect smoothness of his face, that impeccable high, white face, and she hated herself for remembering there ever was a time when they hadn't seen through him, hadn't known him for what he was. Kay hadn't been the only one. With the exception of the matron—and what hold did he have over her to make her turn a blind eye?— each of the nurses had learned to work in fear of that doctor. Jo had split her lip fighting him off in the women's lavatory, Kay had bruises she explained away with an imaginary fall. But that was after his facade had worn away. At first he was all attentiveness, cool and collected and indisputably attractive; the new nurses would get weak in the knees just staring at him. He had brought in little presents too—peanuts or candies or buns still hot from the baker. He could be ingratiating, witty, funny, winning them over with his fine clothes and his fine manners. He was a gentleman, surely, a doctor first and foremost, the savior of the world they lived in, and at first the women gave him the honor, the devotion, the fealty that role demanded.

But he had been right—no one would believe them. He was

a brilliant surgeon, the best in their busy hospital, some said the best in the city. He was from the cream of society, sought after as a speaker, as a teacher, as a dinner guest in the best homes. No one would believe some silly nurse, who probably had a petty grievance. *You know what these girls are, just looking for attention, putting themselves forward. They shouldn't be working anyway, no decent girl would be a nurse. Just look at her, the way she walks—she probably asked for it.* The nurse who had spoken out had been discharged. Kay knew her, knew she had been unable to find work at their hospital, at any hospital. She'd left town, gone back home. The doctor was right—they were no-bodies, easily replaced. Kay could hear him shuffling down the cold corridors even now, his one, tiny flaw—clubfeet not quite corrected, even after half a dozen surgeries—impeding his stride. That seemed ironic—a surgeon with clubfeet. People joked behind his back, but they cast their eyes down when he was near them. *Please, God, don't pick me.*

Once he had caught Jo and Kay at the side door handing food to a woman, a poorly dressed woman who had come silently begging, wet through with rain, hair plastered to her pale, nearly luminous face. He had yelled, "Get her out of here! What do you think this is, a brothel?" And they had seen her belly then, seen it round and firm, her dress so wet and drawn taut against it that they could see the outline of her belly button, turned inside out. They thought it strange that even he would be so vehement, so eager to cast her out into the darkness. The woman had looked at him with something like pity. They say all the great Madonnas were modeled after streetwalkers, after prostitutes paid for their time, to sit placidly with their bastard babies on their laps while paint-ers created images for thousands to adore. This woman could have been one of them. Our Lady of Compassion. Our Lady of Grief. Our Lady of Sorrows.

Be careful of that man—that was all that was said, and then she had disappeared, snatching the roll from Kay's hand, the apple from Jo's. It wasn't the nurses who had spoken, but the stranger, the cold, wet woman. Before she disappeared, she had warned them. She had known him. She had known.

NOT NOW, KAY pleaded with herself. *Stop remembering. Stop thinking.* Kay walked past the empty classrooms where, back when people had had the energy to achieve boredom, forty-six courses had been offered by interred professors. The library had once been active, with books—already infested with bedbugs—borrowed at five cents a copy; numerous committees had met there—the Health Committee, the Entertainment Committee, the Sanitation Committee with their "Swat-That-Fly" campaign. Kay walked by the rodent shed, now ominously closed by order of the Japanese. Without access to the chemicals and traps that had at least kept the population of vermin stable, it was now exploding. Mice and rats were everywhere, in the wards, in the showers. When Kay found a mouse drowned in her mush, she had just pushed it aside, after first carefully scraping the tiny bits of food off its side and eating them. Was there not enough death already without the Japanese promoting this as well? Rats brought fleas, and fleas carried typhus and plague and God knew what else their scientists had created in their laboratories. Kay shuddered at what the Japanese might consider "medical ethics," or who might better qualify as "test subjects" for their experiments than expendable, "homesick" prisoners of war.

Kay thought again of the empty assurances made to the

American women when they had first left Malinta. "Yes, you will get in truck. Yes, you will be with American GIs," their captors had said, but then sent them to a civilian internment camp in Manila, away from their men, away from their work. They were ordered to scrub bathrooms like they were common washerwomen until their head nurse had finally made herself understood: they were nurses, highly trained. If the Japanese would not let them perform their duty for the U.S. Army, let them at least help the hundreds of sick civilians caught senselessly in the crossfire of war. This requisitioned college was where Kay and her fellow nurses had served now for three years. But the Japanese had never recognized the women as officers. How could they? They didn't even recognize them as humans.

It was nearly time for the 1730 roll call when Kay spied a man sneaking surreptitiously from his shanty. She looked away quickly, as if even her gaze might give him away to the Japanese guards. As a primitive form of birth control, married men and women were not allowed in the same shack except between the hours of 1000 and 1400. Partners of pregnant women were either beaten or imprisoned or both.

Kay felt in her pocket and pulled out her meal ticket, a grubby scrap of paper that had to be produced and punched before she could receive her few ounces of food each day. Along the top were three rows divided into twenty columns, each row marked AM, NN, or PM for the morning, noon, and evening meals; along the bottom of the card was room for another twenty days. In the middle of the card, almost obliterated now by dirt and sweat, was a line for her name, her room and ticket numbers, and her signature; to the left of that the words "man" and "child" were neatly crossed out, leaving the single word "woman." Kay remembered rather than read these words now; for several weeks, letters had either swum meaninglessly before her eyes or darted away quickly when she tried to focus on them.

Kay struggled to focus mentally too, to control her thoughts, but it got harder each day. She thought of Dot now. Of meeting her again when Kay first came to the Philippines. They had been through basic training together back home but hadn't seen each other in months. Kay had bumped into her just as Dot came barreling out the hospital side door.

"Dottie," Kay had exclaimed, grabbing on to her arm as the woman seemed intent on storming away. "Dottie Kimble, as I live and breathe."

The woman looked up startled, almost frightened. Then recognition transformed her face.

"Kayak," she said, using her pet name, crushing Kay in a massive bear hug.

"Of all the places to run into you," Kay said, laughing. "What are you doing here?"

The woman's eyes fell, her face flushed red.

"Where've you been?" Dottie changed the subject.

"Hawaii. You?"

"Wasting time out here. Nothing doing. I don't think there'll ever be a war."

"Well, that's a good thing, don't you think?" Kay had laughed brightly.

"Depends who you're fighting for." Dot's face had darkened. Then, in a quieter voice, "I'm—I'm headed home, Kay."

"No! Not now! C'mon," Kay had cajoled. "There are lots of

good positions out here, and you're the best nurse out of the lot of us. You could run lines with your eyes closed. Do you remember that time—"

A middle-aged nurse had stepped round the corner, her hair kinky in the tropical humidity. She had stared hard at the two women and then walked back deliberately, the way she had come.

The color had risen in Dot's face again, but Kay hadn't understood.

"You've *got* to stay in, Dot. We're both out here now. Even if we never see any action, that doesn't really matter. We could have a lot of fun together and—"

"Kay, I *can't*—"

"Nonsense. I'm stationed here. Find me, and we'll talk. I'm so glad I found you again."

Kay gave her friend a hug.

"What's wrong, Dot?" Kay asked as the tears streamed down the other woman's face.

"Miss Kimble," the frazzled, older nurse snapped. Kay hadn't noticed her return. She had sidled up right next to them.

"Dot?"

"Good-bye, Kay." Dot pulled herself out of Kay's arms and ran down the dusty dirt alleyway, through the scrub grasses growing up in between the tire tracks.

Kay stood uncertainly for a moment, following the retreating form of her friend with her eyes.

"Do you know that woman?" the nurse asked. Kay didn't like the way she emphasized "that woman."

"Yes, an old friend of mine."

The older woman snorted.

"And one of the finest nurses I've ever worked with."

"I daresay," the nurse said loftily.

"Hey, what's wrong around here?" Kay took hold of the woman's arm.

"Let go of me," the woman said icily. "For all I know you're just like her."

"Like what?"

"I could have you reported. Have you discharged, like she was. Yes, that's what your 'friend' was here for."

"Discharged? You mean, dishonorably?"

"Yes. She's dishonored her uniform and her profession."

"What are you getting at? Dot's the best—"

"'Dot,'" the woman sneered, smoothing down the front of her white uniform. "I know you're new here, miss, but I wouldn't push your luck. I don't care for that kind."

"What kind?"

"Dykes."

"What?"

The woman had left Kay there, open-mouthed, standing in the heat of the day. Could it be true, about Dot? You heard of such things—here as well as back home. Whispers, really. They said it wasn't natural. They said they weren't human. But they *were* human. Kay knew Dot. Kay loved Dot, everyone in training had. She was a good friend and an excellent nurse. Although imagining the lifestyle was beyond Kay—she couldn't see it, couldn't feel it; she tried to but it stretched her mind too far—that didn't change anything for her. She loved Dot. Not like the smug nurse had insinuated, but with a deep friendship. A bond. A type of love that lasted a lifetime. A love she was not ashamed of.

What had happened to Dot? They had sent her home, "weeded" her out, discharged her, dishonorably, tried to destroy her life. But Dot had gone home before the bombings, before the surrender. Dot had never retreated through Bataan, never cowered like a trapped animal in Corregidor. Dot had gotten out before she was shut up in Manila, like Kay, in a courtyard that stank of refuse and unwashed bodies and rotting food.

Kay thought about food. She always thought about food. There was never a moment when she wasn't thinking about it—about the last thing she had eaten, about the next time she might eat. Last week she had found a banana and eaten it whole, skin and all. She remembered how squeamish she had been back in New York, tentatively touching the pungent *anguilla marinata*—marinated eel—to her lips. (Jo had brought it along for her to try at lunch break, and laughed at Kay's screwed-up face and called her a sissy.) Kay thought of all the things she hadn't previously considered food but would now eat in a heartbeat—tough camotes, an inferior type of sweet potato; *dilis,* a pathetic little fish, only an inch long; sapsaps, a slightly larger fish but one that rotted right away and was unfit for humans; they used to feed it to starving ducks, but now both sapsaps and ducks were gone. Gone too were all domestic animals and unfortunate strays, all leaves, roots, and weeds, anything organic, anything even remotely edible. The previous summer the Japanese had stopped removing garbage from the camp and the internees had had to bury it; but now it lay out in the open, where people poked at it uncertainly with sticks or the tips of worn shoes, looking for anything they could at least try to eat. People came to the hospital begging the nurses for a tablespoon of castor oil; they would smack their lips in satisfaction after swallowing the awful stuff, they were that starved for fat. The interred children were finally ordered away from the Japanese mess halls, under pain of death; even those callous soldiers did not relish eating their meals under the watchful eyes of tiny living skeletons.

Thinking of food didn't help Kay, and yet she couldn't think of anything else. Was there anything else she could do? Was there anything she had that she could barter with? Was there any way she could get a little more food and stay alive a little bit longer?

"You. Nurse. Come."

Kay turned and saw a small group of her fellow nurses being rounded up by two Japanese soldiers holding rifles with fixed bayonets. She walked slowly up to them, raising her eyes questioningly at her fellow female officers, wondering if the time had finally come for the morphine vials they still carried in their hair.

No onlooker cried out in protest. No passer-by demanded to know where the women were being taken. No one came to their rescue, or even made eye contact with their captors, and the girls didn't blame them at all. To do so would be foolish, would only hasten their own deaths. There were no heroics, and no heroes, in this internment camp. Or, if there were, they were the people who had the courage to wake up and do their duty every day, without hope of remuneration or rescue or even survival. The people who secretly possessed glass vials of escape but had, as of yet, refused to use them.

"You come with us. Now."

They came. There was nothing for it. One of the nurses who worked on Kay's floor reached out her hand and took hold of Kay's finger, giving it a little squeeze before the guards could see her, dropping her hand almost instantly. Kay understood. She was saying good-bye. They were ushered into the main

building, then through the main door, kept always locked, out
onto a little lawn, incongruous and green in a city of brown
stone and dirt and rubble.

"Line up," came the barked order. One of the girls crossed
herself slowly, as if she really meant it, as if she knew it would
be the last time she would make that familiar gesture. They
lined up in front of a massive, flowering vine, purple and fuch-
sia and obscenely beautiful in the slanting sunlight; lined up
and squared their shoulders, and resisted the urge to look at
the ground, at their feet, but looked up instead and met the
unfeeling eyes of the enemy. Then the commander himself
came out, walking briskly toward them in dress uniform, with
a Filipino photographer following in his wake, clumsily carrying his equipment and apologizing and trying to keep up.
So they were destined to become yet one more demoralizing
image sent back to America—censored from the newspapers,
of course, but seen by the military. News of their deaths might
make the front pages but never these images, their bloody
female bodies spread out in the green grass, arms and legs
splayed awkwardly, tangled together in a mess of death and
beauty and a clinging, blossoming vine.

"You will take one each."

Kay was surprised. The Japanese were not known for dis-
tributing blindfolds to block out the sight of a firing squad.

She was handed, instead, a delicately designed china cup.

Each girl, in turn, was given the same; only the pattern
differed—Royal Worcester, Wedgwood, Dresden, decorated
with miniature roses, embracing nymphs, blues and golds and
pinks. And each priceless cup was empty.

"We send a picture to your army, show them how well you
are treated. Have tea party with officer."

The commander came in, right among them, holding his own dainty teacup; he alone held a saucer as well. He looked at the camera, pinky raised slightly, impeccable, flanked by disheveled, starving women looking down into the bottoms of their valuable cups, worthless to them without the tea and cream and sugar that would have felt like a meal in itself, that would have helped keep them alive for another day. The obsequious photographer circled the group, bowing and scraping in between shots, smiling and bowing again and thanking the commander for the honor, for the privilege, for not killing him along with the rest of his family. Kay felt nothing, even as she watched the tears roll down the smiling man's face. Then they were done; the cups were collected, and the girls herded back into the enclosure. It was over.

Roll was being called as they walked back into the courtyard; they had been gone longer than Kay thought. They took their regular places and stood silently, motionlessly. Around them, their fellow inmates looked at them, questions in their eyes, but even if it had not been roll call, they would not have been able to talk to them. Nurses could not talk to anyone but medical personnel, under penalty of death. Nurses could not wear pants or (worse) shorts, under penalty of death. Nurses could not speak to patients or outsiders or anyone; or do or say or be anything. Everything was forbidden, everything was under pain of death.

For a moment, Kay was angry—angry that she was still alive, listening to the ever-shortening list of familiar names being read and read and read again. Why hadn't they killed her just now? Why hadn't they killed her on Corregidor? Why had she been born at all? To know a few weeks' happiness with a man she would never see again, a man who had made life precious and priceless and now, without him, made it even more pointless and hopeless? The names droned on—"Gallagher, Aimee. Gallagher, Thomas"—and she looked at the people around her—small children with broken arms slung in scraps of an old, patterned dress, since they had no plaster of paris to make casts; another new wet beriberi case she hadn't noticed at the 0800 roll, the man's arms nearly bursting through the sleeves of his tattered dress shirt; one of her fellow nurses, two rows away, starting to sway from sheer exhaustion, slumping, being grabbed roughly by the middle-aged women on either side of her, propping her up, holding her in position, trying desperately to avoid drawing attention from the patrolling guards toward themselves, toward their children.

What was the point of it all? Why not let them all go? Or why not have killed them all upon capture rather than call roll and make them stand like this for hours and hours until they starved to death or collapsed or went mad? It was mad. It was like a bad dream, or like a good dream dreamed by a sadist. The Japanese had found the most effective way to torture, to maim, to destroy the spirit and the body, all at once: filth and squalor and isolation and—above all else, beyond all else— starvation, always starvation. The girls had missed their evening meal while they were having their mock tea party on the lawn; Kay's one ounce of meat, her five ounces of worthless rice or rancid mush seemed like a feast now that it was denied her. Without it, she was unsure she could survive the night. Or the rest of this day. Or the rest of this roll call. "Jackson, Jacobs, Jamison." She was dying. She was dying and she couldn't even sit down, she couldn't even lie down and die because—why? Why couldn't she die yet? Why couldn't she crack open those vials? What fine thread still tethered her to Santo Tomas, to this world, to humanity itself?

An infant's cry was heard coming from her hospital ward, two stories above. The cry went on and on, interminable, indomitable, floating down to them, the one conscientious objector who could not be silenced, who would defy injustice and inhumanity with his very life, with his unreasonable, reasonable insistence upon being heard, upon being real. The cry continued, resolute, full-throated, and something rose within Kay. She had delivered that baby this morning—among all that death, life had come, and Kay had helped usher it into existence. She had helped that child's mother—had helped her, and two hundred other humans that day—each one of them equal, each equally deserving of compassion and decency and humane care, even if that was all Kay had left to give them. They were all starving, just as the death certificates had proclaimed. But Kay could see to it that, for as long as their bodies endured, her patients would not starve for goodness or tenderness, not while it was still in her power to lift. Or walk. Or even stand, motionless, for hours at a time. "Lambert, Landon, Langley." The baby kept crying, and the sound kept Kay alive. It was as if he were screaming and crying and speaking out on her behalf, on behalf of them all, on behalf of all those forced into silence and submission. But not forever— Kay promised herself that—not forever. She could hold on a little bit longer. She would make it through roll after all. They were up to the *L*'s already.

All she had to do was stand.

7

Jo McMahon

Spring 1945, The Western Front

The major didn't die. He looked like he would, for a day or two, but then his fever broke and the glassy look left his eyes. Suddenly, he knew where he was and what had happened to him, and when he was told about it afterward, he was surprised to be alive at all. Billy, too, could hold his own as long as he didn't move around too much—and especially if Jo could get him anywhere near some steam. "I know I look like death," he quipped, his lips dusky and dark in his pale face, "but I actually feel less like it than before." Jonesy took pride in rationing out the food that Grandpa had won them, wheeling himself around the small tent in his crazy contraption, his leg sticking out in front of him like an awkward battering ram. James asked one day to get dressed—"if you still have my clothes, miss. I mean, I'm not sick, I'm not really injured that bad, just my hands, you know. As for my eyes, well, I can't stay in bed the rest of my life on account of that." So Jo had pulled out the dirty bundle from under his cot, and now he sat upright in bed in his charred field uniform, the burn marks reaching nearly up to the triangular tricolored badge on his sleeve.

Father Hook's visible wounds were slowly starting to heal, but Jo couldn't reach him, not the man inside. His eyes could dart around the tent now, instead of just staring fixedly at one spot, he could answer in monosyllables: "Yes" to "Is the pain bearable?" and "No" to "Do you need anything, Father?" But when Jo would try to draw him out, asking him an open-ended question—or one about his past, whether long gone or recent—he would freeze up, stiffen inside and out, and be gone for hours and hours. Jo had seen shock before, but seeing it now in a priest unsettled her. To her, these were men who were supposed to minister to others without ever having needs of their own. Priests had visited the filthy tenements back home in Brooklyn, bringing closure to the dying; they fed the hungry masses with their God's own flesh; they heard the secret confessions of a thousand hardened sinners without ever appearing to be affected or drained of their limitless resources, of their power to heal. Now here was a man Jo thought should have been untouchable, should have been able to overcome his own shock and pain. He should have shouldered his cross, offered it up cheerfully, like someone whose yoke was easy and burden light—and then dip down into the inexhaustible recesses of his being and offer them all—offer Jo—the words of hope and love and salvation that the whole dying world was aching to hear. But all he was was scared.

Then there was David. Jo had seen typhus cases before, but she couldn't get a handle on this one. Sometimes he would seem to rally. The fever would lessen, he could sleep—albeit fitfully—and he would seem to be on the upswing. Then, especially at night, the illness would come back, redoubled; he would thrash and moan in his long, narrow cot, his thick hair sticking to his sweating forehead. He would call out for his mother, for his gun, for their Scottish equivalents. He would throw back his head and arch his spine stiffly—a sure sign of the end stages of the dread disease—but somehow, in the morning he would still be hanging on, by a thread at times but still hanging on. Now Jo sat down next to him and pushed back his dark bush of hair, revealing a high, unwrinkled brow. Only the dark, indented circles under his eyes betrayed how very close to death he was straying.

"David, David, David," she murmured, closing her eyes, trying to hold on herself, trying to hold on to one of the six men she had vowed would not die, remembering other times she had seen this horrible disease. It had ravaged whole villages in Sicily, the dying mothers bringing in dead children for her to look at, the old men crying and begging the doctors to do something for their wives, their daughters, their grandchildren. *They thought we were gods, that we could cure anything.* Typhus. Plague. Typhoid fever. Jo remembered how, as they pulled out, the Germans had destroyed the Italians' irrigation and water supply—crushing artesian wells, smashing two-thousand-year-old walls, toppling ancient aqueducts. The water became deadly to drink—but what else could the people do that long, hot summer but drink the water that had brought life to their towns and their families for millennia? So they had gotten typhoid first, and then cholera; and then the pools of standing water had brought on the mosquitoes and malaria had entered their hopeless lives as well. Jo remembered the nurses' skin turning yellow from the quinine that protected them, the GIs' pockets perpetually stained from where they hid the pills they didn't want to swallow, pills that could destroy even the hardiest stomach.

Jo's hand was absently stroking the dying man's hair as she found herself humming a theme from *Hänsel und Gretel*. Only a few years earlier—it seemed ages and ages ago now, in this place without a name—she had been studying opera. With Signor Luigi. What a crotchety *bastardo* he had been, but oh how he had loved her voice. He had offered her lessons for next to nothing, screamed at her, cursed at her, done everything in his power to transform her *voce argento* (voice of silver, as he called it) into a *voce d'oro* (voice of gold). But then Jo had started nursing classes and begun working nights; and then the war broke out and Gianni was drafted. Jo's studies fell by the wayside as everything began to crash down around her. She still had the music inside of her, though, even now—muffled and nearly drowned out, but deep down it was still there. It would rise to the surface at unexpected times, like now—"Papageno," "Abendsegen," "O mio babbino caro"—music written in German, Italian, English, the languages that now screamed at each other across the continents, music from a dream world, from a peaceful world, from a world that no longer existed.

> *Abends, will ich schlafen gehn,*
> *Vierzehn Engel um mich stehn:*
> *Zwei zu meinen Häupten,*
> *Zwei zu meinen Füßen,*
> *Zwei zu meiner Rechten,*
> *Zwei zu meiner Linken,*
> *Zweie, die mich decken,*
> *Zweie, die mich wecken,*
> *Zweie, die mich weisen,*
> *Zu Himmels-Paradeisen*

Without even thinking, she softly sang the words now for David—like they were a lullaby, like he could hear her—and her mind wandered as time slouched by, marked only by an increase in hunger, an increase in cold, each moment interminable, endless, unreal. Jo thought of the first war movie she had seen, *Foreign Correspondent,* put out before America had even gotten into the war. She could still see the gloss and the polish, the glamour of espionage, plucky heroines, bravery that unfolded before her eyes in an hour and a half, dressed up in tailored dress suits, high heels, and permanent waves. She thought of the scene where they sneak into the old apartment building and her thoughts shifted to the tenement where she had grown up, where she'd taken care of herself through each of her childhood illnesses. She thought of the smell of oily meals cooking without ventilation, the sound of domestic fights on two floors in three different languages, the feel of the splintery wood of the banister, the hard iron of the fire escape where she would sleep in the summers when the heat of the whole city seemed bottled up in their one room. She hoped the place had burned to the ground by now, rats and all. At the thought of rats, her quick eye caught a shadow as it darted under the canvas. She turned her head, and there, running in and out, was a little mouse . . . two mice . . . half a dozen. There was nothing for them to eat. They were just getting out of the cold, into the cold, back out again, scurrying from dark into light.

She had stopped singing the words in German and switched now into English, just as she had done countless times for sick and injured children of all nationalities trapped in the crosshairs of war, children who had been brought to her bleeding, crushed, and battered, children she could help and those beyond anyone's aid. She had sung soothing strains of lullabies that transcended all language barriers, giving those innocents, if not the healing they deserved, at least a moment of peace and calm and safety in a world gone mad.

When at night I go to sleep
Fourteen angels watch do keep
Two my head are guarding
Two my feet are guiding
Two are on my right hand
Two are on my left hand
Two who warmly cover
Two who o'er me hover
Two to whom 'tis given
To guide my steps to heaven

Jo thought again of that little toddler in Italy, the one whose foot had been lost when a truck ran over it. They had brought her to Jo a few days later to look at the wound, to beg for some antibiotic, and Jo had given it to her. "Who did the amputation?" she had asked in English, looking at the crooked, primitive stitches; the little girl in front of her was wriggling, wanting to get down from the table. Jo repeated her question, knowing her parents' Sicilian dialect would be understood this far south on the mainland. The old village dentist had shuffled forward, fingering the felt hat in his trembling hands. The girl began to cry, and Jo let her jump down from the table, the child steadying herself with her pudgy hands, hopping away from the old man.

"She no longer likes me," he explained, his graying head shaking sadly, the white stubble standing out on his face in the afternoon sunlight, "since I took away her foot."

"What did you use for anesthesia?" Jo asked, knowing the civilian doctors were hard up for supplies.

"Non ne avevamo niente," the man said simply. *We had none.* Jo had nearly thrown up from sheer pity. The plump little girl in front of her, now happily playing with an overturned box of tongue depressors, had had her mangled foot cut from her tiny body while she was fully awake. Jo could see her now-smiling face twisted, as it must have been, in a contortion of pain, could hear her low, delighted babble at discovering a new toy, then her scream of horror and agony and outrage at the injustice of war. Where had her angels been then?

Jo had stopped caring after that girl. She had still cared a little, sometimes—while delivering a baby for a peasant woman perhaps, or helping a soldier get onto his crutches for the first time—but she had cared a little less each day, until now she could run her fingers lovingly through the damp hair of a handsome soldier, singing him enchanted words of love and peace, and feel no more than the captain felt, securing his post; or Jonesy did, counting up his rations and doing short division to see how long they could possibly hold out. Jo had shored up her heart so there were no more chinks where love or feelings could sneak in any longer; nowhere where pain could find a way through. Or, if there were any weak spots left, Jo was working all the time—awake, asleep, thinking, unthinkingly—working to patch them, to solder them closed, to bury her soul alive. That was the only way she could survive, survive the weeks and months and, possibly, years of war ahead of her.

How long had it been since Grandpa had shot himself? Since Queenie had died? The captain came in sometimes, telling her useless, meaningless things about the shifting front, about resupply lines and chains of command; reinforcements would come next week, in two months, from the rear, from smack-dab in front of them. He was mining the field behind the tent in case of a sneak attack by the Germans; he was sending three scouts to the south to see if they could reestablish contact with command. Whatever he said, it changed daily, it didn't matter, it was never the same plan twice; and it made no sense anyway to Jo, whose only concern now was her men. The entire war had boiled down to six lives—those were the only lives she cared about, the only lives she could touch. She was *satisfied* that the major had lived—not glad, or happy, or thrilled, as she would have been had someone told her, as a young nursing student, that she would perform surgery successfully and save an officer's life. No, she was *satisfied*. Satisfied that Jonesy recovered and James sat up, that Billy's airway was open, that Father ate something that morning, that David slept and was stable and his fever hadn't spiked again today. These were her only concerns. And they concerned her only as far as she allowed them to, only as far as her brain and her hands and the nerves that connected them were concerned. But her concern for these six lives bypassed her heart and bypassed her soul. Because if you loved, you could lose. If you loved, you *did* lose. Jo McMahon had lost enough.

Jo got up and walked back into the tiny enclosure she had re-created with those same three sheets—she had washed them and washed them and washed them again, but in her mind's eye she could still see the outline of Grandpa's blood where it had splattered, a distinct pattern no longer visible to anyone but herself, its silhouette seared into her brain. She knew the stains were there and she knew they weren't there and knowing one did not detract from the other in the least. In the relative privacy of her cell, she buried her face in her hands, then rubbed it hard, as if trying to wake herself from this marathon of duty that would never come to an end. She looked at herself in the smudged, blistered mirror that hung crookedly from a nail, and she did not recognize the person she saw. Her ivory skin (so valued among southern Italians) was now lifeless and gray; her hair was tangled and matted, the worst of it hidden out of sight in a disreputable bun. She ran her fingers lightly over her neck, her collarbone, her shoulders—everything was too long, too thin, too bony. She looked down at her hands. The veins on the backs of them were swollen and squirmed like living things when she touched them. There was no part of her that was beautiful, no part of her that was her, no part of her that was even clean or decent. She looked down at her tattered nightshirt lying on the damp ground, soiled with a dozen old bloodstains, the result of not having enough Curity diapers, the only sanitary napkins the girls had been able to find. She hated how cold and how hungry and how ugly she was; the hair on her legs and under her arms disgusted her. She vowed that she would wear the contraband negligee that very night. She would wear it—something fine and silky and lovely—wear it just to be a woman again, not a drudge cleaning up after man's orgy of death and carnage. She would do it. She would.

There was noise outside the tent—not the muffled whispering of the captain's platoon, but talking. Then yelling. Unfamiliar voices, and they were coming closer to the tent. Jo stepped out quickly from behind the sheets just as half a dozen men, Rangers, barreled into the tent. They looked like supermen to Jo, each half a foot taller than Clark—who had followed behind in their wake—the blue and yellow "lozenge" patches on their sleeves marking them out as elite. Here were men who could face anything, overcome anything, no matter the odds; here, finally, were men who could save Jo—and more importantly, save her men.

But as Jo looked at them again she realized that these were not men coming to her aid, coming to get her out of this pit of death and hopelessness. These, instead, were yet more men who would be demanding help of her.

"Doctor," one of the men was yelling. He was covered in blood, but it was not his own. He and another Ranger held between them all that remained of their comrade—he had tourniquets on both legs and one arm (what was left of them), a blood-soaked bandage wrapped hastily around his head. His eyes were lolling backwards, lost in the delirium that is on the other side of pain. Jo took one look at the boy and knew. She shook her head, almost imperceptibly, at his friends, at those who had struggled through who knew what to find him help. There would be no help for him.

"We have no doctor. And even if we did . . ." Her voice trailed off.

"Damn it, miss, we've come this far . . . There's got to be something."

They were rolling up their sleeves, offering blood—as if this kid needed any more blood, he was red from it. They couldn't, they wouldn't believe that there was nothing to be done, that his body was shutting down, that no one—not even a Ranger—could lose that much of himself and still survive. The boy started to convulse, and they yelled again for help, for a doctor, for a man to fix what was broken and bring their friend back to life. And then a woman—a highly trained woman, a woman who could have fixed almost anything but knew that she could not fix this, that no one could fix this—did what no man could do. She climbed up onto the only remaining operating table, her right shoe falling off softly, curling her foot up under her, motioning for them to lay him in her arms. They resisted at first, eyes welling with tears no Ranger could let fall, denying that death would defeat them after all their effort. But the injured man's body was shaking and shaking, and they gave him to her in the end. His wild eyes focused one last time, focused on the last thing he thought he'd find so far from home, on something he never thought to see again—the dark, moist eyes of an American woman, eyes that were gazing down on him like a mother's, like a lover's, like an angel's. He could see she was real—not the phantom of his pain, but real—he could feel her arms, real arms supporting him—and then there was only her, everything peripheral turning into a hazy blur, the war, the tent, even his buddies, who had been more to him than family, disappeared and there was only her. Looking down on him like heaven. Suddenly, he was no longer scared and no longer in pain, and he wasn't even unhappy to be dying (he knew, he knew now that he was dying), because she was there and she was real and she was holding him and now everything, even death, was going to be all right.

"There, baby," she was saying, delicately pushing back a lock of hair that had gotten into his eye. "There, love," and those words were the same words his mother had used and he was safe again. "There, sweetheart," she murmured, pulling him closer to her soft, warm body, and she was his lover, and even with his life rushing out of him, his body responded and he wanted her and he loved her and he would get well and make violent love to her and he would be happy forever because she was not some cheap trick in Paris that helped to pass the time but the woman of his dreams at last, a real woman, and now everything was going to be okay. He closed his eyes and his tired body rested against hers, swaying gently, oh so gently, back and forth on the hard table he could not feel, in the cold tent he could no longer see. The rhythm of her body relaxed him and excited him at the same time, and he was safe, the war was over, they were all going home together. "Baby, baby, baby," she whispered, her lips tickling his ear caked with blood, and his body flooded with pure bliss, with obscene pleasure, with heat and power and might; he was soaring with houri in a Muslim paradise; he was eighteen again, kissing Katie Sue and she had taken his class ring in her tiny hand and she was crying and saying she would wait for him (oh, the joy of it) and that she would marry him when he came home. And then suddenly, without any pain, he was home.

There was silence in the tent. They were men. They could not cry, and they could not cross the line Jo had crossed—they could not do the nothing that is everything, that no man understands, that every man craves and hates woman because he craves it and needs it and cannot give it himself and cannot live without it. Her patients stared, lips parted, lusting after the caresses she had given to this stranger that she would never give to them. The Rangers, hard men of steel and iron, stood in an impotent semicircle around the woman who had given to their fallen brother the only thing she had, the only thing he needed. They looked at her as the dead boy had done only a moment before—as mercy itself, as love incarnate, but above all else, as safety in a world that absolutely terrified them. They looked at Jo and marveled at her, at her softness and goodness and warmth.

But Jo was none of those things, not anymore. The boy was

dead, the part she played was over. She pushed him away from her numb body, the front of her jumpsuit soaked through and warm with his blood, easing her way out from under the heavy weight like a prostitute getting out from under a spent john. Then, with a callousness that made even the Rangers start, she dropped the lifeless thing back onto the table, insensible, his head making a sickening thud as it hit the cold, hard metal.

8

Kay Elliott

Winter 1945, Santo Tomas Internment Camp,
Manila, Philippines

Kay held the limp thing in her hands and did not move. She could not. She just sat there, staring, looking down at it, incredulous, confused, amazed. What did they tell them back home? What did they think it was like over here? She thought of the beheadings, of the impalings, of the firing squads and drownings; of the small children and old women prostituting themselves for food in their desperation, being raped but never paid, never receiving anything for their pain and suffering other than the end of a bayonet or a swift kick into a dark corner where they could gnaw at themselves and their guilt and their shame.

She thought again of Malinta, that mouth of hell that had swallowed them up and then spit them out into an even worse place. For the first time in a long time, her mind wandered back to a time before Malinta, to the nurses crossing Manila Bay under cover of night, the men rowing them out toward Corregidor and the false hope it offered, the burning buildings and ammunition dumps lending everything a lurid, reddish light. Kay could see the tiny craft all around her again—military dinghies and fishing boats, junks and homemade rafts, people holding on to barrels, on to crates strung together with rope, on to nothing but trying to swim all the way out to the island. Tiring halfway. Starting to drown. Screaming for help. And then clawing at anything, at anything afloat, grabbing on to wood, on to metal, their nails scraping the sides, overturning, overloading, bringing everything down with them. "Don't look, miss," the sergeant rowing them had said, and she had listened to him and closed her eyes. But she had felt the rowing stop, felt the boat sway as the man stood up, heard the swish of air as he swung the oar over them, bringing it down hard on something in the water, on something that gave out a low moan, that exhaled as if exhausted, and was silent. Then the boat had seemed lighter, bobbing on the choppy waters, and he had begun to row again, pulling out quickly into the deep, telling her she could look again, it was okay, they would be safe when they got to Corregidor.

She fingered the new fabric now with her skeletal hands. Lastek, the label had said. *They must not use wool anymore.* It was smoother than wool, much more sleek and stretchy; it wouldn't be as rough as wool or rub you the wrong way, leaving scratch marks under your arms or in the crotch. She wondered if it would repel water as well as wool. Wool was good for that.

"Whaddya have there, Elliott?"

"Hmm?" Kay's mind was slow. Slow and stupid. She looked down at the label again, but now the letters swam. *Latesk. Lt. Esk. Lkatse.*

"I saw a package got through, after all this time. Can't believe it. Japs must've let it in, just for show. What'd you get from home? What'd they send you?"

Kay thought of all the things she could have used, of all the things her family might have sent her—that, in all probability, they had been sending her all these years, only to be confiscated by the Japanese half a world away. Cans of tuna fish. Jars of peanut butter. Pilot bread. Evaporated milk. Coffee. Chocolate. Her stomach twisted painfully. Kay closed her eyes, gritting her teeth, struggling to hold on. A full half-minute later she reopened them.

"A bathing suit. They sent me a bathing suit."

"What?"

Kay stopped fingering the silky stuff. *They must think it's still a paradise over here, that this is one long vacation for us, that we get their packages and letters even if they never get ours. They must tell them something to account for that, they must make something up. My family loves me. They would never send me this useless, stupid thing with me dying here and them having so much—butter and cream and eggs from the farm, oh God—they would never forget me. They haven't forgotten me,* she screamed and screamed until her head ached. Or she thought she did. All she really said was, "Uh, huh."

Kay watched as the nurse next to her carefully did up her lips with a little red stub of lipstick. Kay watched her curiously. How had she made the grubby little thing last all this time? For as long as Kay could remember, Kelly—or was it Kathy? Kitty? the names jumped around in her head, interchangeably, she didn't know who this woman was—had done up her lips like this, even here in hell. Kay wondered how she could resist the oily richness of that lipstick, why she didn't just eat it instead. The woman had always been smearing the stuff on, red and greasy and garish now on her emaciated face. She must have had a dozen, a hundred lipsticks on her person when she was taken captive. Why had she brought them?

Who cared how she looked? Did she? Did she notice she still did this ritual, always in the same way, always in the exact same way? Taking time over the right upper lip, getting the slanted curve just right. Then the other half, just as carefully, picking at it with her pinky nail if she drew it too wide. Then slowly, deliberately, the entire lower lip, left to right, pulling it out to the side, the lip rebounding quickly as she released the pressure, replaced the cap, pressed her lips together. Smacking them again and again in a futile kiss until they were perfect, until they were coated, until they were as beautiful and as hideous as she could make them. Kay wanted to slap her stupid, empty face, unreal and freakish, smiling a smile that was just another mask for death.

"Kay?"

Kay looked at her companion, and for a moment she could see her again. For a moment she was herself.

"Kay, honey? Thought I had lost you there for a moment."

Kay thought she had too, but was too weak to answer.

"It's time for our shift, sweetheart. Time to go to work."

Kay rebelled. Every ounce of her. The person she was, the person she had been, all of her. That little girl in Mount Carmel, waking up on a beautiful, surprisingly hot September morning, listening to the birds outside, trying to decide if she would go fishing or hiking or try out that new recipe for sour cream doughnuts—only to realize it was a school day, she would be cooped up all day in class. She didn't want to go. She wouldn't go, she wouldn't. She had been angry then, and she was angry now, she could not move, she could barely stand. The Japanese had relocated the nurses to another building, across the way from the hospital. Just a few paces away, but it would be impossible, it was impossible, the rain had filled the long trench that ran between the two buildings, they would have to wade through the filthy water. She wasn't strong enough, she would never make it, she couldn't; she wanted to curl up where she sat and go back to sleep, maybe she could pretend to be sick and her mother wouldn't make her go to school today and she could make those doughnuts after all.

Her head felt funny for a minute, and suddenly she wasn't a little girl anymore, but she was back in New York, in the hospital. How had she gotten here? Everything seemed clearer, all at once, the fog lifted. The bright lights overhead, the tinge of chlorine bleach in the air, her leather shoes making dark scuffs on the polished wax floors. Jo had walked in. Walked into the break room and closed the doors behind her, then stood silently in front of Kay, staring at the ground. Jo was shaking her head, just the tiniest motion back and forth, back and forth; she was mouthing some words, but no sound came out. When Kay stood up from the table and walked over to her, Jo held out a hand, but not to hold on to Kay. She was warding her off, pushing her away.

"Jo. Jo, honey."

But Jo was frowning now, as if that wasn't her name, as if Kay had somehow gotten it wrong. She shook her head more vigorously, as if troubled by something she saw, playing and replaying it in her head. She waved her friend away, distractedly; Kay was superfluous.

"Jo, what happened?"

It had only been half an hour . . . no, less; they had transported that heart patient to the third floor together, then Kay, scheduled for surgery, had gone to get a quick cup of coffee; Jo had said she was going to show one of the new nurses the wards, teach her the ropes, she had laughed. That had been, what, fifteen minutes ago, not much longer, but looking at Jo now, she wasn't the same woman, she didn't seem to be there at all. Kay gently touched Jo's arm, and she jumped, Jo jumped as if she hadn't seen her standing there at all, had never seen her before. She was scowling at Kay, looking her straight in the eye, looking through her, and then all of a sudden Jo knew Kay, and her face contorted in an agony of recognition.

"Oh, Kay," she whispered. Jo tried to sit down on the wooden bench, but sat up again with a start, it hurt too much, and then Kay understood and wrapped her arms around her and said, "God no, God no," over and over again until she was so blind with anger, with pain, that their pain was one, it had happened to them both.

"My God, Jo, how?"

Jo's mouth was moving, working silently, nothing coming out, she was still shaking her head.

"I'm going to tell," Kay said hoarsely, still holding Jo close to her, feeling her own pulse in her temples, a throbbing *swoosh* in her ears, but even before Jo gasped *no* she knew they wouldn't, they wouldn't dare. The two women had survived the Depression, but only barely; it was not in them to give up a job in a country with ten million unemployed. The hunger and the want of their childhoods paralyzed them still. But they had thought they would be safe together, that they could protect one another, and they hadn't; and then Kay swore, seeing her friend begin to shut down, begin to shut out life, "All right then, Jo, but this ends here. We find our chance. I swear this ends here."

And then, one day, their chance finally came. A maternity case. Not Jo's (thank God not Jo's), but a charity case, no money. It was the poor woman who had stood in the rain that night—she had nearly hemorrhaged to death, but they had saved her, and in the end she had had a boy, a healthy boy, except for his clubfoot, which was rather severe, a bad case of it actually. Several specialists had been called in; they were going to use the case study for the medical college. That was all they had needed. Kay could still see Jo, holding her hand, as they walked into his office. Kay's knees had been shaking, but they were going to do this; she had sworn they would do this, together.

"You will never assault another nurse in this hospital again—" Kay had begun, without preamble.

"What? What is your name? Elliott? You're fired, you'll never work in this—"

"In this city again. Yes, I know. But"—Kay managed the tiniest hint of a smile—"I don't think you'll do anything of the kind, doctor."

Kay could still hear him yelling, outraged. "How dare you? You two are fired, Elliott and McMahon," scribbling their names down on a prescription card. "I will have you trouble-makers blacklisted—"

"If you do"—Jo had spoken up, fighting to keep her voice steady, her fingers squeezing Kay's hand tight—"if you black-list Kay or me or any of us, if we hear you even brushed up against a nurse while walking down the hall, then we'll tell everyone about your baby."

"*My* baby? Are you out of your mind?" The mask was off, he was no longer the man behind the desk, busy with his work, dismissive, annoyed at their intrusion; he was becoming that baser thing, all hatred and hurt and searing, burning pain.

"Your baby, the one we just delivered up in maternity to-night. Born to that poor woman. We wondered that night why you didn't want us to help her, didn't want her around. She knew you. I could see it in her eyes."

"No one will believe you, you've got nothing on me—" He rose menacingly out of his chair.

"We could see it in her eyes—and anyone can see it in your son's feet."

Kay remembered that he had stopped blustering, stopped threatening; he was listening, leaning on his desk, half in, half out of his chair, his upper lip twitching nervously.

"Funny thing about clubfoot," Kay went on, gaining courage. "It's so hereditary. And rare. If that woman wanted to claim paternity, press charges even . . ."

"She wouldn't dare—"

"Wouldn't she? I can't imagine you treated her better than you've treated any of us. But no, somehow I don't think she will say anything. I don't know why. I think she's forgiven you or something—"

He had seemed to relax at that, sitting back down, exhaling slowly; he was regaining control.

"But *we* won't forget. *We* won't forgive. We've told every nurse in this hospital whose baby that is. Each one has that power over you now. All any of us have to do is go to the administrators—or to your wife. They might not have believed us coming to them without any proof. But a clubfooted baby, born to a prostitute you hired—now I don't think that will help your career any, doctor."

The man just sat silently, staring at them out of the slits of his eyes.

"Get out of my office—" he said at last, but Kay saw their aggressor defeated, visibly deflating. They could see it in his face, the slump of his shoulders; his eyes cast down, compulsively taking in every object on his littered desk, not looking up, not meeting the girls' gaze.

Kay remembered her knees had stopped shaking then. She remembered standing tall, next to Jo. All that power had made her feel giddy, made her feel like her head would burst. She felt so very light now that they were finally free of him. Jo would make it, in time—she'd begin to heal. They had banded together and protected themselves at last; as they turned to go her feet barely touched the ground. She hadn't felt the floor at all.

"This is blackmail," the thing behind the desk had called after them, lashing out blindly, spitting his anger at them only to see it fall impotently at their feet.

"No." Kay had put her arm around Jo's waist to steady her, to hold themselves up. Turning toward him quickly, eyes flashing, "This isn't blackmail. This is us winning. You can never touch us again."

Kay could still hear the door close noisily on its hinges.

"KAY, HONEY."

The nurse with the red lips was shaking her now, gently but persistently. This woman had been with her every day since Clark Field, and she was her best friend and a stranger, and now Kay thought her name might be Frances. With an *e*.

"C'mon, baby."

Kay tried standing up, and fell painfully to the ground. Frances (or maybe Emily) helped her get back on her feet, led her toward the door, then outside, handing Kay her duty uniform wrapped up with old twine.

"We'll put it on when we get to work. We've got to cross that ol' ditch first."

They were wearing their shortest shorts as they stepped into the stagnant water, balancing their clean uniforms on their heads, steadying themselves with a rope that had been fastened to the buildings on either side. "No short, no pant," the Japanese had told the women. "Only skirt. Only dress." Kay could see the officer's outraged face, hear him yell at her again as he had the week before during the interminable bowing class they had been subjected to. Eighty percent of the camp dying from beriberi, the rest ravaged by dysentery and fatigue, and they had had to listen to that mad man prattle on about the varieties of respect women owed him, owed to all Japanese, owed to all men.

"Fuck you," Kay said aloud now to the phantom, and her friend, waist-high in water, smiled without looking back, knowing Kay was doing battle with demons in her own head. She was silently encouraged by her friend's show of spirit—but glad no Japanese officer had been there to hear it.

Kay didn't remember getting changed, but there she was in her ward, dried off and in her uniform, her hands shaking. She tried to fill the kettle, sloshing water everywhere. She added the dried guava leaves that helped lessen the symptoms of bacillary dysentery, but spilled half the tea on herself, on her patients. She gave out the last of the medicine to patients with amoebic dysentery; at least she thought it was amoebic. That was what the chart had said back when she could read. Who the hell knew anymore. It was high noon, but when she looked at the old classroom clock five minutes later, it read six o'clock and yellow sunlight was slanting in through the windows.

A baby started crying, then laughing, then it was talking to her in a gruff man's voice. No, it was one of the Kempeitai, the Japanese Gestapo, motioning at her to do something or

not do something, she didn't know which. Then she must have
fallen, because she was looking up from the floor, from under
one of the hammocks where she must have rolled. She saw a rat
coming toward her and thought she had better get up. When
she finally stood up, it was night, and the same doctor was
slumped over his work as when she had first come on her shift.
She thought he was dead, but he wasn't, he was just writing,
she didn't know what. No, when she looked closer, he was dead
after all. She saw the rat again, and she picked up a broom to
shoo him away, and he ran halfheartedly into the adjoining
room, but when she followed him there she stopped and did
not enter.

The room was filled with dead. That was what the Kempeitai had been saying: "No more individual burial." The prisoners were too weak to dig or lift or carry anymore anyway,
so, by default, this was where their dead had gone. On tables,
neatly laid out; on the floor, flung pell-mell—and everywhere
in between were rats. The rats bothered Kay, more than the
mounds of dead flesh, more than the piles of lost companions heaped negligently in front of her. She resented that the
rats were no longer hungry, gorging themselves on a never-
ending feast; they would kill themselves, they would burst
their wicked stomachs with this orgy, but it would never end,
there would always be more and more dead to feed them with.

Kay backed out of the room, bumping into one of the
slung stretchers, disturbing a rat that plopped down heavily
to the floor. She looked at the patient; his fingers had been
gnawed. She looked from stretcher to stretcher, and here, there,
another one, another tail slinking under a sheet, a whiskered
nose poking out from under a withered arm. The rats were not
content with the dead, but had started in on the living, on the

half-living who were too weak to fend them off anymore, patients staring with glazed eyes at the vermin who were eating them alive.

They're not dead yet, Kay thought, something rising within her, a mixture of horror and shock and invigorating madness.

"Not dead yet," she said aloud.

She shook another stretcher, and an obese rat fell out, catching himself with his tiny back nails, scrabbling back onto the side of the hammock. She shook it again and again until he fell, shook himself all over in disgust, and ambled a few feet away.

"Not yet," she said again, moving to another stretcher where a child was crying, trying to shake off the mice that were biting his fingers.

"Not yet!" she screamed, no longer herself, no longer a nurse but a madwoman, darting from patient to patient, shaking them, striking them, hitting them with her broom, with her open palms.

"Not dead yet . . . not yet!"

Now someone was trying to stop her, but they were too weak; she had a strength and an energy born of madness itself, and she was an unholy terror, an impotent angel of death wielding an old palm broom instead of a flaming sword. The mice and rats were underfoot now; she stepped on their fleshy tails, and they chirped discontentedly, moving off slowly toward the Room of the Dead and easier pickings. She passed by the doctor's desk, a sharpened pencil still poised in his left hand, and saw a monster of a rat, swollen beyond measure, calmly eating the man's fourth finger. He was down to the wedding ring. Quick as lightning, she snatched up the pencil and brought it down right through the middle of the gigantic, bloated thing.

It squealed and thrashed and twisted, lashing out and biting her, but she didn't let go. She held the pencil down, its point sunk deep into the teak wood of the table, blood spattering everywhere, and she was laughing and saying to the doctor, "There, Jim, I got him for you—there, Jim, now that's something," and when she woke up, hours later, the pencil was still clenched in her hand.

IT SEEMED TO be afternoon—the afternoon of which day Kay was unsure. Her watch seemed to point to three; unless it was morning, and then maybe it was nine; or maybe it was another time entirely, it was too hard to tell. It wasn't reveille because she hadn't heard the music over the loudspeaker. She wondered if anyone thought she was dead. If anyone was still alive to think she was dead. She thought of sitting up, but it seemed so much bother. She was back in her bunk now, no longer in the hospital. How she had gotten there, across the flooded depression, back up the stairs, she didn't know, she could not remember. It didn't matter anyway. Would it be worth crawling (she would have to crawl, there was no other way) down for the quarter-cup of rice soup that tasted like nothing? For the one ounce of grisly meat she might receive? And what would that meat be? The day before the Japanese had ordered the inmates to kill the last of the carabaos, starving, sickly things themselves. Without weapons, the prisoners had had to tie up the animals and beat their heads until they were dead. Kay remembered an elderly professor hitting the dumb beast over and over again with a rock and crying, asking it, asking God, to forgive him. But in a day or two, the last of the carabao meat would be gone too, and then there would be nothing left. Yes, she had better get up. Better force herself to get up.

Or she would die, right there, in her bunk. She thought about
it for a minute—or maybe for an hour—and in the end she
decided she would get up. In a minute. In just a minute . . .

KAY WAS CUTTING out Christmas decorations, paper angels
holding hands. She had made strips and strips of them and was
stapling them all together to make one gigantic bunting to
decorate the hospital doorways. She was thinking about what
she would get Aaron for their first Christmas together—her
mind ran naughtily along the lines of lingerie, of one particularly wicked, gorgeous kimono that covered nearly nothing
that she had seen for sale in the marketplace. No, she couldn't
do that, not for a Christian holiday. She'd get him something
sensible instead, like gloves. And a tie. *And* the lingerie, last
of all, wrapped up in printed rice paper and a red silk ribbon;
she could already see his face when he opened it. She folded
another piece of paper accordion-style, back and forth and back
again, making the creases sharp and firm with the side of her
short thumbnail. She didn't even need to pencil in the outline
anymore, but started cutting out the head, the wings, the tip
of the angel's dress where it swung out stylishly on both sides.
She thought of Aaron again. He was out on the runway at
Clark Field or up in the sky by now. They had come to Luzon
only a few days before; he to inspect the aircraft, she to continue her work in the hospital ward. And sleep with Aaron.
That was why she had come. That was why she had been born;
she was hot just thinking of him, she couldn't keep her mind
on her work. She was newly wed and in love, and everything
reminded her of Aaron—the smell of the sea, the heady scent
of flowers, the wind coming through the open windows and

playing at her hair under her nurse's cap, blowing the blank sheets off the table, making the long lines of embracing figures fly out and undulate in the Pacific breeze, holding hands, holding on to each other.

Kay had gotten used to the planes by now, hearing them roar overhead. Today Aaron would be out on a test run of a plane that had been acting up. He liked his work. It was a game he played until he came back at night and was undressing her before she could get dinner on the table. Her face went red thinking of him last night, eating his supper buck naked at the table. The murmur of the engines overhead merged with the never-ending calls of insects and birds and other mating things and she was a part of it all, she was full and bursting with it. She thought she was pregnant, but it was too soon to tell. Her body throbbed at the very idea, madly desiring it, desiring Aaron. She would sleep with him until she had given him a dozen sons. She would go fat and flaccid from the pregnancies, she didn't care, as long as it brought him back to her for more, always for more. In a few weeks she'd know for sure, and when she told him about the baby his joy at having her would be complete and he would make love to her but not roughly—delicately, cautiously, unable to restrain himself completely, but with a tenderness even greater than the tenderness he showed her now, a new kind of passion, a reverence, an awe. Three weeks till Christmas. She'd know by then. Yes, she'd tell him for Christmas.

Her best friend, Sandy, walked into the ward, still holding a tray of hypodermic syringes she had been sharpening. (With repeated use, the tips got blunt and the boys complained.) Her red lips stood out in contrast against her pale, freckled face, but her mouth wasn't smiling as usual; it was puckered up into a small, red knot.

"What's up, Sand? You look like you're going to cry," Kay laughed, still glowing inside from her secret. Sandy was Kay's partner in crime, helping her keep the fact of her marriage to Aaron from their head nurse. Kay would have to leave the army when she was eventually found out (no married nurses in this man's army), but they figured that, between the two of them, they'd be able to keep their secret for quite some time. When Kay still got no answer to her question, she came down to earth for one second to connect with the mere mortals who still inhabited her paradise. "Sandy? What is it?"

The red lips quivered for a second, the white teeth biting the lower lip hard, the red paint coming off on them. "It's Pearl Harbor, Kay. They bombed it."

Kay was still smiling. Nothing could tarnish the perfection of her life, of her future, of this shining Monday morning just over the International Date Line. Sandy's words bounced harmlessly off the oblivion of her happiness.

"What are you talking about?" she asked, almost irritably. "Who bombed what?" It couldn't be anything really, just an accidental explosion perhaps, someone smoking too near the fuel tanks again, some fools playing around with unstable explosives, trying to dispose of them quickly in the harbor and blowing themselves up in their hurry. It was nothing, it must be.

Kay watched as a single tear ran down the side of Sandy's pug nose, getting stuck in the little dimple next to her right nostril. "The Japanese, Kay. They bombed Pearl Harbor. They're saying thousands are dead, Kay, battleships, planes, they're all gone."

One minute Kay was a queen, sitting amid her paper cutout court; then the wind picked up outside and blew the angels across the room, robbing her of her subjects.

"We're under attack. I mean, they might come here next, Kay, we're supposed to get our gas masks on and . . ."

Kay didn't hear any more. She wanted Aaron. She needed Aaron. If the Japanese had done this thing, if the unthinkable had finally happened, she needed to see Aaron. She needed to see him running toward the hospital from the tarmac outside, needed to feel his strong arms around her waist once more, needed him to tell her it was going to be all right, that they could win this thing. She needed, at least, one last kiss, needed to say good-bye to him before he flew off into the blue to save the world for their unborn child. But he didn't come. Sirens were going off and people were running and he didn't come. She wore her gas mask designed for a full-grown man; its sides would not fit against her temples no matter how hard she tugged on the straps. She wore it in the heat and the sweat and uncertainty; the nurses were supposed to stay at their posts, to head for the shelters, to not do anything until further orders. The whole time she stood by the window, breathing in air smelling of old rubber and mold, looking for Aaron, aching for Aaron, and still Aaron didn't come.

Then she heard the planes.

She had been listening for them without knowing she was listening for them, but as soon as she heard that discordant noise, different from the American engines she had grown accustomed to, she knew what it was. Before she could see the low-flying silhouettes against the afternoon sky, see them in stark formation over the field, she knew what it was. It was death.

The maintenance building next to the hospital went first. The explosion shook her, surprised her, it was so loud, so close, she could feel the heat on her face. She ran to the other side of her empty ward and looked up. The Japanese planes were pulling up, turning, coming back to strike again. "The planes, good God, the planes," someone was shouting, but they didn't mean the Vals and Zeros closing in on them. The American P-40s were neatly parked in rows on the airfield, not a single one out of place, looking like dominoes waiting to fall. They hadn't been allowed to take off, they weren't cleared, war hadn't been declared yet, and now it was too late, they were going up in flames. The Japanese dropped their bombs like sheets of falling rain, hitting the meticulously aligned targets, destroying one after another after another with an accuracy that was almost effortless. In what seemed like seconds, they were all on fire, their pilots never making it onto the runway but standing halfway there, dumbstruck, unable to move.

There were casualties on the ground, and the girls waited until the last plane had passed overhead and started to circle back before they ran out, kneeling on the burning asphalt in their bare knees, calling out for stretchers, dragging men off the field themselves. The Japanese came back three minutes later, but they had been so efficient there was little left to demolish. They dropped their payloads and then flew off again for Formosa, leaving nothing but smoke and flame in their wake.

"Have you seen Aaron?" Kay was asking, asking everyone—the injured she was treating, fellow nurses, his drinking buddies, the men in his command, men who had never heard of him. She saw the wreckage of a twisted B-17 burning in front of her. That was what he had said at breakfast, wasn't it, that he would be test-flying one of those? She couldn't remember, she hadn't been paying attention. No, it couldn't have been his, he couldn't be dead. Her belly ached, and she was sure she was going to throw up, but then she caught sight of him—*thank God, thank you, God*—he must not have gone up after all. She saw him rushing around the burning airfield, yelling orders, hoisting men onto litters. He didn't see her through the smoke, and she couldn't get to him across the field, but she was crying—crying and crying for sheer joy amid all that death and wreckage that still didn't touch her, that still wasn't real because he was alive. He was alive, and as long as he stayed alive she knew she could face anything—anything at all.

KAY ROLLED ON her side and fell off her bunk. Then slowly, inch by inch, she started crawling toward the dormitory door, toward the staircase, toward the courtyard with its irresistible aroma of rotten food.

IT WAS CHRISTMAS EVE and they were evacuating, pulling out, leaving everything behind. They seemed to be losing. *How could we be losing? We are the greatest army, the greatest nation on earth, and yet we're running.* The nurses packed up their injured, their supplies, everyone was on trucks, in ambulances, they were headed toward Bataan, wherever that was, from there to some island, some stronghold, someplace underground, she had heard, a place where they'd be safe. They'd have to go through the jungle first. The women had pulled the mosquito netting from the beds, covering the injured, stuffing the extra nets into sacks, into truck cabins, into pockets. They would need it where they were going. Kay had seen Aaron that morning, but just for a second. She hardly recognized him anymore, his hair long and disheveled, dark circles under his eyes from sleepless nights spent strategizing with fellow officers, with command, trying to find a way out, trying to save the men. And now not just men but women too, the nurses caught in the crossfire. And not just any women. He had to try to find a way to save Kay.

She was making it worse, she knew she was, just the fact of her. He had too much to contend with already without his heart walking around outside his body, imagining—he couldn't think of it, he never thought of anything else—the Japanese taking his wife from him, raping her, then casting her aside, a bayonet run through her belly. But he had his orders, his duty, they were his first priority . . . almost his first priority. He struggled not to look at her now as she boarded her truck. This was too much to ask of any officer, of any man—to put the lives of his men above that of the woman he loved. To march his men toward uncertainty and death was bad enough without having his wife hanging on to his arm all the while. So Aaron had tried to shore up his heart, to push Kay aside, to become distant and aloof, but he had failed, failed miserably to protect himself, failed to turn off his soul. The one or two times they had managed to steal away together he would make love to her desperately, exhaustedly, and fall asleep holding on to her, his arms and legs wrapped around her for dear life, until her arm fell asleep under his weight and still she lay there unmoving, embracing him, enfolding him as if she could protect him, as if she would never let him go.

But they were moving out. During the day the trucks rattled down the crazy trail, jolting them, bouncing them along the way. They had to get to Bataan, to Corregidor, before it was too late. It was slow going. They crossed paths with other units, with other soldiers; got bogged down, held up by villagers, by refugees, by missionaries coming down from the hills to ask what all the fuss was about. The roads were washed out, impassable with mud or stranded carabaos or children begging to stand on running boards, to hang on to the backs of jeeps, anything—*Take us with you, GIs.* When they found U.S. wounded they would stop and set up tents and operate, and the Japanese would spot the red crosses from above and zero in on them as if they weren't off-limits, as if the Geneva convention didn't forbid it. Japanese planes would hone in and strafe them, and the injured they had just put back together again would be blasted apart, and the nurses would stand outside and scream at the sky, shaking their fists and cursing. Then there came the day when the guerrillas who had fought alongside the Americans knew the game was up and went back to their villages, to their own wives and children, to die with them instead of with the white soldiers. No one tried to stop them from going. And then Aaron had told the officers to rip off their insignia, to take everything off that marked them out as special targets for snipers. The second lieutenant nurses were to do the same; his wife was to do the same.

They were bombed in the jungle, and Kay knew by now to keep her mouth open—the concussion would be too much for her ears if she didn't. They patched men up, and the Japanese tore them apart, and it all seemed one long nightmare; even in her dreams Kay was smearing the men's blood on their foreheads in the shape of an *M* just as she did in real life. They had run out of tags, and this was the only way to keep track of who had had morphine and who had not.

They had some Filipina nurses with them, nurses who had served with them at Clark and, before that, alongside them in

Hawaii. Now one of the majors was telling them to go, that they were no longer needed, to try to make their own way back to whatever island they came from, thanking them coldly for their service. The nurses cried, begging the men not to leave them. They wanted to come with them to Corregidor, not be left to be raped and tortured by the Japanese. They pleaded that they were Americans too, that they couldn't be abandoned like this. But the major was adamant—for him, America had suddenly shrunk to forty-eight contiguous states. He was not responsible for them, he declared; they were not "real" Americans, after all, they would have to make do.

Then the nurses from Kentucky, from Texas, from Louisiana and Maine had sat down and refused to move. *Take us all or leave us all*, they had said. Kay had done it too; she'd put down the suturing kit she was taking into surgery and sat down on the muddy ground with her fellow nurses, crossing her arms. She had seen Aaron looking at her when she glanced up defiantly for a second, and for that second he seemed to smile at her with his eyes, to love her even more than he already did. But in another second, the look was gone, he was one of the officers again, mad at the obstinate women—or pretending to be mad at any rate. The major had yelled at the girls, kicking down a lean-to in his anger, but in the end he had had to take them all, had to load all the "god-damned" women back onto the trucks and move them all out, turning from this minor defeat to the major ones that loomed ahead of him in Bataan. The small Filipina nurse next to Kay in the truck had taken her hand in hers and kissed it.

But that had marked the beginning of the end. Shells had rained down on them nearly every day after that, often several times a day. They had lost a lot of vehicles; many of them were

walking the long way south to the peninsula. The injured cried
out as the remaining trucks and jeeps hit potholes, jarred them,
shook them, reawakening their pain, reopening their wounds.

Then Aaron had been hit by shrapnel—not killed, only a
minor wound, really, but in this jungle of dirt and sweat and
infection it hadn't taken long before he couldn't walk without
her help. Then until he couldn't walk at all.

Kay had gotten him onto a truck, changed his dressings
more often than they needed to be changed, poured sulfa onto
them; but she watched as the raw, pink edges of his injury
turned red, then purple, spreading out over his abdomen. His
color was all wrong too, he was all over sweat from the heat
and humidity and his fever.

"We're almost there, sweetheart," she would say, smiling
a little too brightly, walking alongside the ambulance, easily
keeping up with its turtle pace. "Nearly to Bataan. They'll have
a real hospital set up for us by then, nothing to worry about,
dear, nothing at all. They'll have everything ready."

What would they have ready? They could clean the wound
there, surely; could give him fresh water to drink and she could
sit by his side and fan him to keep him cool. But what could
they really do for this? What could anyone do for an infection
once it took hold of a man? *This is 1941 and dear God, we still
don't have anything for this, nothing in the whole wide world for this.*
The nurse in her thought Aaron would die, and the woman carrying his child (she hadn't bled now for three months) knew he
would never die, that he could not die, not before their son was
born, not before their dozen sons were born, and grew up, and
stood around their father, still handsome with his white hair,
each boy half a foot taller than his dad.

Kay looked around her, and all of a sudden she was back

on earth. From the moment she had stepped off the gangplank at Pearl Harbor—back when that name had just been a port of call—she had lived with her feet off the ground, in a world set apart. That dream world was now shattered. She found herself dirty, disheveled, dripping with sweat. She was hungry and thirsty and so tired that she wanted to lie down in the dirt road and sleep and sleep and never wake up. And with a revelation that was startling in its suddenness, she realized that everyone around her felt the same way, had felt the same way for weeks, for months now, as they tramped through this jungle toward death. She hadn't realized it before because she had been special, she had been safe, she was in love, and nothing could ever separate two people who loved each other as much as she and Aaron did. Nothing, that is, except death. Now she knew that death could do that, that death had separated millions of lovers before her, would separate millions more long after she and Aaron were gone and forgotten. She was nothing special after all. She had loved a man for a few months only, and now he might be dying, and there was nothing she could do but walk beside him, staying with him to the end. At least she had that—she would hold on to that. She would stay with him to the end.

THE KAY STARVING to death in Manila pulled herself painfully down the dark stairwell. Something was in front of her, blocking her way. She nudged at the heavy mass, and it moved only slightly; she put both feet to it, groaning and pushing with all her might, and the bloated corpse fell away from her, down the stair, into darkness.

THEY HAD MADE it to Hospital No. 2 in their southward retreat, but when they got there the hospital was out of supplies and they told Kay to try farther on, at Little Baguio—they might still have something there. Little Baguio was on their way anyway, everyone was heading south. Corregidor was the last hope; the Japanese were only five miles behind them—well armed, rationed, and equipped, a quarter-million strong, pushing quickly down from the north. Kay looked around her at the stretchers and litters lined up and ready for transport—four thousand were waiting here, she estimated, probably at least as many were waiting ahead of them at Little Baguio, the last outpost before the tunnel. How would they manage to bring them all? How could they all fit? Well, what did it matter as long as there was room for Aaron? She'd get him something—*What, exactly?* her mind asked her, and was silenced—and then get him on a transport, get him to this Corregidor everyone kept talking about, some kind of stronghold. She'd get him there and then everything would be okay. Somehow. It had to be okay.

At Little Baguio she got some fresh bandages (washed and dried out on a line in the sun, but better than nothing), the last of the powdered sulfa, and a canteen of potable water, but that was it. They were out of everything, they were mobilizing, they had their own wounded to deal with plus the wounded the retreating forces had just dumped on them. America was pulling out, dragged down by eight thousand bloodied soldiers pulling at her pant cuffs, slowing down her retreat. The buses never stopped honking, even though traffic south was at a standstill. Refugees pounded on the sides of the vehicles and climbed onto the roofs, everyone was screaming, everyone was crying, *Please, GI lady, take my child, take my baby.* Kay looked around her and knew that this was hell. No need to die first in order to see it—man had created it right here, for himself, for the living. *God have mercy.*

She had fought for a spot under a gran'folia tree, and now
Aaron lay there in its shade. He had a fever, but she wished it
was something acute, hot and fiery, something to make him
call out, something to fight against, even if only in a delirium. Instead, he just grew weaker and weaker, "sleepier and
sleepier," he called it, trying to smile. He wanted to rest, to lie
down, to sleep—*Kay, dear, lie down with me, let me sleep, darling.*
But Kay looked into his sunken face and knew that if he gave
in he would never wake up. She had to get him to Corregidor.
She couldn't lose him yet.

Bud, the ranking medical officer, walked over to her, to the
rest of the nurses straddling the wounded, tying off bandages,
splinting broken limbs.

"Hey," one of the girls called, but he didn't respond with
his usual wisecrack and bucktoothed smile; instead, he looked
sheepishly at the ground, then at the hat in his hands. He
swallowed, his Adam's apple bobbing awkwardly; Kay was
amazed it could squeeze past his tightly buttoned collar.

"General King just surrendered Bataan."

The ground they were standing on. Bataan.

"Officially, it goes into effect at midnight tonight." Here he
swallowed painfully again. "Practically speaking, girls, it goes
into effect the moment the Japanese get here."

Kay looked around her, at the nurses from Little Baguio
who were strangers to her, at the nurses who had disembarked
with her that very first day when their ship had dropped anchor
in paradise. Each woman, in her own way, was steeling herself
for what would come next; she could see it in a hundred tiny
gestures. One redhead bit her lower lip and inhaled sharply. A
chubby brunette straightened up, sore after hunching over the
wounded for hours, her freckled hand rubbing resolutely at the

small of her back. An older woman nodded her head sagely, as if she had known this was going to happen all along, as if the worst finally happening was a kind of relief, in itself. Several women folded their arms across their chests or raised hands protectively to their throats.

"Ready or not, here they come," one of the girls quipped. Everyone tried to laugh.

"The orders are for you to move out, immediately," the officer continued, stiffly, the toe of his boot digging absently into the dirt. Kay wondered why he was making such a formality of all this—*Yeah, sure, move out, we know the drill by now, Bud.* One of the head nurses started calling out orders: "Triage the new patients, load them onto the buses. Ambulatory patients will be assigned a green tag, those needing surgeries upon reaching Corregidor will get—"

Bud cut her off. "No, not the patients. *You* are to move out immediately."

"What?" the nurses laughed, derisively. "Yeah, right."

When they still didn't take him seriously, when they turned back toward the stretchers instead, toward their patients, the young medical officer raised his voice to them for the first and last time (he would die just two hours later).

"This is a direct order from headquarters. Refusal to do so will be punishable by court-martial."

They turned and stared at him, incredulous. Then, in a smaller voice, an apologetic voice, the voice of an older brother saying good-bye to his kid sister for the last time, "The Japanese are fucking three miles behind us, girls. Don't die right here, in front of us. Please, get in the buses."

People were arguing. A big-boned, short-haired nurse was yelling at Bud, and then more officers walked over and repeated what he had said, but now the Japs were closer, only two miles off. Buses were at the bottom of the hill, waiting for them, they'd have an escort to board, to get through the crowd. Someone was saying she wouldn't go; another had her head in her hands and was crying in the middle of the road, her elbows propped up on her knees. Kay heard someone ask if she had time to go get her underwear off the line, and when they said she didn't, Kay sank to her knees and held on to Aaron's hand until his fingers turned white.

"Easy there, baby," he mumbled groggily, looking up at her. She loosened her grip slightly. He hadn't heard what the commotion was about. Weak as he was, everything other than Kay was extraneous, was just random light and noise. She was all that remained. He smiled the shadow of a smile, and his watery eyes looked adoringly at her.

"I won't leave you, Aaron, I won't ever leave you."

His dazed eyes looked around him, looked past her for the first time in a long time. It took him a while to focus. "What's happening? Are we moving out?"

"I won't leave. They're sending the nurses away without the wounded. It's not right, I won't do it, I won't leave you."

Aaron wrinkled his brow as if trying to take it all in; for a second, Kay saw what he would have looked like as an old man, rubbing his cleft chin thoughtfully, his pale stubble making a homey, bristling sound.

"They're sending off the nurses," he repeated, slowly. "That must mean we're surrendering soon—"

"They just did. I mean, we just did. Surrender. Bataan anyway."

Aaron sat up, or tried to sit up. He made a violent lurch forward, then fell back.

"And you're still here? Bud, Bud," he was yelling, and his weak voice forced into a yell was throaty and broken and hoarse. "Bud, get my wife on a truck." Bud was still in a confrontation with the raging nurse, who was gesticulating wildly, but Kay noticed lines of women officers already starting downhill, getting onto the buses.

"No, Aaron, I won't leave you. Not ever."

"Listen," Aaron began. She was ready to resist him, to resist the whole U.S. Army, to cut and claw and scratch for the right to stay by Aaron's side. No one could force her, no one could make her leave with threats of court-martial or imprisonment or even death.

But she was not ready for—

"Listen," Aaron began again, quietly. "Look at me for a minute, baby."

And he smiled.

It was his peace that undid her completely. He looked at her and the nightmare around them disappeared, and he smiled like a holy mystic who had just figured out the secret of the universe and it was all some wonderful joke only he knew the punch line to.

"We found each other, babe."

"No, Aaron, no—"

"We found each other and we had each other, if only for a little while."

"Stop it, Aaron—"

There was an explosion and the women refugees screamed, but it wasn't the Japanese, not yet—just the American GIs blowing up their ammunition dumps.

"I won't listen to this, Aaron, I won't," and she pulled off his old dressings crawling with ants, dumping sulfa powder onto the oozing, blackening sore, crying and gulping air now tinged with gunpowder, wrapping and rewrapping the new bandages, tying them off, undoing the knots, retying them.

"I've got them too tight, let me try it again—"

He grabbed her wrists and held them firmly.

"Kay." He said it with such force—she knew in an instant what this man was made of. She had sold him short. She had not guessed at the strength and the steel inside of him; she knew, given a chance to live, he would have made an honest worker, a strong father, a faithful lover.

"Kay." He said it with such gentleness, thinking only of her, of her safety, of his life meaning nothing as long as she made it out safe.

"But—but the Japanese don't take . . ."

She was stammering now and shaking her head; this couldn't be happening, this couldn't be real. "They don't take injured . . ." She couldn't finish—her breath was already coming out in queer little bursts, like a child holding her breath until she couldn't hold it any longer, breathing out and in quickly, holding her breath again.

"Kay." The world fell away and she was melting into his eyes and they were on the beach again and making love and the harbor in front of them was silver in the moonlight.

"Go, Kay."

The buses were loaded, even the angry head nurse had made her slow way down the steep hill. They were honking their horn for her. They were leaving.

"Go."

Her breath was coming in shrieks now as she unshouldered her musette bag, stuffing his hands with the sulfa bottle, with the last of the food, with her canteen.

His blue eyes lit up one last time, and he smiled again and said, "I had you. I'm the luckiest guy in the world."

She was halfway down the hill when the main ammunition dump ignited; its concussion knocked her off her feet, but she was up again in a moment. The inside of her lip was bleeding from kissing him so hard, she could taste the salt, and then she was running again, running down the hill, she had always been running, she had to go faster, she could never go fast enough.

9

Jo McMahon

Spring 1945, The Western Front

They could use some Italians. Italians were fun. To Jo, they had never seemed to take the war very seriously. Sure, they could shoot and fight and bleed to death as well as anyone else. Back home in their sleepy, medieval villages, the Fascists had probably whipped them up into a frenzy that was patriotic enough at the time, abetted by the liberal application of liquor and women willing to send them off to war in truly traditional fashion. But by the time Jo's medical corps encountered them, the Italians' hearts had gone clean out of the thing. They were not opposed to violence, of course—in fact, memories of knife fights, of family vendettas, of watching their fathers' blood trickle into the gutter after a duel fought over a wayward sister, held for them the same golden glow of nostalgia that a turkey dinner with all the trimmings would bring their New England counterparts in the U.S. Army. But those acts of violence had been understandable to them, had been facts of life. They had been swift—vengeful, passionate, brutal, yes, but swift, the work of a moment, a blind rage, a burning and a fire, an explosion in your head and then a release. But war—prolonged, calculated war—had not been to their liking. North Africa had been hell. Retreating through their homeland—watching it be ruthlessly destroyed by ally and enemy alike—had been hell. And the Germans had been hell to work with. Germans might think themselves half-gods, divinely appointed to disseminate their Aryan seed, the free world might think them usurpers and butchers, rallying around a fanatical leader, but the Germans just bored the Italians to tears.

The Germans were no fun, they found no joy in life—they were all for rules, for order, for method. They looked down upon the Italians as inferior, as barbarous; the Germans never got their crude jokes, even those who spoke Italian. Listening to their ideology, it seemed the Germans wanted to rid the world of everything the Italians thought worthwhile—corruption and easy living, theatrical flourish and wanton revelry, lying back in bed with your best friend's wife, drinking his wine, watching his vineyards ripen in the sun, watching your son ripen in the soft, supple bump of her belly. The German officers' talk of eugenics and genocide fell on deaf ears; besides, the Italians were homesick, they were hungry, they wanted to go home. When the Americans finally caught up with them, they were throwing down their weapons and throwing up their arms just as soon as they could be sure the GIs had the Germans covered.

Jo thought of those first Italian POWs they had met—cheering, waving, whistling at the American nurses, holding out their hands for cigarettes, jostling each other for a chance to see them better: *Ciao, beautiful woman, I love you, I kiss you.* They had taken some Germans captive that same day, some of them seriously wounded. Queenie had argued with a patient eighteen inches taller than herself, asking him to lie down, to get onto the table: *Sir, we need to operate, to start the anesthesia.*

In broken English, the officer had defied her, saying he could endure the surgery while still conscious. Pain was for weaklings, for Americans, not for a man such as himself; then he had yelled at the scared Bavarian farm boys and music students from Berlin to rise up out of their cots and kill their nurses, to destroy their oppressors, to fight to the last man. Queenie, wearing the disapproving expression of an elementary school teacher, had said, "Bloody hell," and strapped the anesthesia mask to his face, holding it there until the *überman* had fallen in a heap on the floor in front of her as she yelled for the orderlies to get him the fuck up. The Italian patients had laughed, and a few of them had started to applaud.

Jo missed the Italians. She had been called upon to act as translator. They understood most of her dialect, they smiled even when they didn't: *Giusepinna, cara mia, io voglio tanto tanto bene.* They couldn't keep their minds on what the American officers were trying to get across—the terms of repatriation, their legal status for the duration of the war. "We eat? We have cigarettes?" they would laugh, slapping each other on the back at their good luck. "God bless America."

Jo remembered one Italian soldier she had met early on; she had asked him the usual string of questions in Italian—his name, where he was from—and, in a perfect Brooklyn accent, he had asked her for a Lucky Strike.

"You're American?" Jo had asked, astonished.

"Listen, sister, I was over here visiting my aunt when all of a sudden we up and join this war. I couldn't get home, and my aunt didn't want me getting shot for being an American, see? So I end up getting conscripted into their army." Jo's face had showed her amazement, and he had laughed out loud. "I've been shooting up into the air for months now, just waiting for you guys to take me prisoner."

Jo missed singing to the Italians. She was shy about her voice with almost everybody else—she had never sung for her parents; once or twice Gianni had come to hear her practice at Signor Luigi's, but the men and women she worked with always seemed whiter, always seemed "more" American than she was. Why that should make a difference to her about her singing she didn't know, but it did, and her *voce argento* had been silent around them. But one of the Italians had caught her humming Puccini when she hadn't even noticed she was doing it, and at the end of her shift he had somehow elicited her whole story from her and had her singing every piece she knew in Italian. (He didn't care so much for the German operas.)

> *O mio babbino caro,*
> *mi piace, é bello, bello.*
> *Vo'andare in Porta Rossa*
> *a comperar l'anello!*

When she spoke of wanting to buy the ring, the Italian soldiers had smiled blissfully, but talk of throwing herself into the Arno had sent them into absolute ecstasy.

> *Mi struggo e mi tormento!*
> *O Dio, vorrei morir!*
> *Babbo, pietà, pietà!*

She could still see their adoring faces, the older men actually crying, propped up two or three to a bed, the guard

assigned to watch them with his gun slung carelessly over one
shoulder, playing poker with the orderlies and cursing when
he lost. His work was easy—no one was trying to escape here.
Where on earth would they go?

But they had gone, reluctantly, to some other place of de-
tention, to different cigarettes and different rations and (they
hoped) different women to flirt with. Jo looked around the
tent now, and everything seemed gray without them. The mud
floor had dried and cracked into a gray, powdery mess; her
patients' skin was a paler shade of gray. Her hair was streaked
with it, the linens tinged with it; the sky outside was a solid
sheet of it. The weather was petulant, dangling the hope of
spring in front of them one day, ramming winter down the
back of their shirt collars the next. Puddles froze and thawed
and froze again.

The Germans hadn't found them yet, and Clark's men hadn't
encountered any on their patrols, but whether the enemy was
advancing their way or completely surrounded them or had
passed them by weeks ago remained a mystery. The Rangers,
after hastily burying their comrade, had been in a hurry to
leave (to "get away from that crazy nurse," one of them had
muttered, spitting). Two of Clark's best men had gone with
them, to reestablish contact, to get them back into the goddamned war and out of this limbo. But they had left five days
ago now and still no word. The world turned. And it was gray.

Jo thought of another monotonous steel-gray morning, but
one that had been monotonous in a different way, in a much
busier way: she had been wrapping and plastering heavy orthopedics, hanging the casts, moving the never-ending stream
of broken men farther down the line. Nearby, just outside the

open tent flap, she had noticed half a dozen men in a semicircle, apparently questioning one of the new recruits. The young man had looked nervous, smoking a cigarette and smiling ingratiatingly. "C'mon, guys, quit foolin'," she had heard him say. Then more men had joined the group, some of them officers. The other men saluted and stepped aside; then the officers were questioning the newcomer, an orderly who had joined their unit only a few weeks before. A nice kid, from all Jo could make out; she had never had to ask him for anything twice.

"I don't know what you're talking about, this is crazy—" he was saying.

Then the low murmur of his interrogators' questions.

"Of all the goddamned nonsense, who's been saying that?" His voice was high now, irritable; he looked like he was going to cry, or punch someone, or both.

"I've never even been to—"

He was cut off by another question.

"I'm from Cleveland Heights—"

"Yes, right next to Cleveland."

"In Ohio, goddamnit, what do you take me for?"

"God Almighty." He was keeping his temper in check now, but barely. "Bordered by Pennsylvania, West Virginia, Kentucky, Indiana, and a little bit of Michigan, for Christ's sake."

The officers straightened up at that, rubbing their chins. They looked solemnly at one another, eyebrows raised. The kid looked from one to the other of them, hopefully—

"Okay now? Satisfied? Can I get back to work?"

One of the officers nodded his head, and the others started to widen the semicircle that had been slowly tightening around him. The orderly relaxed his shoulders almost imperceptibly and exhaled; he wiped his forehead with a dirty handkerchief. Almost as an afterthought, one of the officers—a major— looked over his shoulder at Jo and said, "Miss?"

"Yes, sir?" She slowly lowered the heavy cast she had been working on.

"We have reason to believe someone around here is not what he—or she—seems to be."

"Sir?" Jo had found deference the easiest way to deal with the brass.

"I know I can trust your discretion, miss, so I'll be blunt. We think there is an enemy agent under cover here, perhaps in your own unit."

Jo stared at the major, then at the orderly, then back at the major; she waited.

"Is there anyone you can think of who has acted suspiciously in the past few weeks? Think carefully, miss."

Jo had been so busy, so overwhelmed with work, that she wouldn't have noticed if Queenie had shaved off all her hair, but she just answered, demurely, in the negative. "No, sir, I haven't noticed anything unusual."

The major shook his head, as if he were a detective following up on a lead, unwilling to give up the scent while it was still fresh. "Isn't there *anything,* miss," he asked, throwing up his hands, "anything at all you can think of that a Jerry wouldn't know? I mean, they're smart, I'll give the bastards that, they're well trained. They know the starting lineup for the Dodgers and Superman's girlfriend's name and U.S. geography better than my own kids back home. Can't you think of *anything?*"

The officers all looked at Jo expectantly; the baby-faced kid sitting on a barrel looked at her and smiled impishly behind their backs. She was too busy for all this cloak-and-dagger stuff. Probably someone had it in for this kid; he had swiped someone's chocolate or someone's girlfriend, or even just cut in front of the wrong person in chow line. Of all the silly comic-book nonsense—

The men were still looking at Jo. She would never get back to work at this rate.

"I don't know," she began, looking up as if she were searching the lowering clouds outside for an answer. Then, exasperated, grasping at straws, at anything—"Ask him to sing 'Happy Birthday.' Everybody knows that." Then Jo went back to her work, apologizing to her patient for the wait, for the colossal waste of time.

Her back was turned, so she could not see the kid's face.

Because the boy on the dented barrel stopped kicking his heels aimlessly, his smile melting from his features. His eyes became wide and terrified for a moment, then narrowed, giving him an almost inhuman visage. Jo heard someone yelling, but she couldn't understand the words; and when she turned around she saw he had snatched the sidearm from the sergeant standing next to him and had emptied three shots into his chest before they gunned him down, still screaming, his free hand clenched, blood spattered over his freckled face. Then he stopped moving on the ground, but he was still staring at Jo with hatred, with fixed eyes that froze and glazed over but didn't close. They had found their leak.

Jo's mind was wandering today. They were out of medicine, they were almost out of food. Her patients slept fitfully; she felt more like a hall monitor than a medical nurse. She sat up with people; she noticed if they lived or died; she held a hand, when they wanted to, when the pain was too bad. Her body was stuck in space, but her mind wandered.

One of the men's helmets had rolled under a cot, and she stared at it now with her head cocked to one side, looking at its dull green luster, crisscrossed with scars and scratches. Her thoughts ran to that shell-shocked patient she had had a few months back, the one who could never catch his breath, who always thought he was suffocating. He had been in a house in the French countryside, he told her, freezing and begging for food with some of his buddies. They had been separated from their unit, and the family there had taken them in. Then the family's little boy had burst through the front door, saying the Germans were coming down the road, *ma mère, mon père.* It was fields all around, not so much as a tree or a hedgerow for them to hide behind. The Americans were trapped—and the family along with them, for harboring the enemy.

The quick-thinking *femme au foyer* had said, *Get below, we'll bury you in the coal in the cellar until they leave, it can't be long. Dépêchez-vous! Hurry up!* And they did. They buried the soldiers under the coal. *Take a deep breath, boys, and cover your face with your helmets, they'll dig us out again all right.* The Germans came, and they didn't find the GIs. But they hadn't come this time to search the house or scavenge for rations and then leave, but to set up a temporary headquarters, a reconnaissance station. Three days later, when the Germans finally left and the Americans rolled by afterwards in their dull-green trucks, the same housewife had hailed them by flapping her white apron above her head and saying, *Come, dig up your dead soldiers, they're down in my cellar, get them out of my coal.* But not all of them were dead. The one boy lay there on the cold, frozen ground of the farmyard when they hauled him up (at last), coughing and gasping for breath, his face black, spitting up dark phlegm and gritty blood. Try as they might, they couldn't reason with

him, couldn't get him to open his eyes, couldn't get him to let
go of the helmet he still kept clamped in front of his face so
he could breathe.

Jo looked from cot to cot, her eyes searching the faces of the
six men in front of her, looking at them, looking right through
them. Father Hook, his hair needing a trim, the fringes starting to curl around his ears; his freckles standing out starkly
against his pale skin; his eyelashes so fair they seemed transparent, thick but colorless, shielding his little boy eyes. Major
Donahue, weak and exhausted, perpetually scratching at the
scar on his right side. His hair was dark and his eyes were
dark and he desperately needed a shave—*and* antibiotics, to
knock out the lingering infection that kept him too weak
to sit up. The major sighed, and rolled over, and started to
scratch again. Jo looked at Bill—*Billy,* she mentally corrected
himself—propped up with pillows, with rolled-up blankets,
with the men's uniforms folded up and stuffed beneath it all,
so he could breathe. He really was bald, she could see that now.
Everyone else looked disheveled and hairy, even herself, but his
egg-shaped head was taut and shiny. His small eyes were closed
behind his gold-rimmed glasses, and he was breathing fast,
fast, always too fast. Across the aisle from him James sat up in
bed, his knees pulled up to his powerfully built chest, his face
averted. She had taken off his bandages earlier in the week.
The skin had healed—it was no longer raw and oozing—but it
had formed into rounded lumps of flesh around his cheekbone
and eye socket. His fingers tentatively explored the new terrain
of his face, following its crests and valleys, fissures and cracks,
as if by doing so he might stop it, might make his real face
come back. And David. David should have been dead. From
everything she knew about medicine he should have been

either dead or better by now, but not still dangling, stuck in a half-world between life and death. The typhus had to come to a head soon, but something—a secondary infection, a mutation of the illness itself, maybe his own strong constitution—kept him from healing and kept him from dying and left him just hanging on. Jo looked at him now, lying still (too still) on his right side, his thick eyebrows shadowing his eyes, his mop of shiny black hair contrasting with the cool whiteness of his skin beneath. She remembered an old lithograph of Endymion she had seen once, eternally beautiful, eternally asleep, cast into endless slumbers so the goddess Selene could come to him and make love to him and give him fifty daughters he would only see in his dreams.

"Miss?"

Jo snapped out of her reverie.

"Yes, Jonesy."

Looking at him from across the tent, Jonesy looked incredibly prosaic—his features were enormous, disjointed; he was bucktoothed and big-eared, his nose seemed to take up half his face. There was nothing ethereal about Jonesy.

"Anything I can do for you, miss?"

"No, nothing, Jonesy. Thank you, though. I guess we just have to wait."

"Begging your pardon, miss, but, wait for what?"

Jo didn't answer. He hadn't meant her to. This was all they did. Wait.

Was there any hope left? That was the question anxious family members had asked her at that receiving hospital uptown; the question soldiers had asked her as they carried in their wounded buddies, bleeding and unconscious; the question she

asked herself every day. The problem was, she didn't know how
to answer it now any more than she had known back then. It
was the same conundrum the nurses had always been in. If a
soldier was dying, should they tell him he was dying? Should
they give the soldier that final chance to make his peace with
his God or his demons or the agony of his unfinished, trun-
cated life? Or would he, poised on the knife's edge between
life and death, hear a nurse's words as prophecy? Would his
psyche oblige? Would his heart stop through the sheer power
of suggestion? Would the nurse be doing more harm than
good? Was there any hope left? She didn't know. She had never
known.

And what role, after all, was faith supposed to play in all
of this? If someone had asked Jo outright, she would have said
that it was her faith that sustained her. The only trouble with
that was, for a long time now, she had been unable to feel her
faith, to access her faith. She could pray with words—hollow,
empty things rattling around in her head—or pray with her
very suffering, but the prayer itself was no longer a part of her.
It didn't seem to be coming from Jo McMahon at all. She was
too numb or paralyzed, or had become, somehow, immune to
the awesome, terrible power that prayer used to hold for her.
Maybe she was just too tired. Tired or hungry or cold. Maybe
this black emptiness was prayer, true prayer. Maybe what she
had mistaken for piety back in the civilized world had in reality been the effect of clean sheets and central heating and at
least one square meal per day. Maybe her own goodness and
generosity had only ever been the result of shaved legs and
combed hair and hot showers with plenty of lather—nothing
to do with her, with the person who took credit for those

things. Maybe God was in the emptiness, in the cold and pain and despair. Maybe finding Him there would be faith. Maybe even imagining He could be there was hope.

She looked again at David, and her heart lurched, and she said, "Goddamn, that's all I need—not that, not now." She shook herself and walked briskly to one corner of the tent. "Maybe you could do something for me after all."

Jonesy looked up hopefully, like an ugly bull terrier.

"Are you any good with radios? Ours is broken, but I'm not sure how bad it is. Maybe you'd like to look at it."

Jonesy willingly took the offered machine, its outer case cracked in two, turning it over and over in his hands.

"I'll have a go at it, miss." His face was glowing. He was already lost in another world, a boy tinkering with a new toy. She handed him an old screwdriver, and he took it without even looking up, gently tapping at the box, shaking it, lifting it to his ear, and rattling it again.

Jo needed something to do. She had to keep busy. She knew that much.

She emptied the bedpans and straightened out sheets and blankets. (But she shouldn't have done that—the sweet, unwashed smell rising off of David made her head swim.) She boiled water for coffee, but they were out of coffee, so she waited for it to cool a little and gave the men hot water to drink instead. James wouldn't speak to her, wouldn't look at her; he shielded his face with his hand when she came near. But when she asked Father Hook for the hundredth time if there was anything she could do for him, he didn't immediately say no.

"Father? *Is* there anything?"

"Would you—would you mind sitting by me for a moment?"

Jo pulled over a packing box and sat down, slowly.

"I've been—I've been going through a very rough patch," he began. Jo took his pulse and put a hand to his forehead automatically, but he actually smiled a tiny smile and said, "No, no, miss, I don't mean that. I don't mean I feel any worse physically. It's more like, I've been through a very dark place. And—and it was awful," he said simply. "But I think I'm just the other side of it now. I realize where I am, and what's happened, and how you've been here all along, helping, and me not doing anything—not seeming to be doing anything anyway." He got all tangled up in his words and then smiled, ingenuously, at himself. "But God bless you, miss, for that."

He still looked terrible—pale and disheveled and sick—but the lost, vacant look in his eyes was gone. Very quietly, Jo asked, "Do you want to talk about what happened, Father?"

His face clouded for a moment. Then he sighed, resolutely. "No, but I guess I should, just this once anyway."

There was a long pause, so long that Jo thought he had changed his mind. Then, all of a sudden, he started, midsentence.

"And we were jumping, just—just like we always jumped. The younger guys were getting scared—'getting religion,' they used to call it, asking me to hear their confessions, even the ones who weren't Catholics. The older men laughed at them and cursed, but it was okay, we all knew we were the same underneath. Everyone believes in God just before they jump. So we did—I mean, we jumped. I don't carry a gun, you know, so they always try to keep tabs on me, always try to have one or two guys pretty close to me, to cover me when the fire starts. The bigger their sins the more valuable I seem to become," he said, smiling wryly. There was another pause before he started again, in a lower voice this time.

"It was night, and there were a lot of wind gusts as we got closer to the ground. I got all twisted around—I didn't know which way was up for a while. Then, all of a sudden, I was pretty close to a couple of guys, close enough to hear them yelling to each other. They were cutting their lines, they were getting out of their harnesses—we were coming in fast over the water, you could see it shimmering beneath us. They wanted to be free of the chutes before they hit so they could swim without getting tangled up in them. Then it came to me all of a sudden—I guess it was seeing the buildings so close by—and I yelled to them not to do it, that it wasn't water, it was asphalt. Asphalt can shine like that, miss, when the moon's out. But it was too late and they hit, I mean, they must have hit, miss, at, like, sixty miles an hour."

A tear ran down his baby cheek, and Jo thanked God for it. *Please, God, let him tell the worst of it, let him let it go.*

Jo reached out her hand and took his, and he didn't pull back.

He smiled a little, self-consciously. Then he went on, sniffing and rubbing his nose with his sleeve.

"Like I said, it had been really gusty. Somehow my chute got pulled up again—no, more like pulled up and out to one side, not toward the buildings, but—there was this row of trees, really big trees, you could see them black against the night sky, and I skimmed over one—not all the way, as you can see here." His free hand moved and rested lightly on his belly. "I remember crying out, it hurt so much, but I was surprised when I touched down on the ground, I mean, I was okay, I was alive, and in the end I came down so soft. It was like landing on a mattress."

Father Hook was staring right through Jo. She was there

but she wasn't there; she was the conduit that made it possible for him to speak, but he could no longer tell he was talking to her, no longer tell she was there at all.

"And then—I looked up. And—everyone else was still up there."

His tears flowed freely now, down the sides of his pug nose; he was crying, silently and freely.

"They were up there, screaming, all of them. They were stuck—they were—impaled by the branches. The branches were going right through them—they were struggling up there, the moon was out, you could see them—thrashing around, screaming, they just kept screaming . . . Good God, miss," he ended, shuddering, noticing Jo all of a sudden, coming back to her from the hell where he had been trapped, releasing the vice grip he held her hand in. "Good God," he repeated in a small voice, staring straight into her eyes, a scared boy, crying in the night.

Jo leaned forward and wiped the tears from his face.

"It's over, Father. It's all over."

"They died. They died, and I wanted to die too."

"But you didn't, Father. You're here. You're okay." Then, repeating it again, deliberately and slow, as if speaking to a very little child, as if her saying it would make it so, "It's over."

Jo was a mess. She knew that. Not just her physical self, but the Jo underneath—she knew how bad off she was. She saw her dead brother, and she'd come close to killing herself, and she knew the worst, most likely, still lay ahead of her. She felt that she had no courage and no strength left, no certainty of her future, of her patients' future, of the future of the whole damned world. But the only thing she was sure of—as she got up and made her way, achingly, toward the front of the tent—

was that she had just acted as a nurse. That that had been important. She had sat with a patient for a few moments only, but
she knew what she had done, what she had been. She had been
a nurse. And she was surprised how that still made her feel.

Up until then she hadn't been sure she could still feel anything anymore.

Jo sorted through the last of the rations, looking for something they could eat. It had grown steadily darker until she
had to light the small spirit lamp she had found earlier, packed
away. Now, in the soft glow of its light, she turned the cans
around and around in her hand to make out the labels: an open
B-unit can (stale biscuits and hard candy, minus the sugar and
coffee they had already scavenged), one can of meat and vegetable stew, one can of meat and vegetable hash. She felt she
could eat both cans herself and still be hungry, and here she
was trying to figure out how to feed the whole tent on just one.
She would need to leave the other one for tomorrow.

She settled on the hash and reached for the can opener, hung,
as always, on its rusty hook. She remembered the time, back
in Anzio, when she had been holding a post-op patient's hand,
soothing him with her soft words, with her soft touch, and one
of the new nurses had been complaining that she couldn't find
the can opener. Jo could still hear her voice, grating and irritable, jarring even if you hadn't just come out of surgery. Jo had
stood it as long as she could before finally swiveling around in
her chair and facing the young girl: "Could you be a *little* quieter? We hang it right here," and she had felt her patient's hand
go limp in hers almost simultaneously with a sharp round of
gunfire outside. The new girl had hit the floor, still whining,
and Jo had looked down on her contemptuously, but when she
turned back to her patient her heart stuck in her throat. There

was a new row of bullet holes running through the canvas just behind the bed where her patient had been propped up, intubated, trying to learn how to breathe. A row of neat holes with the setting sun burning through them now—a row ending where Jo would have been sitting had she not turned around at that exact second. The machine-gun fire had gone right through the canvas, and then the man's neck and his severed head was on the floor. Jo was holding the hand of a decapitated body. She had stood up, dropping the lifeless hand, tripping over the still prostrate form of the new girl. Jo had run outside, on the far side of the tent, and thrown up, thrown up until she couldn't anymore.

Jo nicked her finger with the sharp edge of the lid. She sucked it, and it tasted like salt and smelled like dog food. She began scraping out portions of mash into metal bowls but ran out and had to divide it up all over again. There was no chance of heating it up—their oil stove had run out of fuel that afternoon. Clark thought he had heard something a few nights back, so now that the temperature had edged just above freezing, fires were off-limits. There was a greasy, oily film on the indistinguishable mush in front of her and she was so hungry that she would have been happy to just have that, to lick the inside of the can, the sharp lid. Cut seven ways, there just wasn't enough. Cut six ways, maybe each man would get a mouthful. She cut it six ways.

She shivered as a cold gust of air hit her. Her back was to the tent flap, and in the split second it took for her to decide to turn around after getting the last of the hash off of her spoon, a Luger was clamped to her head.

Even as she felt the man's left arm come across her neck from behind, pulling her toward him, she held on to the food, managing to put it down, carefully, on the desk in front of her. As if she were outside of her body, looking at the scene unfold, she was pleased, she was proud. She hadn't dropped the food.

With her two hands free now, she tried pulling down on the man's arm. It was strong and hard like iron beneath the dark wool; the most she could manage was to wiggle enough to get her chin down, to wedge it between his grip and her bruised throat. She coughed, and swallowed, and took a quick breath. The tip of the barrel was pressed against her temple. So the Germans had come. She had always imagined them coming—in North Africa, Italy, France, here. In her dreams they were powerful, supermen, tall and dark and merciless. The man was whispering orders to her now in a hoarse voice, not daring to raise it, but Jonesy looked up from his work and opened his mouth. The man tightened his grip on Jo and held his elbow out fiercely to one side, exaggerating his hold on her, repositioning the gun against her skull. He was warning Jonesy, threatening him with Jo's life. Jonesy didn't have to know German to understand. He shut his mouth and stared, mutely. Billy blinked and quickened his shallow breathing; Major Donahue struggled to a sitting position, as did Hook—Jo noticed the priest's face tighten in pain as he sat up too quickly for the first time. (She hoped, abstractedly, that his stitches would hold.) James turned toward the noise and asked what was going on. Hook tried shushing him, but he asked again, louder this time, and the German sounded angrier.

"James, just sit quietly," Jo said in a voice so level it surprised her. "Don't speak."

"But what—"

The German was repeating himself. It was the same phrase, over and over, slowed down, over-enunciated for them; he was breaking it down into syllables, into small, phonetic chunks. Jo thought one of the pieces sounded like the English word *why*.

She looked down on David, just in front of her; his eyes were open, but whether he could see her, could see his enemy, she didn't know—his expression remained unreadable.

Jo's ankle hit the leg of the desk and she turned it, involuntarily, stumbling slightly and bumping into the man's torso. She could feel him wince, feel his grip momentarily weaken, hear his sharp intake of breath.

"You're hurt—" Jo began.

Again, the man began his recitation, but this time he was struggling through it, mumbling some of the words, starting over.

Jo tried turning to face the man. He nearly shouted at her in warning, catching himself mid-yell. His voice sounded like it was in pain, forced. Jo felt his body trembling. She bet everything on the hunch that he would not shoot her outright and, with a sudden effort, twisted around in his arms. She was terribly close now, right up against him, her head level with the little skulls on his collar. She felt him switch the pistol to her left temple, now on his right side, felt him grab her tightly around the waist, pulling her fiercely toward himself, all the while telling her something she could not understand, something he needed her to know. Jo wished she was wearing something with a red cross on it, a duty uniform, anything.

"Nurse," she said, trying to point to herself, but her hands were pinned down at her sides. Then, brushing the edge of the desk with her fingers, she felt for the stethoscope, grabbed it, banged it against the desk to get his attention.

"Nurse. I can help."

The man stopped speaking, glanced quickly at what was in her hand, and asked her a question.

"I'm sorry. I don't understand German," then, struggling, reaching, *"Ich spreche kein Deutsch. I think."*

He loosened his grip slightly, just enough to pull away from her for an instant, enough to look down into her face, to gauge her. Jo looked up into his blue eyes, spastic and squinting in pain. With her head tilted back, his cleft chin was right in front of her, she could see the tiny flecks of golden stubble on it. Again, she looked at the little skulls on his collar—they reminded her of Halloween, of children dressed like skeletons, of pumpkins carved like death masks, lit up with fire, and laughing. The gun was still against her head as he released his hold and took one step back. Jo could see that his great coat hung open and that his uniform beneath was a deeper black— drying blood, a great splotch over his belly. Jo exhaled quickly and reached for the desk drawer. In an instant, his death grip returned, he was almost yelling.

"Oh, good God," Jo complained, stamping her foot in her impatience. "Here, you open it." And she motioned for him to pull out the drawer. He did, and she reached inside for the rolls of bandages, piling them up on the table. She pulled the tiny spirit lamp over and fell to her knees, pulling aside the strips of bloodied cloth. All at once, he was in distress over something, grabbing her hands, forgetting about the gun for a moment, then remembering, clamping it back in place but continuing to plead with her all the while.

"I don't understand," Jo said, pushing his free hand away, struggling to see. "Could you just keep still," she said more to herself, knowing she was as unintelligible to him as he was to her.

She was cleaning his wound now, patting at it with gauze in the half-light, washing it with the cold water she had boiled earlier, still sitting in its freezing teapot. He kept getting the gun between her and the light. Exasperated, she grabbed the Luger from him—but just to thrust it back into his other hand, pushing both up against her head. "There, fine, shoot me if you have to, but just stay out of my light."

He stopped complaining after that, standing there meekly, eyes cast down. It struck Jo that that was exactly the kind of thing Queenie would have done; and, for the first time, she realized she could think about Queenie without her heart breaking, think about her and even smile a little, just like she was alive, like she would come through that tent flap soon and get a kick out of Jo telling her how she'd wrestled a gun from a German only to give it back to him.

Jo covered the wound with gauze, then began wrapping it. The long strips of bandage had to stretch around the man's back, then back again, cross over and over. Jo laid the side of her face against him as she reached behind him, passed the roll from one hand to another, pulled it back, switched it around again. When she pressed against him, she could feel him trembling. He still kept the gun to her head, but it hung awkwardly now, unsure of itself, as if it stayed there because it couldn't think where else it should go. Jo finished and stood up. The man still held her, but loosely, the gun merely a token, brushing her shoulder.

"You should give yourself up," Jo began automatically, but she was uncertain even as she said it; she was unsure of what Clark would do to an injured German, to someone he could more easily persuade to give him information. The Geneva convention would mean little to a man like Clark. Jo shuddered; she had not believed it could be like this, that the enemy would have a face, that she would care. The German shook his head slowly, unable to understand her words.

"All right, then," Jo said, looking around. Then, "You must be starving." She glanced down at the food, and he followed her gaze.

"Guess I can split it seven ways after all," and she picked up a bowl to give to him. He did not move. He was staring into her eyes, an incomprehensible expression on his face.

"Go ahead, it's all right," Jo coaxed, smiling. "Back home, I had to skip meals regular."

Still he didn't move.

"Afraid these men here will jump you?" She smiled again. "I think you'd be okay without the gun, mister, but if you can't give it up—" and she scooped up some of the food and held it up for him. He ate it hungrily. She fed him again, a tiny speck getting stuck on the side of his upper lip; she scraped it off and fed it to him again. There were only a couple of ounces of hash on the plate, but time seemed to stand still as she fed him. They had always been there, a man and a woman, locked in that bizarre embrace, a loaded pistol hanging impotently between them.

Finally, Jo glanced down. She came back to the here and now. Clark's men could come back at any moment—a realization that sickened her.

"You'd better go," she said, and found she was whispering.

He took a step past her, heading for the back tent flap.

"No—" she called, reaching out a hand in warning. The man hesitated, looking back at her, puzzled.

"Damn it all to hell, how do you say it?" Then, guessing,

hoping the English word was anything equivalent: "Land mines that way. Land mines."

"*Landminen?*" the German asked, startled, eyes wide open.

Jo closed her eyes and silently thanked God. "Yes, you understood me. *Landminen.*"

The man hurried toward the front of the tent; then he stopped, turned around, and strode resolutely back to Jo.

"*Sie sind der letzte wahre Mensch in Frankreich.*"

And he kissed her.

He pulled her toward himself, and she could feel the gun again in his closed hand, but it was the handle this time, and he was holding her close and kissing her. She could hear the ticking of his wristwatch near her ear and the men rustling uneasily in their cots. She was distant and cold and detached— and then a spring broke within her, a cog, a wheel, a dam that had held her back, kept her unthinking, unfeeling, alive and yet dead all these months. The shackles of her self-preservation fell from her, and with a power that was overwhelming, it all came back to her at once. Her love for Gianni, her agony at his death, at the death of everyone she had cared for—she could hear Grandpa humming his tune, and see Queenie laughing as Jo saluted and the truck pulled out into the night. She was holding that boy's hand and his head was looking up at her from the floor, and every sight and every sound and everything she had witnessed but not felt came rushing back, the good along with the bad. So she kissed this man, her enemy, the figure that had haunted her dreams since the war began, and she found that he was just another human being, lost and maimed and alone; he was cut off from his friends, from his countrymen, just like she was; he was starving and cold and searching, just like her. Her hand reached up behind his head, and she found she had to stand on her tiptoes to press his eager mouth to hers but she did and she wanted him. She *wanted* again. She felt. And then he was gone, rushing out the front tent flap, and Jonesy was calling out for Clark, for anyone, sounding the alarm.

Jo picked up the nearest bowl, and it felt weightless in her hand; she checked it twice to make sure something was in it, that it wasn't empty. She sat by David's bedside for a full five minutes, but try as she might, he wouldn't cooperate, he wouldn't eat. The delirium was coming back, he was angry at her, he called her something vile in Scottish that didn't even need a translation. She could hear her voice—it was hers, yet it wasn't, it was too calm and too quiet. Jo wanted to scream, but she just whispered answers to James as she put the bowl into his hands—yes, the man was gone; no, she hadn't been hurt, he'd just been someone cut off from his unit. The second bowl went to the priest, his face dark and scowling; maybe he had been insulted by the liberty the German had taken, or maybe he was in physical pain, Jo couldn't tell. Major Donahue ate, and Billy ate, and after she had convinced him to stop yelling, to stop banging metal against metal—*Do you want to bring the whole German army down on us?*—Jonesy had eaten too. Jo was still whispering, she was hushing the men if they talked. She didn't know what she was listening for, but she was. She collected the bowls and washed them out in the far corner of the tent, by the back flap that led to the mine fields; then she dried them, and the whole time she was taking little half-breaths, breathing shallowly, straining her ears in the silence. She nested the bowls into each other—one after another after another—and she felt she was going mad, everything hinged on this, on stacking the bowls perfectly, geometrically. She put them down and picked them up again, and then she heard it.

It was laughter. She didn't know whose at first—she had never heard him laugh before—but it was an ugly sound, sinister and knowing. There was a low mumble, another quiet laugh, and then, "She's got a light on inside, we can search him in there," and then Clark came in, smiling—God, he was beautiful, she hated him, she wished he was dead. Then some of his men came in, carrying something heavy and long between them, dark against the darkness outside the tent. One of the men lost his grip for a moment, and the thing they were carrying shifted—it was a body. An arm fell down by its side, and she could see the wristwatch on it, hear it ticking across the tent, across the universe that separated them, and she dropped the bowls, all of them clanging discordantly against each other as they fell, shattering the silence, and she screamed.

"Don't you touch him!" She had never screamed so loud, it rose up out of her, uncontrollably, the hatred burning her throat like acid. "Get away from him, you get fucking away from him."

She could see Clark's dead eyes spring to life for a second, grow large and startled, then confused; she even saw him take a step back.

"No, God, no." She was sobbing, worse than when Gianni had died, tears were running down her cheeks, tears of searing agony. She rushed forward, bearing down on the confused men, scratching at them like an avenging fury, tearing the burden out of their hands, holding on to him, on to the black coat, on to the red collar.

Clark recovered. "Get him the fuck out of here, get him out," he was yelling, and he tackled Jo from behind, pinning her arms back. She threw her head back against his chin, and he cursed as his lip split open and he fell to the ground with her, trying to get his weight on top of her, spitting out blood and yelling, "Get him out!" again. Jo fought and fought as the men quickly reversed, dropping the body and dragging it back outside by the heels. She struggled until her strength failed her completely, until she went limp in Clark's hands, weeping and crying out and then just whining, pitiably, like a whipped dog. He let go, pushing her away from him with his boot, a look of horror and disgust on his face, an impassable gulf separating them. Then she curled up and just lay there, shivering, a white skull pin clutched in her bloodied hand.

10

Kay Elliott

February 1945, Santo Tomas Internment Camp,
Manila, Philippines

*P*lanes *today. American. Could tell from the sound. Please, God,*
let them come in time.

KAY AND THE other nurses jumped off the back of the truck
and stood outside the impressive-looking building. "That's
Santo Tomas," Sandy said brightly, tucking in a stray curl with
a bent hairpin. "The big university here. I read about it in a
travel brochure once. Imagine actually *wanting* to come here,
Kay." Sandy looked worriedly at her friend, who was gazing up
blankly at the balconies, the clock tower, the cross rising high
above it all.

"Why is the cross still there? Why haven't the Japanese
taken down the cross?" Kay asked, squinting now in the sun.
Maybe it's too high. Maybe they can't get to it yet.

The girls stepped toward the main entrance, but the Japanese motioned with their bayonets for them to turn around, to
go to another building across the street. SANTA CATALINA, the
sign read. GIRLS' DORMITORY. The nurses entered the main
floor. Before being rushed upstairs, Kay caught a glimpse of

figures in long linen gowns, smooth-looking and cool, worn by some native women perhaps, but for what purpose? What was there to celebrate in wartime? Who would dress up like that to go to hell? A moment later, it registered: of course, they were nuns, sequestered and imprisoned, just like everyone. *Nuns never have anything else to wear.*

The officers confiscated their musette bags, their belongings—they searched them and returned them, then questioned the women one by one.

"I need to come with this one," Sandy said, helping Kay to her feet.

"Why? What is wrong with this one?" the guard asked, motioning, pointing at Kay's belly, at her head.

"Nothing, nothing at all," Sandy replied, her red lips smiling sweetly. "I'm her best friend, I can answer any questions you have for her. She was born in Mount Carmel—"

"What wrong with her? Why she not talk for herself?"

Sandy bit her painted lip to keep from saying, *Because you bastards killed her husband, killed her baby's father, you probably ran him through the middle and left him to bleed to death in the jungle, you sons of bitches.*

All that came out was, "She's a little tired out from the trip, that's all."

They stayed in the dormitory six weeks. They were allowed downstairs to eat twice a day—never with the nuns, they never saw the nuns again—usually rice and carabao and papaya, the first fresh fruit they had had since before the tunnel. No one came in and no one went out—the thatched *sawali* surrounding their building made them an isolated island, cut off from the rest of Manila, from the rest of the world.

"Why do you think they're keeping us here like this?" one of the nurses asked, worriedly. "Do you think they're saving us for concubines?"

"I don't think so," Sandy said practically, rearranging her victory rolls, which were limp from the humidity. "More like a 'silent debriefing,' I'd say. I don't think they want us going into the big camp right away, telling everyone what we saw out there." The girls shuddered. "As if we could ever forget."

Kay started bleeding their third week into isolation. It was only spotting at first. She kept telling herself it would stop, it was nothing. She would lie down and rest some more. Sometimes you bleed a little when the baby burrows in, when it gets settled in for good. She couldn't lose the baby now, not now—in the jungle, in the tunnel being bombed, bumping along in the back of trucks, in jeeps—but not now, she couldn't lose her son now. But there came a day when it was unmistakable—she was bleeding out. The other nurses heard her crying behind the thin, rattan screen, crying and wailing and bleeding her baby away. Then Sandy was there, saying, "There, there now, honey, it'll be okay, you'll be okay," but she wasn't, she wasn't okay, she never would be. Kay's heart was splitting open. The baby had been the only thing left to hold on to, to keep her together; now she was losing that, she was losing herself.

"Baby, baby," Sandy soothed, oblivious to how the word stung, changing the gauze pads, gauging the blood loss, eyeing the insects in the corner of the filthy washroom. "Who knows what we're going into out there," Sandy said, lifting her eyes in the direction of the prison camp. "You couldn't have had this baby, it might have killed you. I bet there'll be precious little to eat for one out there, let alone for two. Don't cry, baby, it's for the best, it's for the best, really."

But Kay was gone—she was lost herself, there was nothing left for her now. "That's all I had," she stammered as the nurses quickly changed the sheets, washing her dirty feet before getting her into bed, trying to save their hemorrhaging friend in a cesspool of filth and infection and tropical heat.

"That's all I had," Kay repeated, starting to shake uncontrollably. "Now I've lost Aaron. Now I've lost him for good."

ONE OF THE planes flew low, buzzing the camp. The Japanese were yelling for everyone to get up, to get out of the courtyard, but Kay lay where she had fallen, mistaken for just another dead body. With her sunken eyes and protruding bones, it was hard to tell.

Ten planes flew over. Kay counted them carefully on her fingers as she looked up through the palm branches. *Thank God, thank God,* she thought over and over—not that they'd made it in time to save her or her baby, or any of them, really. They were dying too fast in the camp for that. Just, *thank God* they existed, they were real, they were finally here. They were from another world. A free world. A world the internees had all but forgotten.

Something fell from the sky, and one of the kids ran out and got it. He had it in his hands a whole ten seconds before the Japs got there, grabbed him by the back of his hair, and lifted him off the ground before tossing him aside, confiscating the thing, hurrying inside with it. But the boy was all right when he got up—he was a little scrapper, Kay had set his broken arm twice herself—and he'd had time to read the note wrapped around the pair of goggles the Americans had dropped. The news spread like wildfire throughout the camp. They were threatened with death if they were caught talking about it, but who could talk about anything else? It was only February, but the note had said, "Christmas is here. We'll be in today or tomorrow."

11

Jo McMahon

Spring 1945, The Western Front

My uncle's a colonel," Jonesy said, holding out a roll of bandages. Jo was changing Father Hook's dressing. The inflammation was coming down; the wounds were pink around the edges, but not purple, not black. He could eat, he could drink—he was going to make it.

"Is that so?" Jo concentrated on his words with difficulty. Her skin hurt; she wondered if she was getting a fever. Everyone else had rolled down blankets and unbuttoned collars, but Jo felt colder than ever.

"In the catering corps."

"That's ridiculous. You're making that up."

Jonesy smiled his ugly bucktoothed grin. "No, miss, it's the honest truth. Worked his way up to the top. You should see his uniform too. Struts around like a peacock—I mean, it's really something. Just like those big men in the newsreels. He just omits saying what branch he's in. Anyway, everyone's so intimidated by all that shiny metal they daren't ask."

Jo smiled, but then her skin crawled. She rolled her shoulders, and every goose pimple rubbed painfully against the inside of her shirt. This felt like fever coming on.

"Thanks for helping here, Jonesy. I think I've got the rest."

"Miss." Jonesy rolled his chair back toward his bunk.

Jo's knees ached as she crossed the tent.

"How are you feeling this evening, Major?"

"Tired, miss."

"Yes," Jo sighed, checking his wound, taking too long, staring at it, through it, drifting for a moment.

"Will I be all right, miss? Is anything wrong?" he asked anxiously, half sitting up.

Jo came back. "No, you're fine, Major. The wound's healing nicely. You've got a mild infection, that's why you're so tired. But you don't have any fever to speak of, and you can eat, so that means we put you back together okay. As soon as reinforcements arrive, they'll hit you with so much penicillin you'll be up doing a jig before you can say 'Jack Robinson.'"

The major looked relieved, sighing heavily.

"I won't forget this, miss. You saved my life. I am not an unimportant man," he boasted, smiling broadly. "Any promotion you like, any assignment, I'll pull the strings, you just say the word."

Jo looked down at the man absently scratching at his potbelly. He was serious, she knew; he really meant it. To him, the world of bureaucracy still existed, still mattered. He thought she would be impressed, would care how many gold stripes or bars or leaves adorned her dress uniform. Hell, he probably thought she still had a dress uniform—something other than the blood-soaked, washed-out, olive-green jumpsuit she was wearing now, the one she had swiped from the mechanics' supply shed back in Tunisia so she could straddle the stretchers without worrying about her skirt.

"Billy," she began, turning to the major's bunkmate and sitting down on his cot.

"You remembered, miss. *Billy.*"

"Yes, finally. Anything you need before turning in?"

"No, ma'am—I mean, no, miss. Breathing was a lot better today, I think the worst is about over. I mean, this was a bad spell, miss, coming after that bronchitis and all, but I'll be out there fighting again before you know it."

"You'll be going back home to your girl and your air warden job, if I have anything to do with it," Jo corrected.

Billy looked crestfallen. Jo wanted to move on, to check on James and David and go to bed. She was exhausted, she was getting sick, they had eaten the last of the food. *Goddamn it, do I have to hold their hands every step of the way?* Her eyes started to ache from behind.

"Listen, Billy." She focused on him, on his big, hurt eyes. "They can take care of you better back home. You won't get so sick, so you won't have these attacks, so you can get out there and do important work that needs to be done, stateside." He still looked devastated. Then, stretching, reaching for snippets of something she'd heard somewhere—a movie? a poster?— "We're all in this together, Billy. Fighting back home is just as important as fighting out here. More so in your case, 'cause you'll be one hundred percent back home and really able to do some good."

He looked thoughtful at that, and she jumped at the chance.

"C'mon, you're ready to get off your back, aren't you?"

"Y—yes, miss."

"You're ready to get back to helping our side win, right?"

"Oh, yes, ma'am—I mean, yes, miss." Now his face was lit up again, shining.

"Well, then," and she patted his foot reassuringly as she

stood up. She crossed the tent, mumbling under her breath, *Goddamn.*

James turned his face away from her as he heard her approaching.

"I don't need anything, miss," he said quickly, dismissing her.

Jo was tempted to take him up on it—take the easy way out, get five more minutes of sleep. Then she walked up to the side of his bed and asked, "Mind if I sit with you for a minute?"

His face was averted at a sharp angle, his body tense and taut. He didn't want her there.

"If you want," he grumbled.

She sat down.

He pulled his knees up to his chest, wrapping his arms around them so she wouldn't touch him, so she couldn't even brush up against him by accident.

She looked at him, and she didn't know what to say to all that brokenness and rage and fury. And then it just popped out.

"You're beautiful, James."

"*What?*"

In his shock and disbelief, he forgot and turned his disfigured face full toward the sound of her voice, toward the sound of those ridiculous, incredible words.

"You are—really."

"I'm—I'm a monster." The pain was so palpable when he said it that it was like a living thing, a serpent lashing out, biting and hating and biting again.

Jo laughed.

"You're laughing at me?"

"No, I'm sorry, I'm just laughing at how wrong you are. Right now, you can only see—well, not see, really, more like feel—that you're ugly. But you're not. A four-by-four patch of your skin is badly burned, I'll give you that, and you might never see again, that much is true. But you're just focusing on that. On that tiny little part of you. It's a part of you, James, not all of you. The rest of you is perfect, beautiful—and even if it wasn't, I bet there is stuff inside of you that's beautiful too."

His face looked a little less dark.

"It's kind of like . . . remember the morning you woke up all over chicken pox? It happens to all of us—one morning you're fine, the next you're blisters all over. Big, wet, glassy ones too—remember?"

James nodded. "Sure."

"Were you a monster then? Were you any different inside?"

"But that was different! That was kid stuff. You were better in a few weeks, good as new."

"Yes, it was a little different, James, but listen to me." Jo was hot, then cold, then hot again, her ears starting to ring; she'd take her temperature when she was through with this, but she had caught on to something and didn't want to let it go. "It wasn't as different as you think. You looked in the mirror that morning and saw something that looked scary, but you knew it wasn't you, not the real you, inside. Well, if you could see yourself right now, yes, you were burned pretty badly around one eye, but the rest of you, the real you, is still the same."

James turned away again, but not from shame, not from rage. He put a fist up to his mouth and pushed hard.

"And I don't just mean you're beautiful inside, James," Jo

added, rising stiffly from the cot. "Hands down, you are the most handsome man in this tent."

Then his tears came.

But by now she had come to her last patient, to David. And he was dying.

Maybe she was catching typhus from him. Maybe her fever was coming from that, from spending nearly all her spare time by his bedside, trying to force her sickest patient to live by sheer willpower. But now it seemed too late. His pulse was wrong and his color was wrong, and when she touched his brow, it burned and she didn't need a thermometer to know it was 105, 106. He was leaving—it was nearly over. *The seizures, then he dies,* she thought absently. *Then he dies.* She had sworn he wouldn't die, but she wasn't God, she wasn't even a goddess, she wasn't Selene coming to him in his sleep. Then her heart lurched and she thought, *Go ahead, fall in love with him now, right before the end, he can be one more dead person you can love, one more living person you can lose.* She tried reasoning with herself. She knew nothing about the man—maybe he was a lecher, maybe he was a politician with a plump wife and six kids back home, maybe he was a sadistic butcher from a small village who beat his lover and drank. But it was no good. She couldn't imagine it away, imagine him away. Why this dying man, racing away from her as fast as he could, why he should be the one her heart got snagged on—now, at the end—she didn't know. She couldn't help it. And she couldn't help him.

Jo covered her face with her hands. It was getting late. He would need her later; she had been running on adrenaline for so long, but now she was almost out. She needed to lie down, to collapse for only a few minutes so she could wake up, get

up, and watch this man die. She walked into her tented space
and looked at herself in the mirror. There was blood on her
face, dried blood, someone else's. How long had it been there?
Hours? Days? She rubbed at it, violently. It bothered her, it
made her feel filthy. She started to rip off her clothes, all her
soiled, dirty clothes, took them off and threw them in a corner.
There, I am done with that, I can't stand it anymore. There was
some cold water in a jug, and she poured it over herself, over
her hair, started to rub the old remnant of a soap bar into a
weak lather. She was washing herself, washing her hair, un-
coiled now and dripping; she was shivering from the water and
from her fever and from knowing she was losing David. She
shook until she hurt. Kissing the German had turned her soul
back on, but it was raw and bleeding and nothing could turn
it off and it would kill her in the end. But compared to the
numbness she had felt for so long, she was glad, in a way. She
was ready to die. But she would wash her corpse first.

Jo didn't remember falling asleep. Her clothes had gotten
wet where they fell, and she had hung them on a hook; she
hadn't had anything else to wear, so she had put on Queenie's
negligee while her clothes dried. She remembered that much,
and brushing her long hair and putting it up in a towel. The
men had been quiet, had fallen asleep, she had put the blanket
around her shoulders while she waited. She didn't remember
falling asleep.

She awoke to screaming. She didn't know where she was
at first, because it was so dark in the enclosure. She was half-
sitting against some packing cases on the floor; the blanket
had slipped off her shoulders, the towel was gone, and she was
colder than she could remember being in a long time. The

screaming was terrible—*A man's,* she thought, *from the sound of it, but they must be doing something awful to him, torturing him, cutting off his leg without anesthesia.* Then her head started to clear as she heard Jonesy calling out, heard the other men talking excitedly together; she knew where she was all of a sudden, back in the tent, she must have fallen asleep. *Good God, that would be David, the end is coming, the end is here.* She stepped out into the tent—she had left the spirit lamp burning, she noted disjointedly, she'd have to be more careful next time. For one second, she saw David's spine arch unnaturally, his heels and head rammed down into the rough canvas of the cot. She took a step toward him, and then the tent flap shot open and Clark came in, followed by his men. The captain walked directly up to David; he drew his sidearm, hissing under his breath, "I'm going to shut him the fuck up."

It was going too fast—no, on second thought, it was going too slowly; it was like watching a movie in slow motion. Jo noticed everything, could see Jonesy struggling to get out of bed, hear Father Hook ordering them to stop in the name of God. Even some of Clark's men seemed uncertain, hanging back; one asked, pulling at his sleeve, "Captain, are you sure? Are you sure, Captain?" But the others were panicking, looking worriedly over their shoulders at the tent flap behind them, as if the Germans were right outside, as if they were coming in at any moment, as if it were already too late.

"It's us or him," Clark said grimly, picking the pillow up off the floor where it had fallen, putting it over the muzzle of his pistol, lifting both toward David's head. And then, for a split second, he looked over his shoulder before pulling the trigger. And he saw Jo.

Jo didn't understand why Clark just stood there, rooted in place, staring at her like he had never seen her before, but she didn't wait to see how long it would last. Almost without thinking, she threw herself protectively over David's body.

"Get her the hell off of him," Clark ordered.

Jo tried hushing David, holding his face in her hands, trying to get him to focus on her, to notice she was there.

"Darling, sshhh, darling," but David was still yelling. He had stopped convulsing, but he yelled at her, yelled at the whole world, yelled at death that was dragging him down, dragging him away. Jo felt the cold, hard fingers of one of the soldiers close around her arm, but she held on to David, willing him to be quiet. And even in his delirium, he responded to the weight of her body on his as any man starved for a woman would. Jo strained to listen with everyone else for sounds of the enemy outside.

But they didn't come.

They never came.

They waited, and David passed out, or fell asleep, but the Germans never came. The men eventually left, one by one, Clark last of all. His men had looked sheepish as they filed out, but not the captain; he glared at Jo's bare back as she still held on to the man, waiting for the last of them to leave, for it to be safe again. Clark left, and she slipped off of David. She would sleep right there, keep her arms around him and sleep there, on her knees; if he even began to stir, she would quiet him down before anyone came back. David would be awake a dozen times before dawn, she knew that; she would be right there, though, she could save him—from Clark, anyway.

But David slept all night and Jo woke to sunlight in her eyes, sneaking in from the air vents in the top corners of the tent. She was so used to getting up in darkness, in grayness, that the sunlight flooded her senses at first and dazed her. Her hair—loose and tumbling—had gotten in her eyes and, in the bright light, shone like burnished copper, like spun gold. Then, all of a sudden, she could see again—someone had moved her hair, things came back into view. She was still kneeling by David's bedside, one arm flung protectively over him, but she was being supported now by something, by someone. She felt someone's arm holding her up, keeping her from slipping onto the floor completely—someone who had just removed, with great delicacy, the single curl that had strayed toward her eyes.

Jo closed her eyes, then opened them again; then she saw David, apparently focusing on her.

"David?" She was in disbelief—he seemed lucid, he seemed able to hear her. Then, quickly checking his fever with her hand, feeling nothing, registering nothing—"David." And she was incredulous—his fever had broken. He was alive. He was going to live.

"Thank God," she sighed, closing her eyes again, throwing her head back, exposing her delicate neck and throat; her chest heaving, bare down to the sternum; taking in deep breaths, drinking in deep draughts of air, of sheer relief. Jo stood up slowly, rubbing the small of her back, taking in the rest of the room, taking stock of the rest of her patients, just as she always did.

The first thing she noticed was Father Hook. He was staring painfully at his clasped hands—that was odd. And everyone else too—what was wrong with them? James seemed okay, but why was everyone else looking at her like that, like they were starving? She reached up and scratched her head, great masses of untamed curls getting in the way.

"Why is my hair—"

Then suddenly remembering, realizing . . . "What am I wearing?" she gasped, running for the partitioned room.

DAVID GOT STEADILY better each day. Clark's men found a supply of German rations while out on reconnaissance; they tasted just as bad as American rations, but they were food, they could eat again, all of them, even David, as much as they wanted. Jo still hid her fever; it was only 102, and that didn't give you seizures or the shakes or anything. She masked the fact that she wasn't eating by always being around food, opening cans, dishing it out—the men were so happy to eat again they didn't even notice.

One of the men on the patrol came in one day—Jo remembered him as the one who had pulled at Clark's sleeve, asking him if he was sure.

"Excuse me, miss, but we found some other stuff when we found those rations. I thought you might want it."

And he had carried in case after case—dark black, carefully labeled—of enemy medical supplies.

"They were just out there, miss, and nobody was using them. The Germans must have—no, sorry, miss, I forgot, I'm not supposed to say what all we saw out there. But Cap—some of us were for leaving them, miss, but some of us thought they might come in handy. Seeing as how you've had to make do."

Jo fingered the cases almost reverently, undoing their clasps, looking inside.

"Good God, yes," she said. She had been having to make do for so long now, the idea of having enough was almost beyond her.

"I'd best be getting back, miss," and he was out the flap before she could thank him.

Jo had memorized basic German medical terms during their boat ride over, but that seemed a very long time ago now. *Let's see what I can remember.*

Hauptbesteck. Torso trauma? Yes, she was right, there were the dressings, the gauze, the clamps, the surgery kits. *Sammelbesteck*—right again; ear, nose, and throat. She lifted the small *truppenbesteck,* a catchall for runners, small enough to fit in the nose of a motorcycle sidecar. And there were plenty of *verbandkasten,* smaller first aid kits, and Yankauer masks for anesthesia. She handled the thick stacks of tags—*kranke* for the sick, *verwundete* for the wounded—edged with yellow (group those with the same illness together) or green (any transport will do). Jo was amazed by it all, amazed she could remember any of it—they had had to pass a test on it. ("What are they going to do if we fail?" Queenie had asked. "Have us swim home?") They had even had contests among themselves to see who could spell the names of the German hospitals— *verundetennetz, hauptverbandsplatz,* and the one Jo had won five dollars for spelling correctly, *truppenverbandplatz.* Jo's hands were greasy from just opening the lids—everything was covered in Cosmolene to prevent rust. Luckily, the American had carried in a case of isopropyl as well. Jo could use that to rub off the greasy jelly when she needed to.

David got better. Jo felt worse and worse, but David was better—all the men were better. David ate like he had never tasted food before, he grew strong, he sat up in bed and smiled, and his brogue was just as she had imagined it from his ramblings, with a trilling burr in the back of his throat she hadn't expected at all. He didn't remember much after he had gotten sick. Typhus had swept through their camp, their cheery, orange tents becoming thick with the dead, with the dying. He had letters to write, he said, to his people back home; he hadn't written in so long, they would be frantic for news. Jo offered to write them for him but told him they were out of paper; then she remembered all those medical tags. So right over impossible-looking questions like *"Knochenverletzung?"* and *"Wundstarrkrampfserum?"* Jo wrote instead, "Dear Mum, I am all right, I love you." His dictated letters were simple, direct—they were to his mother, his baby sister Kit, his older brother Bumpy.

"Bumpy?" Jo asked, raising an eyebrow.

"His real name is Duncan, lass. Should I not call you 'lass'? Is that not right at all?"

She wanted him to call her "lass," she loved the way it sounded. So why, instead, was she answering, coolly, "Most everyone around here calls me 'miss.' You were saying about Duncan?"

"Aye—miss—when he got mumps his whole neck swelled, big bumps." David demonstrated obligingly with his hands. "And the name stayed ever after."

The man was all over smiles; she never thought he'd be so happy, having watched him die for so long, never imagined that his cheeks could be rosy, that Endymion would laugh. It seemed strange to be writing right over those German words describing death and dying with words so full of peace and love. "I have had the typhus, Mum, but thanks be to God I am recovering. Thanks be to God, and thanks be to—what is your first name, miss? Aye, that is lovely, that—and thanks be to Josephine McMahon, Mum, you pray for her too, when you pray for me, it is a hard place we find ourselves in with all of our comrades lost. Only God's grace, and your love, sustains us."

The letters to his siblings were jovial, asking about fishing and golf and whether the fair had gone off all right in September and what the price of grain was and how much Highland wool was selling for and how school was going for Kit and whether Bumpy had fallen in love again since his last letter. Jo wrote them down, each letter composed of half a dozen tags; she dated them, and kept them in order, and promised to mail them when they all got back to the hospital, back to the world.

One day David paused during dictation as Jo stared through the hard, packed ground in front of her, reliving, reviving dead memories, and the weight of it must have showed on her face because when she looked up, pen still poised, David was staring at her and his eyes were moist.

"It's been hard for you, miss."

Jo tried to smile, but she just pulled one lip out to the side, unconvincingly.

"Have you no family of your own to write to? No lad serving out here, might be?"

And Jo covered her mouth, covered half her face. She had lost so much. How do you put that into words, convey the magnitude of that?

"I don't have anyone. No one is left—among the living anyway."

And she turned quickly, hoping to catch a glimpse of him, but Gianni wasn't there. He hadn't been there for weeks; he had abandoned her the day she had chosen to stay with her men instead of going to him. Her dreams were empty; his ghost was gone. She had lost even that.

She felt a strong hand take hold of hers, muscular and

weather-beaten; she could feel the tiny ridges of his fingertips, almost smooth with wear. She looked into his blue eyes; they were a dark blue, a living blue, so unlike Clark's flat turquoise. She looked into them, and they were like a summer sky at twilight, a pool reflecting the Evening Star.

"Not everyone, miss. You haven't lost everyone."

THE DAYS PASSED. Jo felt she should be rejoicing more. Her men were well, David was well, but she couldn't shake her fever. Jo thought again of her parents, both gone with the influenza. She had had that one short note from her mother, scribbled in a schoolgirl Italian, saying she was nursing Jo's father through a bad case of it. Then a second letter, from one of their neighbors. The flu had taken her father, and her mother had worn herself out caring for him. Jo's mother was too weak when she caught it herself. She hadn't lasted a week.

One night Jo's fever spiked and she couldn't hide it. Jonesy volunteered to lie awake in case anyone needed help—she was to go to bed.

"After a breath of air, Jonesy. I'll just step outside for one second. We've been cooped up for so long and the weather's turned warm. I just need some air." And she was out of the tent before he could argue.

For so long Jo's world had been defined by the canvas boundaries of her tent. She stood outside now, in the unknown darkness, a swollen moon just rising out of the trees. It was perfectly quiet, the small breeze swirling about her ankles making no sound at all. It was too early for insects or the chirp of mating frogs; not even a twig snapped. She could hear her heart pounding in her ears; then that subsided too, and she stood in the dark and the quiet and didn't even breathe.

Then she heard the radio. She hadn't known that Jonesy had fixed it; he must have been waiting to surprise her. He was crazy to be playing it so loud, though, and big band music too—he was nuts. She turned to scold him, but her ear popped and she realized the music wasn't coming from the tent but from farther down the worn path that used to separate post-op from surgery, from the tents Clark and his men slept in.

Jo was confused.

Since their arrival, the patrol had slept in their individual tents—small things, useless against the wind and rain, green blankets propped up with sticks, no more. But now, in front of her, the tents were gone, and in their place stood a full-sized tent, as large as a mess hall, as large as the surgery tent had been. Where had they found it? How had she missed the familiar sound of stakes being driven in? She knew from experience that tents were no easy thing to set up or tear down. She was walking toward it now, the night air split in two by clarinet and horn. They must be drunk, they must have found the tent and found some liquor somewhere—there was no other explanation. That or they just wanted to die.

The radio grew louder. She could make out the song "I'll Be Seeing You." She knew all the words by heart—everyone did—she could hear voices inside singing along. People were laughing, she could have sworn she heard a woman's laugh, but that was impossible, the whole thing was impossible. *I'll find you in the morning sun and when the night is new, I'll be looking at the moon but I'll be seeing you.* Jo was standing in front of the tent flap now. She was shivering in the balmy air, her shoes caked with dried mud, her jumpsuit unable to keep her feverish body warm. She opened the flap slowly and stepped inside the tent and her coldness left her—a warm, wet wave of heat and comfort engulfed her, and her painted toenails were visible in her open-toed shoes and the long, white hem of her dress licked playfully at her ankles as the flaps closed behind her.

The tent was beautiful. Christmas lights hung down like chandeliers from the center tent pole like they had on base, back in the States, the night before they left for the war. It was warm in the tent, deliciously warm, with the warmth of sixty, of a hundred bodies. Bare shoulders, the glimmer of jewelry, lamé that looked like it had been painted onto the women wearing it. Clean-shaven men in their dress uniforms neatly pressed, freshly starched. Their cologne reached her nostrils, and Jo inhaled deeply as the men turned to look at her approvingly and she curled up her lip in a provocative smile. She took in the rest of the crowded room in one glance.

Queenie was at the baccarat table, laughing and drinking and cheering with everyone else when she won. People were dancing—the music had changed, switched to Goodman's "Sing, Sing, Sing," and the place went mad. She saw Gianni twirling a petite blonde in a pink dress. She was a good dancer, but she could barely keep up with his lead, she never stopped spinning—underarm turn, pretzel, behind-the-back backward pretzel, inside-out turn . . .

Grandpa was playing darts and drinking something out of a snifter; he was dressed in a Confederate uniform that had been tailored just for him, the yellow braid standing out at his waist and embroidered onto the turtle dove gray of his sleeves. The doctors were all there, and the nurses too, gathered around a table heaped with hot food. There was smoking all around, enough cigarettes for everyone, the tent was filled with tobacco smoke, and Jo sniffed it in greedily—it had been so long. The Italians were singing now along with the clarinet, *dah-dah-dah-dah-dah-dah-dah-dahdah,* and laughing, clapping along with the crazy tune, swing-dancing with each other, and laughing again.

Then, from the back of the tent, walking straight toward her, she saw the German. He took off his hat as he came up to her, and she thought for a moment that there was going to be trouble, that they would take him prisoner, but the sergeant who came up to him just gave him a slap on the back and offered to take his greatcoat for him, laying it atop the piano, folding it neatly in half so it would fit. The German's face was tanned and smooth, and he smiled at her, a deep rich smile. The crow's-feet at the corners of his eyes made it perfect. He was wearing gloves, but he took them off so he could feel her hands in his. And the music changed again, becoming slow, rhythmic, and melancholy—"You'd Be So Nice to Come Home To," which shouldn't have been a sad song yet it was. The German held her close, pulling her toward him, but he had no gun in his hand this time. His left hand was holding on to hers, his free one slowly inching down from her shoulder blade, where it had started, to her waist; she could feel him rubbing the smooth whiteness of her dress, the tiny seam, the hidden side zipper. He smelled gorgeous, and she closed her eyes and melted against him. The dance floor was so crowded, they were all packed together, no one could move, no one wanted to—she opened her eyes and looked into his, still smiling. The tiny hairs on his jacket stood out smartly, the wool had been brushed; she looked down at his boots, the jet-black tips shone from the polish. *You are the last human being left in France,* he said again, but this time she understood him, and she got up on the balls of her feet to kiss him again, to make it happen again and again and never stop, this was heaven, she was home.

But just before their lips touched she heard Queenie give a little scream, throw down her cards angrily, and walk out. Jo craned her neck around to see what had happened, and she saw Gianni push the little blonde away from him. He was yelling at her in Italian—she was no good, *go away, you stepped on my feet.* Jo looked down at the ground for a second, but it was muddy now. Her partner's boots were sunk in it, she could feel it squishing between her toes. The lights started to flicker, and the music went off and on—it was "You Belong to Me" one second, and the next it was an Allied news program, and the next it was Axis Sally telling them their sweethearts back home were untrue, would not be waiting for them when they got home, if they ever got home. Things were spinning too quickly now. Jo could only see glimpses of it. The surgeons had on their caps and masks and were pulling surgical gloves over the sleeves of their dress coats; the radio had cracked open and was lying on the floor—someone was stepping on it, but Axis Sally kept talking, kept crying, kept laughing at them. The lid of the piano was closed, but she could hear it playing, a marching tune that sounded German. Then the back flap opened again and women—made-up, lips red, in high heels and filthy jumpsuits—were running, screaming, as a figure approached. As it brushed up against them they disappeared.

"No," Jo tried to call out, but her voice was gone. The Italians tried tackling the dark figure, but they vanished as soon as they touched it. Gianni ran up to it—Jo was screaming inside for him to stop—but as soon as his first punch landed, her brother split into atoms, into nothingness, was gone. Jo wheeled around, but the nurses, the dancing couples, were gone. Grandpa drew his saber and raised it above his head, but dropped the sword and held a hand to his heart and collapsed, disappearing when he reached the ground.

"Don't touch him, don't you fucking touch him," Jo whispered hoarsely, grabbing on to her dance partner, pushing him away from the phantom. Then, just before they went out for good, all the lights shone brightly for one moment and in their light she could make out who the figure was. It was Clark.

He switched on his flashlight in the darkness, and Jo realized that her arms were empty. The German had vanished when the lights went down; it was dark now, the moon was rising just over the piano. The hem of her dress was soiled, but she had on sturdy shoes, she could walk through the mud, over the cold, hard-packed ground with no problem now.

"What are you doing out here?" Clark asked, and each word was so real it was like cut glass, tearing into her.

Jo backed up. She had a military jacket on over her dress; the wind picked up and her skirt billowed around her. She backed up and then started to run, not toward her tent but behind it, toward the field; she knew now that was where all the others had gone, where they were waiting for her. She wouldn't let Clark stop her; he would try to, she knew that—he was always in her way.

"Stop," Clark called, and at the sound of his voice the tent was gone. It had never been there. He was running around the empty pup tents she had negotiated perfectly without even seeing they were there.

"Stop."

She was terribly cold, she was freezing, the wind ripped right through her dress. She had lost her high heels as they scrambled up the hill; her jacket was gone. There was nothing to this dress, it was lighter than air, she had no stockings, no underthings, she was barely wearing a slip, showing sickly white now in the light of the waning moon. Clark was right behind her, she could hear him panting; she was almost to the top of the hill, though, she'd make the field before him. Then she heard him cock his rifle and yell, "Halt!" just as she crested the hill.

She stopped.

"Don't go any farther, you goddamned bitch," but it sounded like he was crying, Clark was crying, crying and pointing his rifle at her and trying to get her to stop. Jo looked down. Something cold and hard and very thin rested against the front of her bare ankle. *That's called something,* Jo thought, burning up in her fever, in her delirium, *something like trick. Or tick.* No, she had it. *Trip. A trip wire.* She stood there, shimmering in the moonlight in her transparent dress, in her stolen jumpsuit, stood there and looked at Clark and thought how beautiful he was, he was a god, she would like to give him fifty daughters, no that was someone else, she was mistaken; he was crying and had a gun on her. *I wonder why, I thought we were on the same side.*

Then the fever consumed her and she lost consciousness before she hit the ground, falling backward, the trip wire shining impotently in the rising wind, her white wrap becoming caught up in it for a moment before flying away, over the minefield cheated of its harvest of death.

JO DIDN'T CATCH typhus. Clark carried her back, and they laid her in James's bed, and her fever came down, but not for a day or two. By then she had forgotten her dream—or her nightmare—her time spent with all those who had died, with those she had almost joined in the minefield behind the tent. She could eventually eat, her appetite coming back all at once;

she was a few days behind everyone else in saying, "God, this stuff is awful, can I have some more?" She got out of bed but had to walk around nearly doubled over, she was so weak. The men made her sit down as much as possible. She smiled at them—they were so strict with her now that she was their patient.

"We're fine, miss," they bragged. "We don't need you at all."

Even James got out a stick and started pacing out the room, and soon he could carry food and water, as long as no one moved his stuff.

"Where is the goddamned can opener, Jonesy?" he would yell, and then Jonesy would apologize for moving it: "It's right here. Sorry, I won't forget again." James brought the full bowls of food and took away the empties. Jonesy and Billy (who was good for short spurts on his feet) insisted on dealing with the bedpans, though. "We don't want you tripping over something with them," they hinted, darkly, to James.

Father Hook heard David's confession one day, and Jo asked if he'd hear hers too.

"What, *yours*?" the priest asked, incredulous.

"Why, yes, Father."

"I can't imagine you'd have anything to say, miss. You're— you're an angel."

And the young boy looked up at her with such devotion, such faith and confidence Jo hadn't the heart to spoil it for him, to bare the secrets of her soul, to tell him of the lust and the hopelessness and the pain and the anger that had nearly destroyed her, so many times over. *Let him believe in me a little while longer.*

IT SEEMED TO Jo that there was a lot of commotion outside the tent, more noise than she had ever heard before.

"Yes, miss, the patrol made contact," Jonesy said. "They're sending trucks for us soon. The bridges were out—that was the delay. But it's safe to talk and all now, miss, the Germans are a good many miles from us. I think they're pulling back at last."

Jo heaved a great sigh. *At last.* The trucks would come, her patients were stable enough to be transported. She'd get them back to a hospital, to a real hospital—not a field or an evac hospital but a real one—get them treated and then . . . then . . . well, maybe then she'd have time to acknowledge that knot deep inside her chest, the one that swelled and expanded whenever she breathed, whenever she paused, whenever she looked inside herself. It felt like nothing she had ever felt before. She thought it could be happiness, and if it was, was it because of David? Her feelings for David? If it was, she didn't have to think much further ahead than that right now. They'd sort it out later, together, when they got back. *Sufficient for the day is the evil thereof,* Sister had always said.

David practiced walking around the tent.

"Look at us, miss," he would laugh, sweating from the exertion. "Two people in the prime of life, bent over and hobbling like a *guidshir*—sorry, miss—like an old man, a grandfather."

Breathless, he'd sit down next to her and talk about how they would be leaving soon. "Tell me more about yourself."

"We'll have a long trip back to the hospital, don't forget, David, and lots of time to talk then. Besides, you've gotten everything out of me already. What about you? What will you do after the war? You know, before your fever broke, I imagined you were—no, never mind about that. What will you do, though, really?"

He looked at her, like he was looking inside of her soul, and

she could feel it and it was warm and comfortable; they had
known each other forever.

"Well, miss, I used to think I'd go right back to the farm,
my father's farm. He's dead now, God rest his soul, but my
mum still lives there, and Kit. Bumpy moved off to the city,
he likes that kind of life best. But, aye, miss, if you could
see it, just once. We raise sheep—gentle creatures, miss, you'd
like them, the finest in the county. Walking them up to the
high pasture as the sky turns pink with the dawn. Breathing
in God's good clean air—no gunpowder, no smoke like here,
miss—and the last stars going out above you and—and just
praying and singing inside yourself for the sheer joy of being
alive, of being free and whole and alive, miss. And the air so
still and clear, and the hills all around you opening into the
plains down below, and the lake shimmering far off on the
horizon and the birds already calling to each other, calling for
their loves. Have you ever seen anything like that?"

Jo was mesmerized. It was like poetry. It was a moment
before she responded, as if in a dream.

"No, never."

"Can you imagine it, miss?"

"Yes. Aye," she laughed, "when you describe it. It sounds
like a fairyland, one I used to read about in books. David,
I grew up in a box, twenty feet by twenty feet, with twenty
boxes to a floor, piled up five, six floors high. They freeze in the
winter and stink in the summer, and it's all concrete and steel,
and streetlights and car horns outside, and there's no green and
no lakes and no big, open sky like you say."

"It sounds awful, miss. If you don't mind my saying it."

"I don't mind, David."

They were holding hands.

"You said you used to think that was what you wanted, David. Have you changed your mind? Are you off to the big city, like your brother?" she teased.

David's face clouded for a second.

"That depends," he said seriously.

"On what?" she asked, still smiling. "On the price of wool? On the state of the crops? Are you afraid pastoral life will seem too tame once you come home from the war? It might at that, you know."

"Oh, no, miss."

"Well, what then?"

He patted her hand and stood up.

"I'd better be getting back to practicing."

And he walked back and forth, back and forth, until he was out of breath, until he had to lie down.

THE DAY TO leave came at last, and the rains came with it. The trucks were lined up outside, waiting; the orderlies ran back and forth carrying the stretchers, running lightly when they were empty, plodding along when they were loaded down with the weight of their patients. They had to go slowly in the sucking mud, and that made things worse. Their ponchos were glued to their bodies—they were soaked through. The men with eyeglasses couldn't see a thing. Jonesy immediately made friends with the two orderlies carrying him; he was so happy to see new faces, to ask questions, to answer them, he was so delighted and obliging it was all he could do to keep from jumping off the stretcher to help them. Major Donahue immediately took charge, making sure each new face knew his rank, knew they were dealing with an important person. "Look lively, son, don't drag your feet, come on now, move along, that's right—now that's more like it." James walked out under his own steam, refusing everyone's arm except Jo's. "Feeling sorry for a blind man," he fumed at the orderlies. "Puny little voice he had too, bet he was a puny little man. Am I right, miss? Aren't I bigger than him?"

"Oh, much bigger—and stronger," Jo said, smiling.

"That's what I thought. I wish I could punch him right in the nose."

"Well, I'll hold him still, right in front of you, and tell you when to swing."

Then, for the first time, she saw her patient smile.

Billy walked out to the truck, hovering over the young priest. Even in a short time, he had developed a penchant for caregiving.

"Now watch out, men," he said, spreading a poncho over Hook's head to keep him dry, stumbling in the mud, bumping into the orderlies. "Be careful now, this is a very delicate patient, severe injuries—*and* a priest too, so you'd better watch out or you'll all catch it."

"Billy," Jo said, grinning, "I think you'd make an excellent nurse."

"I might at that. Now don't laugh. Maybe they'll have male nurses one day."

All the men but David were loaded. Jo wanted to rip off the poncho the orderlies had given her. It was doing no good, it smelled of strong chemicals and mold. She headed back to the tent. *For the last time,* Jo thought. *The last time.* So many weeks spent there, so many losses sustained there. This had been her world. But she could leave it now. She had done the good she set out to do—she had saved the lives of the six men she had vowed to protect. She was leaving with them. She was leaving with David.

She walked into the tent. It looked strangely lonely—just the sawhorses standing there without their stretchers, the sheets ripped down, her enclosure gone. She stared at where it had stood and, a moment later, couldn't even envision it, as though it had never been there at all. Two orderlies were talking with David, taking out his stretcher without him; of course, he was well enough to walk from here to the idling truck outside; it was only a few paces, she'd hold on to his arm to make sure. He was standing with her now, alone in the tent—the first time they had been alone together. Jo looked at him, at his eyes sheltered beneath their thick brows, at his black hair swept back from his forehead; his face was pale but glowing, as though lit from within, lit with a secret joy of his own. He looked taller than he had before, and stronger too, in his woolen jacket, HD embroidered in orange against a blue background on his sleeve. His kilt was gone. Jo wondered whose pants he had borrowed; they were too short for him, barely coming to his ankles. Jo smiled at him, and he smiled back. And then he put on his doughboy helmet.

"You won't be needing that in the truck," Jo laughed. "We're heading back to the hospitals, soldier, not on into battle."

"You're heading back to the hospitals," David said, and her heart stopped.

"Don't joke, David."

He looked steadily at her in reply.

"David, come on. Get on the truck."

"I cannot go with ye, miss."

"Of course you can. What do you mean? You've been lying

in bed with typhus for God knows how long before I even saw you. You're weak as a kitten. I mean, you've only been walking around a few days and—"

"I cannot lie abed, miss," he said, slowly shaking his head, keeping his voice low and gentle, as if trying to spare her even now. "There are so many worse off than I, out in the field. I cannot stay back."

"David, this is nonsense." Tears pricked her eyes. Then, stamping her foot, "I order you to get in that truck."

And he smiled at her, a mischievous smile that was almost all eyes.

"Aye, you have some fire in ye, miss," and he was beaming. "That's a good thing. I shouldn't love a woman without some spit and fire in her, and that's the truth."

Jo was speechless.

"And although you do outrank me, miss"—here he stepped toward her, softly touching her shoulder where her insignia should have been—"I'm afraid that's one order I cannot obey."

Jo felt nothing. It wasn't the cold, frozen numbness she had known for so long but, rather, she was feeling everything so much, so intensely, that none of it could register. She had never even conceived of this—that he would do anything but go back with her to the hospital, to safety. She would help him get fully well, recover, and then, in the course of time, with enough time—well, then, anything could happen. But now—

He was in the middle of an eloquent speech. She heard something about light and a bit about power and mountains and glory and love conquering all. He must have practiced it a thousand times. It was perfect, but she couldn't hear it— she was trying to memorize his face, his eyes, the way his lips moved when he talked. She could have done that on the journey back, over the next couple of weeks, but now she had to do it before he stopped speaking. She couldn't do it, couldn't possibly; there wasn't enough time.

David ended his soliloquy.

"—every man here is in love with ye. And I am no different."

He had both hands in hers now; she was rubbing her thumbs against his fingertips, against his knuckles—there wasn't enough time to memorize how they felt, she couldn't do it in time.

"The first thing I saw when I woke up from the typhus was a beautiful creature, an angel with copper hair, holding on to me. I didn't know who you were, didn't know how much you had done for me already. I just knew I was alive, I wasn't dead—I felt so peaceful and warm—and I had this great sense of gratitude. I knew, I absolutely knew, that someone had saved me."

Jo inched closer to him, she wanted his smell, the feel of his hair, she couldn't get it, she couldn't get it all in time.

"You saved me, miss. Aye, God saved me—and my mother's prayers saved me—but God and my mother's prayers got me you, got me to you—and you saved me, Josephine," and as he called her by her Christian name for the first time he seemed to savor every syllable, as if they were delicious, as if just pronouncing them delighted him.

"You are an angel, a beautiful guardian angel." Here he touched the tendrils of her hair, wet and sticking to her face. "You have given me everything. And I have nothing to give you but my heart. And this—"

And he was pulling off the great ring his father and grandfather had worn before him.

"This will be too big for your wee hand," he said, smiling, putting it into her right palm and curling her fingers around it. "But keep it for me. Keep it without promising anything. Keep it so I can know it goes with you—that my love goes with you—so I can hope, one day—"

The truck horn sounded outside, jarring and cruel. Time was speeding away. They would be parted in a moment, in just a moment, there was nothing she could do to stop time. David's eyes were deep and calm and knowing. He kissed the open palm of her left hand.

"God bless you, Lieutenant McMahon. Even if I should die, my love never will."

And Jo turned away, turned without saying a word, because she couldn't, because she had to, because none of this was happening, it was all happening at once.

The rain had redoubled. There was no wind, just a relentless downpour that made it difficult to see, difficult to breathe. She walked up to the ambulance. An orderly inside was holding out a hand to help her over the tailgate, but she just stood there, rooted in place, looking into the rear of the truck without seeing it.

It was an absolute deluge. The new men were eager to pull out.

"Forget something, honey?"

Then, as if waking up suddenly—

"Yes."

She ran back into the tent. David looked up and took off his helmet. Then she was in his arms, kissing him.

"Damn you," she said desperately in between kisses, coming up for air. She was exposed, she was naked, she was raw and open to the world, but with that vulnerability, her passion and her heart and her fire came back to her, she ignited—she was Jo again.

"Stay alive, David. Just stay alive, just live," and she was vehement, almost angry, her kisses burned.

Then just as suddenly, she ran out into the rain, jumping into the back of the ambulance without any help. The orderly banged twice on the outside of the cab, and the truck lurched into gear, tires spinning for a second before rattling off, leaving two thick gouges in the mud track behind it.

12

Kay Elliott

February 3, 1945, Santo Tomas Internment Camp,
Manila, Philippines

Twenty-four cents a day. They used to spend twenty-four cents a day on each of us for food. Two whole bits. There used to be enough food to buy a quarter's worth of food for every man, woman, and child in this place. And we thought we were hungry then.

I am writing this down. It looks like scribble to me, I don't recognize any of the letters, but these are the words I am saying, inside, whether it looks like it or not. We are not allowed to write at Santo Tomas, our diaries are burned, we'll be shot if we're caught writing, but I am going to die anyway so this is my final act of difiance. Do you spell that with an e? I was going to go back and fix it, but it's not there anymore, none of the words are really there, or they are and I can't see them. All right, I'll just mean it with an e, that'll have to be good enough.

The planes flew over, and in the dark of the blacked-out dormitory Kay heard Manila being attacked. She wondered what the Americans would find when they finally got to Santo Tomas. The inmates were locked in. Even those out in the courtyard who looked like they were dead had been scooped up and dumped just inside the door. Kay couldn't see anything from where she was lying, scratching pen against paper. Some-one had told her the stairwells were packed with barrels of gas-oline. *They're going to burn us alive,* she guessed, *if the Americans get here. Maybe before the Americans get here.*

The Japanese shot at the prisoners if they got near the win-dows, so it was hard for anyone to tell what was going on. The courtyard was empty—that much they knew. The Japs had set up signals and machine guns on the rooftops, which made them a military target, but when had they ever followed any convention? Kay liked to imagine that somewhere—in a small fishing village perhaps, far from all this—a nice, plump Japanese woman was bouncing her baby on her knee, singing him a funny lullaby about dragons and magic kites, because other than her, they all seemed madmen to Kay—cruel, hard madmen. Destroying just to destroy, because the rest of hu-manity wasn't human, wasn't like them. *No, they won't think twice before burning us in here like trapped rats.*

Kay remembered the Japs talking a lot to the nurses about rats. In the infirmary they had wanted the women to inoc-ulate everyone against some kind of "plague." They had a new serum. They said it would protect the inmates against it, against malaria too. *Good God, what did I give out in those shots?* Looking back now, she didn't know. One of the mission-aries had told her later—after she had done it believing what the Japs had said—that in China the Japanese had dropped a ton of fleas infected with plague, real bubonic plague; they had done it without hesitating. Turning the "worthless Chi-nese" into guinea pigs for their biological weapons. If they died during the course of their experiments, so much the better—one less lab rat, that was all. *God forgive me for what I may have done.*

Kay wondered what was happening in the rest of the world. There was no way to tell. She imagined the world was still fighting against the Axis powers—but what if they weren't? What if Hitler had taken Europe, taken Britain, (*good God*) what if he had taken America, and not recently but years ago? What if the world was already dark? What if this little, insignificant speck on the map was the last thing they were fighting over? Then it would all be over. The Japs and the Germans could start picking over the remains. They could start killing each other.

In that one letter Kay had from Jo, they still were fighting, back then anyway, crawling across Italy, heading north to France, to Germany itself—were they crazy? Kay remembered every word by heart, she had read it through so many times.

Dear Kay, I hope this reaches you, that you are being treated well in captivity, that you come back home, or come join me here at the front. To be fair, we're not always at the front, sometimes we're a little behind it, sometimes a little in front of it, but we seem to hover right around the center here, getting quite a beating at times and then picking up the men, picking up the pieces of this tragedy—and war is a tragedy, hot or cold, wet or dry, Pacific or Europe or Indo-China. But you're famous, did you know that, Kay? It was an ad for war bonds, I think, no, here it is, a homefront "Work to set them free" campaign in the paper, you know what they're like, no, maybe you don't, I guess you haven't seen them yet. Well, there's a mean-faced Jap in the foreground (do they all look that sinister, or is it just for the posters?) and, behind a barbwire fence, there's an artist's rendering of what he thinks "nurses taken prisoner in the Pacific" look like. Well, you'd be glad to know you're still glamorous, Kay, with a fresh permanent in your hair, and you're wearing the most outlandish getup imaginable—starched cap and white uniform (like at our commencement, remember? real fancy dress) with white pumps and (get this) bright white stockings, no runs in them even; and the whole silly thing's topped off with a Florence Nightingale cape from the last war. I never saw anything like it. I know you would laugh if you saw the picture, Kay. (Queenie says hi, and is laughing next to me now, just looking at the paper, she says she wouldn't be caught dead in it.) We both say, keep your chin up, let us finish up over here, and we'll be right over to visit you next.

The fighting was much closer now. Kay wondered what the Americans were using. Maybe tanks? She liked to think tanks. Rolling toward them, crushing stone and rubble beneath their tracks as if they were nothing. Coming toward them. Toward the enormous rat trap soon to be set ablaze.

Kay pretended to write, not even noticing that the pencil stub had slipped from her hand. Not even noticing that her hand had stopped moving.

I hope they get here, I hope the Americans crush this place, that they tear down these walls, that they break through the gates of our hell. I hope they come here and finally end all this madness.

"The Lord was going before them in a pillar of cloud by day to lead them on the way, and in a pillar of fire by night to give them light, that they might travel by day and by night."

It's night now. Just follow the light, boys, you'll find us.

Peacetime

13

Jo McMahon

June 21, 1945, London, England

Jo scratched at the collar of her dress shirt. It had been especially tailored for her, it wasn't too tight, but she was unused to it—to the beige tie that had to be worn just so, to the formal brown jacket, the fitted skirt. She sat there, in that quiet room, listening to the clock on the wall tick incessantly. The floorboards were so glossy they looked like there was a layer of ice on them. The windows in the room were shut tight against the sun outside; Jo felt stifled. She readjusted her collar and wiggled uncomfortably in her seat, her stockings itching her legs, her high-heeled shoes hidden beneath the hard-backed chair, one foot tucked demurely behind the other.

The door opened and a woman with a bad complexion said she would be seen now. Jo stood up quickly, and the sunlight glaring down on car windshields below shot up and hit her in the eyes, blinding her for a second. She clicked carefully across the shiny floor and entered the small, smoky office.

"Lieutenant McMahon," said the captain at the desk, half-sitting up as she entered and saluted. He made a brushing gesture with his free hand in response.

"Sorry about the mess," he said, smiling, putting down his

coffee mug, pushing an enormous pile of papers aside to make room for it. "There's so much to do, and only so many hours in the day. Who knew winning a war would make so much paperwork?"

He grinned enormously at his wit, and Jo smiled politely in response.

"So, miss"—he was checking a list in front of him—Jo saw names messily crossed off in blue, others with large red check marks next to them—"ah, yes, now I remember. Well, dear, we have some good news and we have some bad news."

The "dear" gives it away.

"The good news really is tremendous," he continued patronizingly, as if speaking to a very small child. "Looks like you were busy across the channel, huh?" He handed her a tiny cardboard box like it was a birthday present. She opened it.

"The Silver Star," he proclaimed, as if she needed a refresher on military insignia. "That's amazing. I mean, I don't know, but you may be the only woman to have ever received this."

No, not the only woman, she thought.

"There will be a pinning ceremony sometime," he said vaguely, waving his hand in the air, looking again at his chart. A buzzer went off, and he said, "Not now, Bessie," scowling as if Bessie could see his disapproving face.

"You can ask my secretary the date as you go out."

He seemed to have dismissed her, to have forgotten about her, about the bad news he still had to give. He was counting under his breath and shaking his head, as if the sums weren't coming out right.

"Can I ask who recommended me, sir?"

"For this? Uh, sure, no problem," he said in a tone implying the opposite. He clicked on a switch. "Bessie, see if you can find out who recommended this woman for the Silver Star, I don't have it here. And have my lunch sent up, will you? I'm starving."

Jo sat quietly, hands folded, looking at the man. He was running to fat; he must have had a desk job the whole war. He never looked up at her, checking and rechecking his charts. The bald spot on the top of his head was shiny. It reminded her of Billy. There was a clock in this room too, noisier than the one in the waiting room; the clicking sound was so loud, she wondered how he could stand it.

"Oh," he said, as if just remembering something, crossing off another line with satisfaction. "You're also promoted to first lieutenant. You *must* have been busy," and the way he said it sounded suggestive this time, as if being promoted was not exactly a good thing, was somehow questionable.

Jo looked around the small office—a smug room, she decided; there were diplomas and medals and fake swords crossed above his head. The room was littered with books, with pamphlets, with a half-eaten sandwich; there were orange rinds peeking out from under his desk, his area rug peppered with pencil shavings and ash.

Jo cleared her throat.

"The bad news, sir?"

"Oh, oh, yes," he said, his voice growing serious. He put on the glasses he had been reading without only a moment before. Jo imagined the thick frames were just for effect, to try to make himself seem formidable.

"Miss, there seems to be some question as to your—uh, how do I say it—fitness?—to continue nursing, at this time."

"There's no question about it, sir."

"Now, I know what you're going to say, that you're fine,

that you can keep at your post, and I highly commend the sentiment, but—"

"Excuse me, sir." His eyebrows rose in surprise at the interruption, his glasses slipping a notch lower on his nose. "I meant there was no question. I am *not* fit to stay on in nursing. I have been saying that since I got here."

The man seemed genuinely surprised.

"You're not contesting it? You're not going to put up a fuss?"

"Sir, I have asked the matron since the day I arrived to please find some other kind of work for me. A desk job. Paperwork. Anything. But I can't help these soldiers, sir—"

Her voice trailed off, and she looked vacant for a moment, lost.

"I'm sure you've been through a lot, miss—"

What do you know about what I've been through?

"—and no one can blame you if you're ready for a change."

Jo felt her eyes prick; she would not show emotion in front of this man. He wasn't worth it.

"Sir, it's not that. I love nursing. I love the men. It's—it's just this."

And she extended her arms in front of her, palms facing downward, and her hands shook, trembling uncontrollably. The man's face went white, as if this were the worst thing he had seen in the war, the worst thing he had ever seen.

Perhaps it is, Jo thought.

"Shell shock, sir," Jo said simply. "Battle fatigue. God knows I've seen enough of it in others to know it in myself. I am not able—not competent—to care, to give medical care, sir. I've been saying that since I got here."

Jo slumped back in her chair, seeming to forget that he was there for a moment.

"I—um—I don't know what to say, miss—perhaps, being a war hero and all now"—he smiled weakly—"we could arrange to have you sent home?"

"No, sir." Jo sat up straight in her chair. "No, sir—I mean, please, no, sir. Not until we win in Japan too. Not until we're all going home together."

I have to stay here, until I know where David is, until I know what's happened to David. I have no one back home. No one to go home to.

Jo's fire lit up the dingy room for a moment and seemed as if it might even ignite the smoldering embers that lay dormant in this captain, who hadn't even bothered to give his name. Then his lunch came in on a tray, with two kinds of drinks clinking together in their beveled glassware. He looked at it, then at Jo. He had to bring this interview to an end—it was after twelve already.

Bessie put the tray down heavily, right on top of a stack of papers marked "State Department."

"The name was Donahue, sir."

He looked blankly at his secretary. *Really, she should do something about her skin.*

"The name you asked for. The person who recommended her for promotion."

Bessie stamped out, her orthopedic shoes making no sound on the hardwood.

Of course it wasn't Clark. Jo had known that, but she had had to find out.

"There's your answer to that then. And, um, miss, if you're sure about the way you feel"—he glanced longingly at his tray, resisting the urge to look under the silver lid; it smelled like turkey—"there are a few canvassing jobs here yet, raising money for the Pacific campaign. It's not really too involved—just door-to-door stuff, asking for donations—"

"I'll take it," Jo said quickly, standing up.

He felt there was something more he was supposed to say to this woman, something else perhaps that he should do for her; then he looked again at his meal. Perhaps turkey with dressing.

"Bessie, will, uh, make all the arrangements, miss."

"Thank you, sir. Thank you for keeping me on."

Jo turned resolutely and walked toward the door.

"Miss," the captain said, already putting his napkin on his lap, "you forgot your star."

JO STEPPED OUT into the sunshine. Her feet hurt in her pumps as she walked quickly down the sidewalk thronged with pedestrians. There were so many Americans—officers, enlisted men. A group of Navy sailors, arm in arm, passed by her, whistling loudly. It was hard to believe this was London—it looked more like Fifth Avenue back home. Jo looked at the city and saw it but didn't see it. There were the parts that looked like postcards, like snapshots in a travel brochure, looked like she had always imagined they would—bakeries and pubs and flats, St. Paul's, Piccadilly Circus—juxtaposed against bombed-out rubble, shells of former homes, sandbags piled high, knocked over, ripped open, and pouring out into the street. She cut across Hyde Park and looked up at Wellington Arch, the Angel of Peace descending on the chariot of war being driven by a small boy. Who was he? Hitler as a child? Hirohito? The dictators of a year ago, of a hundred years ago, a thousand? What did it matter as long as the angel descended? Came down and stopped the runaway horses, stopped the madness. *Angel of Peace. Look out for David.*

"Look out," a cabby yelled at her angrily, and she stepped back off the pavement. She had not heard from David. *How could I?* she reassured herself. The war in Europe had only been decided a month before. Who knew where he was, how long it would take him to get back to civilization, to her? How long it would be until his family heard from him, until she did? And how would he even know where to find her? All he knew of her was Brooklyn; surely he would eventually look for her there, not in London. But she just couldn't go back, couldn't leave England, not yet, not with David still out there somewhere. Anyway, London was a hell of a lot closer to the Scottish Highlands than Bay Ridge.

She was glad she'd be out of the hospital finally, glad she'd be going out, doing something again for the war effort. Her field patients had all healed up and moved on. Many would be home by now. Jo glanced at the American papers being sold in the street and saw the *Queen Mary* had docked yesterday, laden with American troops. They'd be storming New York. They'd all have hangovers by now, like New Year's Eve and Mardi Gras and Independence Day all rolled into one. Jo didn't miss it, though, didn't wish she was there. She was glad, of course, that the boys were home—at least until they moved on to Japan—glad that the war in Europe was over and reconstruction could begin over here. But she couldn't leave yet.

She reached into her musette bag—not her old canvas one but a newly issued leather satchel, highly polished and smooth—and pulled out a penny.

"Here, son," she said to one of the paperboys, and opened up the paper.

She couldn't take it all in, the parts of the war she had missed—the last desperate push into Germany, into Poland, into deep crevices the free world was never meant to discover. She read strange words like "Dachau" and saw pictures of emaciated men, of piled corpses—*but this is evil for evil's sake*—and her eyes welled up and spilled over. When she could see again, there were heavily garbed Soviets on the page in front of her. She had left the theater of war before the Americans met up with them. Their uniforms, their faces were foreign to her—she had forgotten they were even in the war. But their civilian casualties were in the millions. Jo looked around her, at the tube entrances caved in, at the libraries and schools leveled—she looked at the devastation England had sustained, the loss of 60,000 noncombatants—innocent women and children, old men, old women, bombed in their sleep, buried alive, never to wake again. Then she tried to multiply that awful figure to imagine a million Russians dying, then ten million, then the twenty million they were estimating now, even as the reports kept coming in. Jo looked at the pictures—there were happy servicemen kissing girls in the streets, naked Gypsy orphans crying on the side of the road, Axis spies being shot like dogs, Allied spies being killed like martyrs. There were crowds cheering in Manhattan on VE day and crowds cheering in Milan as Mussolini and his mistress hung upside down on meat hooks. Jo couldn't take it in, couldn't understand it. It was peace that still reeked of war and death and starvation and torture. How could it ever come right? How could God fix it? How could the world ever recover from this? And it wasn't over yet. Japan, the Pacific—that war wasn't over, not by a long shot. What was it like, really like, over there? She hadn't heard from Kay since before Pearl Harbor; she didn't know what had happened to her, whether she had gotten any of Jo's letters, whether she was still alive. What brutality would the American forces face there now, taking the Pacific one bloody island at a time, pushing into the very heart of the enemy? *Please, God in heaven, not any worse than this.*

Jo had folded the paper, was walking along the streets again, looking but not seeing, picking up her feet to avoid the potholes, the sandbags—now useless and littered everywhere—following the streams of humanity as they detoured around craters, around workmen removing piles of rubble from the road. She stopped to tie her shoe in front of an Anderson shelter—and from that vantage point, saw the bright plaid of a kilt in front of her. Red and white, green and blue—there were two, no three. When she had been upright, the men had been indistinguishable from everyone else on the street, but from below they were unmistakable. Jo stood up and hurried after them.

"Please, please," she called. There were too many people, too much noise.

Then, remembering David, his smiling eyes, trying to teach her Scottish.

This is how you say hello, miss . . .

"Aye, aye, min," she nearly yelled.

The three men stopped dead in their tracks, two housewives with parcels bumping into them and glowering before moving on. The river of pedestrians flowed past them.

"Good afternoon, miss," they said smiling, bowing to her right there on Apsley Way.

"Thank goodness I've found you, I've had the most awful time—"

They smiled patiently—they had all the time in the world.

"Can we be assisting ye in some way?"

"You see, the British aren't always that helpful when it comes to Scots—"

"Aye, miss, we've taken a notice of that before."

"I'm sorry. I'm not making any sense, I know. I must seem ridiculous, just coming up to you like this. My name is Josephine."

"Good afternoon," they said again, in unison.

"Good afternoon. Could you please help me? I need to find someone."

"A Scot perhaps?"

"Aye," she nearly yelled again, and they laughed.

"I mean, yes," she said, blushing.

"He looked something like us, and ye met him in the war, and ye lost contact with him?"

"Yes again. You see, I'm American Army; we don't have any way to trace him. And you all are supposed to be a United Kingdom, but good Lord, there's England and Australia and Canada—"

"And us, miss."

"Aye," she couldn't help saying again, in her excitement. "And none of you seem to know where anyone else is," she ended breathlessly.

"We could take ye back to our captain, miss," they offered. "We're headed home soon ourselves, but we would be happy to escort ye. What was your young fellow's name?"

And that was that. Jo was walking with them down the same street, but now it was summer, Jo noticed the heat and the sun and the smells—there were flowers in the vendors' stalls, in flower boxes, flowers coming up between the cracks in the pavement. The sky was a glittering blue, bluer than it had ever been before. The men asked questions and answered them, and the lilt of their voices brought David back. They would help her really bring him back—find him and bring him back to his mother. And Bumpy. And Kit. Bring him back to her.

They gave her cold water in tiny paper cups when they got to their captain's office. The captain—a great big man, too large for his kilt, for his tiny office—was friendly and formal and obliging. He got on the phone, he sent messengers, dispatched telegrams—no trouble was too much to take for young love. He wrote down her address in London and in New York. *A lot of the men are unaccounted for, but not to worry, miss, it's just the paperwork, just the backlog, we can't process it all, can't write it down fast enough.* Jo was happier than she had been in a long time; no—a slow smile transformed her face—happier than she had ever been before. The men looked upon her benevolently, like a sister, like a friend about to marry into the family. Of course she loved David—was he not a Scot? To them, there was nothing more to it than that; it was the most natural thing in the world.

Then the office was closing. Jo glanced up at the clock, the tiny, quiet clock that hadn't made a sound, looked accusingly across the street toward the church bells that had chimed out the hours without her hearing them. She had been there all day, drinking little cups of water and talking about David and being blissfully happy. She stood up, apologizing for taking up their time, but they were all smiles—that was nonsense. *God be with ye, miss, invite us to the wedding.* Everyone laughed.

As they were leaving the captain's office his secretary handed him a sheet of paper. "Just come over the teletype, sir, the new list."

He glanced at it, and Jo kept smiling, but the captain's face clouded for a second, for a second too long.

"What did you say your man's name was, lass?"

He hadn't called her "lass" before, and she wondered why he did now.

And there, under the "Mac" section, overburdened on that list of Scottish names, was "David MacPherson, missing in action."

EVERYONE KEPT SAYING how difficult things were when, really, they were so simple. It was impossible to get good beef, the woman in front of her was complaining. *That's nothing,* another joined in. *Can you get sugar? Real sugar? No, I didn't think so.* Then there was the lack of dry goods to discuss, the lack of fresh eggs, of rawhide and muslin and new music records from America. But it was so easy, if you stopped to think about it. You slept in beds. You woke up. You washed your face. There were things to eat, real things, things not scooped out of cans, half-frozen and rancid. You could stay inside. Or go out, walk for miles and miles and miles, and no one knew and no one cared, and as long as you were back in the dormitories by midnight, no one even noticed. Never, not once, did anyone try to kill you. No bombs, no planes, no mines. Busy streets full of busy people, shaking their heads and commiserating about the interrupted tube schedule or the wait at the post office or the thousand other civilian worries Jo could no longer understand. It was all so easy, so terribly easy.

She walked down the bustling sidewalk, turned quickly,

and headed for a quieter part of town. Shiny black wrought-iron fences ran endlessly on and on before her, making neat shadows beneath them in the scorching sun. Jo readjusted her cap, tucking in a loose hairpin; her hair was dyed now, back to her original copper; the threads of white and gray were gone.

The houses around her were palatial, regally set back from the road, their lawns an emerald green. Groundsmen trimmed hedges, pruned back masses of rhododendron and azalea, watered flowerbeds, and filled birdbaths. Some estates seemed virtually untouched by the recent war—she could see the topless Daimlers pull up, deposit their precious cargo of debutante and earl, duchess and industrial magnate, before being waxed down thoughtfully by a chauffeur with six boys working under him, sweating in the noonday heat. Jo walked a little farther on—she refused to solicit at any home displaying mourning, curtains drawn, women walking past the windows in their widow's weeds. There was a Georgian mansion flanked on one side by an Italianate monstrosity and, on the other, by the gutted remains of a burned-out shell. It amazed Jo that everyone carried on as before. The families of these houses must have shared invitations to dinners, to dances. Their servants would have met at the hedgerows to smoke and exchange gossip. Then, in an instant, their domestic staff—the butcher boy bringing in the chops, the mailman lingering a second too long to flirt with the second housemaid, the gardener bringing in the last of the lilacs and hoping they would do—were gone forever, annihilated, with nothing left to show for it, for their lives, for their loves and jealousies and petty hatreds and silly dreams. Jo looked at the rubble for another moment before pushing open its neighbor's ornate gate and starting down the long, immaculately raked gravel drive sedately curving away from the site of destruction as if from some embarrassment, some social foible, something best left forgotten.

Life must go on.

The sun poured down, and as Jo walked her mind raced. *Missing in action. That's worse than killed in action. Of course it's not, how can you say that? Killed in action is the worst, it's final, there's no hope there, nothing. But killed in action is final, that's the point. Your heart can break, you can die, kill yourself even, but you know what's what. Your life is ended. He's gone. Missing in action, now, now that's nothing. Truly nothing. You can be missing because you're lost or because you're stranded or trapped or prisoner or anything. You can be missing because you're dead and no one found your body, or because you're alive but no one's looking for you, or simply because someone typed an* M *when they meant to type a* K.

Jo imagined David in a prisoner-of-war camp in northern Poland, still shivering in June. Or starving in Germany, held by some rebellious outlaws unwilling to surrender, about to take out their anger and rage on an Allied prisoner. She saw him hanged in Dresden, drowned in Munich, lost in Russia. His typhus came back and he died on a transport ship, buried at sea before they remembered to pull off his leather identification tag. ("What was his name? Who knows? No one will miss the poor devil.") As soon as Jo convinced herself he was alive (lost or starving or sick, but alive), doubt came in and whispered that he was dead. Then, when she had almost accepted that reality, preparing her heart for death, hope would creep back in and buoy up her heart, a sickening, feeble kind of hope that was worse than despair. Then the entire vicious cycle would begin again.

The lady of the house was not at home, the servant said. Jo thanked him politely, walked back up the drive, headed toward the next house, then the next one after that, like an automaton, walking senselessly in the sun. Jo's head ached from the heat, it ached from thinking, from not thinking—this was all she did, chasing her own thoughts, waking, asleep, in the terrible in-between land between waking and sleeping when she couldn't tell dream from reality. David was a brave man, not a coward, but he died a thousand deaths in her mind. And just when she was about to kneel at the grave she had dug for him and weep with her head in her hands, she would hear him call to her from beyond, from where he was trapped, waiting for her—and her mind would start to race again.

Jo felt the crumpled ball of paper in her jacket pocket as she walked. She didn't need to read it—she had memorized the address a dozen times over.

"This is the only address we have for him, lass," the Scottish captain had said in slow motion—she had watched his mustached lips move as if in a dream. "We sent word to the farm, but the family moved off with the air raids. This is a relative of his, an uncle here in town. You might try him."

The captain's voice had been so sad. Jo had wanted to comfort him, to rub the top of his head like a small boy, to say it would be all right, not to worry, but her heart hadn't started beating again since he had said David was missing. So Jo had taken the address and later thrown it away; then, on her knees, had searched for it again amid the orange rinds and eggshells, smoothed it out, read it, memorized it. She would go and see the uncle, her only link to David. No, she wouldn't. Yes, she would.

Her feet had led her there while she debated with herself. Her mind said, *Clearly you cannot do this,* but her hand reached out and rang the great bell. No sound reached her ears behind that mass of mahogany and iron and steel, but in a few minutes the door was opened by an elderly servant who betrayed no emotion, standing motionlessly in the door, eyebrows politely raised.

"Good afternoon, madam."

Had she aged as much as that, in the war?

"Good afternoon. May I speak to the lady of the house?" That was their line, what they were supposed to say.

"The lady?" The servant's voice betrayed the slightest hint of inflection.

Jo swallowed. Her throat was dry.

"Or the man of the house. Really, it doesn't matter."

"Whom shall I say is calling?"

"Lieutenant McMahon, United States Army."

He inspected her for another minute, examining her dress uniform carefully, as if she were a phony.

"If you will step this way?"

Jo had expected it to be dark and cool inside the colossal entryway, but it was flooded with light from above. Skylights shimmered in the full blast of the sun—on the panes of glass, on the ivory marble of the staircase, on the ornately carved tile work beneath her shoes, radiating out like a sun. Jo raised her hand to her eyes; the glare hurt them.

"In here, madam."

Jo was grateful to be ushered into a comfortable library, dark and soothing to her spinning head. The servant brought Jo's card—first carefully centered on a polished silver salver— over to an old man with bushy hair and even bushier eyebrows. He had been surveying a top row of books, craning his head back. Now he took the card, rubbing the small of his back through his tweed sports coat. He looked nothing like David. Maybe the address they had given her was wrong.

"Lieutenant McMahon, sir." The servant withdrew silently.

"Hello, miss," the old man said simply. "Will you sit down?"

Was there the hint of a lilt in there? No, he had called her "miss," not "lass," he had said, "Will you sit down," not, "Will ye." She was imagining things. This was a mistake.

"Thank you, sir."

Jo sank into the cold softness of leather; there was a wooden blind blocking out the light from the garden—Jo could make out chinks of green and red and yellow in between the slats. There was something metal—or perhaps it was water—outside but it reflected the sun and she moved her head back and forth surreptitiously, trying to get away from its piercing light.

"Can I offer you a drink?"

"Water, please, sir."

"Just water? I thought perhaps brandy? Whisky?"

"No thank you, sir. I've walked a great deal today. And it's much hotter now than when I started."

So much more sun.

"Of course." He handed her a heavy crystal goblet, so unlike the small paper cups the Scots had given her on the happiest—on the saddest—day of her life.

Jo sipped the water, but it tasted funny, like metal.

"Can I help you with something?"

Jo thought of the Scots she had met in the street and how they had wanted to help her too, how they had wanted her to find David, to marry him, to raise fine Scot boys who could raise hell like their father.

"Miss?"

"I'm sorry, sir." Jo shook herself, as if trying to wake up. "I am an American Army nurse, and right now I am soliciting funds for the Allied Pacific campaign."

I have to get out of here, this is not David's family. Even if it is, what am I to them? An interloper, a stranger, they owe me nothing. I am nothing.

"You're not acting as a nurse right now? I mean, here in London—"

The door from the garden burst open, and two young people came barging in. The light was blinding, and Jo squinted painfully.

"You certainly did nothing of the sort and you know it," one was laughing.

"I'll beat you with a stick—" the young man threatened, and that seemed to delight the girl, who was laughing and hiding something behind her back.

"Children—" the old man chided softly. "We have a guest."

The children who weren't children but nearly as old as Jo came up short and looked shamefaced for a second before breaking into smiles.

"Oh, thank goodness," the girl said, beaming. "I'm so relieved, I thought you were Mrs. Youngblood or somebody awful like that. She does scold so. You look nice," she ended ingenuously.

"My niece," the old man introduced, apologetically, "and one of her many admirers."

"Begging your pardon, sir, but 'admirer' my foot. This little whippersnapper of yours has—"

"Now, children, children, you're wearing out our guest. Katherine, go see if your mother can come down. Let her know we have a guest from the United States Army with us."

"No, not really, how exciting—" and their eyes grew wide and they were about to pounce on her, to hit her with a barrage of questions, but the girl's uncle shooed them out of the room.

He closed the door to the garden they had left open in their exuberance and pulled the cord of the blind so that the light slanted down, onto the Oriental carpet, away from her eyes.

"Another glass of water? I know my dear sister would be most interested to hear anything you have to say."

"Yes, thank you. I must have gotten a touch of the sun today, sir." As she took the refilled glass her hands shook and dribbles of water fell on her skirt, on her stockinged legs.

Women did this, she knew. Found the family of a beau they had in the war, or even the family of a complete stranger who had died—you could access charts, you could get people's names, their next of kin—and passed themselves off as their son's fiancé. They got money that way, a place to stay sometimes; they could pawn off an illegitimate grandchild, or the bastard child of a complete stranger. *Look, he has Johnny's eyes, the dimple is just the same. We'll set you up somewhere, dear, get you started in life, just let us keep the baby.* Those women made Jo sick, feeding off the dead like ghouls. She wasn't that, she could never be that. She had come because she had to, had to find out if they had had any news, if they knew anything about David at all, but now she knew it was wrong—she shouldn't have come. The Scottish captain had her address, he would let her know as soon as he heard anything.

Jo finished drinking. The water still tasted funny—this was sunstroke coming on. She carefully placed the glass on the side table, using both hands. She let them fall to her sides, then remembered and clasped them squarely in front of her. She always did that now to hide the shaking, or crossed her arms across her chest; once, when it had been bad, she had had to actually sit on her hands, but that had only happened once.

"You were saying you are a nurse."

"Yes, sir, I'm a nurse."

"From the United States."

"New York—sir."

She had paused in between "New York" and "sir"; she didn't know why. It seemed to have some meaning, she wasn't sure.

Another door (there were so many doors to this room) opened quietly, and a small woman walked in. She was wrapped in a black lace shawl, clean but well-worn. Her face was kind and open, but her eyebrows pinched together a little in the middle, as if she was worried about something and trying not to show it.

"My dear girl," the old man said, putting his arm around his sister and helping her into a chair. "This is a United States lieutenant, come to see us."

The old woman smiled, her face breaking into a thousand creases. *I hope I look like that when I'm old,* Jo thought fleetingly. *If I ever become old.*

"Hello, dear," and there was something so kindly, so welcoming, in those two words that Jo wanted to kneel down next to her and bury her face in the old woman's lap and let her pat her head.

All at once a shadow passed across the woman's face. "She hasn't come about—" her voice quavered, and she looked worriedly at her brother. For a second it was as if all the light in the woman's face had disappeared and was replaced with cold, a shivering cold.

"No, no, Clotilde, how could she? She's here raising money for—was it Japan, child?"

And Jo didn't mind being called "child," not by these people, by these wonderful, warm people. She could stay here forever with them.

"Yes, sir."

The woman in the antimacassar chair looked relieved, as if she would have slumped back in relief if the highback hadn't stopped her.

"I think of those children over there—you'll excuse me, miss, but they all seem so young to me—you seem so young to me—like children running around with scissors and I wish I could stop them."

Jo wanted to stop them too, wanted to desperately.

"And it must be so hot too. So terribly hot. Too hot to bear, really."

The woman didn't seem as if her mind was wandering, but more like she had given all this a great deal of thought, had thought it all out.

"She's a nurse, also, dear."

"No, not really? Do they have you canvassing besides doing your rounds?"

"No, ma'am. It's not that. This is all I'm doing right now."

She could have left it at that, but the woman's eyes were looking into her own with something Jo couldn't define. She had to tell her. Jo was speaking before she even realized what she was saying.

"You see, I was in the war, right up in it." Her voice faltered for a second, and she hated herself for that and moved on, quickly. "It was quite hard, parts of it, ma'am, and—I'm ashamed to say it, ma'am." Jo's eyes fell, were following the intricate pattern of the rug, up and down and around. "I'm, I'm not fit—my hands, ma'am." She put out her hands like a girl in school, shamefaced, waiting for the ruler to come down. "I'm very shaky right now, ma'am," and Jo's voice trembled and she wanted to cry. This was ridiculous. She had to ask them

for money to make this seem legitimate, ask them for a couple
of pounds, for anything, for spare change, for enough to send
over a Hershey's Tropical Bar, candy-coated, guaranteed not to
melt in the jungle sun.

"You were a nurse near the fighting, miss?"

Jo nodded her head. The room blurred, but she got the
tears back down, she got them down in time, her face was still
dry but her cheeks were burning. Even if they were David's
family, she wouldn't tell them, tell them how he had suffered,
how he had nearly died from disease and filth. She wouldn't
make them relive it over and over again—as she did.

"My dear, we owe you—all you nurses—so very much."

Jo folded her hands, then stuck them under her armpits,
crossing her arms hard across her chest.

"You see, my boy was wounded, taken care of by an American nurse."

"Oh, I'm sorry, ma'am." This was her out—she'd be telling
them in another minute if she didn't leave now. "I don't ask for
funds from families that have already lost someone," and Jo
got up, too quickly; the room tilting.

"He's not dead, dear. Just—just missing."

The woman in front of her became blurry, weakly smiling
at Jo through a haze. She was no longer one of David's rela-
tives, or anyone in particular anymore. She was just a mother
who had lost her child, the saddest thing in the world. There
were a thousand like her, a thousand thousand. For weeks now
Jo had been hearing, *My son . . . my nephew . . . my cousin . . .
my brother is dead . . . is missing . . . is injured.* Jo had told her
matron that she was bleeding these people dry, that they had
given too much already, but the response was that every bit

helped, went to Japan, went to end the war once and for all. *Please, God, for good this time.*

Jo noticed that the old woman had been talking all this time.

" . . . and I think—it sounds ungrateful, I know, no one understands me when I say it—but missing in action is worse than killed in action, don't you think?"

Jo made a desperate sound, a groan and a gasp at the same time, choking down a sob. She turned toward the door, but there were so many, so many more doors than she remembered. They all were closed, they all looked the same—which one did she come in by? One flew open, and the young girl came bounding back in, sandwich in hand, her young suitor no longer with her.

"Thank goodness you're still here, it took forever to get rid of Tommy. I want to hear all about the war. My brother was in the war, did you know?"

Jo reeled away from her. There was a shrill ringing in her ears, it sounded like the mosquitoes back in Sicily, the ones that would sneak into their tent and hover over their faces at night. A tiny sound, small and metallic, growing steadily louder.

"Emile, do something, she's gone white all over—"

The old man was advancing toward her now, hands outstretched. The woman had risen and was walking over too, taking small mincing steps as if her shoes were too tight, steadying herself with the chair, with the back of the sofa. How could Jo not have noticed their eyes before, how large they were, how very large? They were enormous, like saucers. She had to get out.

Finally, she pulled open the right door. She was blasted with sunlight, she was swimming in it, it was hot and stifling, she was walking into a furnace. She heard the sound again, but now it was louder, like a teapot. No, it was more like a tune. Someone whistling a tune. Jo looked up. The curved stairway went up forever, went up to heaven itself, there was nothing but power and majesty and light, so much light, too much light, Jo was blinded. There were two hands inside her throat, and they were squeezing her trachea shut.

Then the whistling grew louder, a man was whistling, a jaunty, rollicking tune; he was tripping down the stair and straightening his tie and whistling. Jo's ear popped, and the whistling grew louder, then stopped altogether as the man noticed Jo and smiled.

It was David.

Or it wasn't David, because he didn't seem to know her, to recognize her, standing there dazed and dumb, staring up at him, standing in the middle of the burning tiles and gazing up at him in confusion and terror and wonder. His smile kept curving wider, and he winked at her, saucily.

"Hello there, beautiful."

Jo reached her hand out to steady herself, but there was nothing there and she fainted. The sun went behind a cloud, and it was like a light switch had been turned off all at once and Jo crumpled in a heap on the floor, on the lifeless tiles, still warm but dull now without the light of the sun.

JO WOKE UP on a chaise longue, the family crowded around her. She could see them now. They were no monsters; their eyes looked concerned, that was all.

"Get her some brandy," someone was saying, and Jo swiv-

eled her jaw until her ear popped and the words were no longer
garbled.

"I'm sorry," she said weakly, trying to sit up.

"You know," the David who was not David was saying,
"I should be very flattered, having a beautiful woman faint
dead away at a line like that. Makes me believe I've really got
something after all." There was something different about this
voice: it was David's, but it wasn't. The brogue wasn't there,
or if it was, it was polished, hidden. "But whatever came over
you?"

"You're—you're Bumpy," Jo whispered, remembering a line
from one of David's dictated letters.

"I beg your pardon, miss—"

"You're Bumpy and Kit and—wait." Jo shielded her eyes,
straining to remember. "You must be Uncle Emily."

"What?"

"How could she know that?"

Jo's eyes welled over in explanation.

"Who is she—"

"Wait a minute—could it really be?"

"My God, what was the name on that card?"

The young man snatched it off the tray.

"J. McMahon. J. Josephine. *Jo?*"

"You have your brother's eyes."

THEY ATE DINNER. It was like a dream, but they ate dinner,
all of them together, like they would have if David had been
there, if he had brought her home to meet his family. Jo never
stopped talking—the food on her plate went cold but she
never stopped talking, she couldn't. Here, at last, were people
who knew David, who loved him, who could share in her love

and her pain and her sorrow. Now that they knew who she was, she told them everything—she told them too much. She wasn't allowed to divulge where she had been or who she had served under, but God, she didn't care. She told them everything, she couldn't stop herself—the names, the dates, the places—they were starving for information. She told them all about David—everything she could remember, everything—and saying it made it real, made him alive again. But she told them everything else too, because they would care. She could see in their eyes that they did care, they loved David, they would love her given half a chance.

She told them about Queenie, and she told them about Grandpa and the German and the cold and the rain and the ice. She dropped the Ranger's head back onto the table again, and she cried this time, and she screamed somehow too, although she never raised her voice. It was like she was burying them all, one by one, her comrades, her friends, laying them down to rest in peace, *Please, God, after all that, let them rest in peace.* They looked at her in horror, in awe, some hiding their emotion, some crying openly. Tears ran down the face of the old butler who no longer scrutinized her as a stranger, who had bounced the man Jo loved on his knee before she was even born. And the war was over but it wasn't over, it would never be over, not until David came home, until all the countless lost Davids came home. And of course they never would.

They retired to the library (there were only two doors, there had only ever been two doors) and Jo looked at a framed picture in the hallway and stood stock-still. It was David, the real David, her David—but David as he had never been for her. She had only ever known him as sick, as delirious, as one step removed from death. But this black-and-white photo came to

life in front of her—he was healthy and well, one rubber boot
sunk in a stream, the other on a bank lush with grass. He was
holding up a catch of fish and laughing at the cameraman as
if he had just told a joke. His eyes were glittering with it, sup-
pressing his smile, his bubbling laughter, just long enough to
pose for the shot. He was young and healthy and happy, and Jo
put her fingers up to the glass reverently, touching it, touching
him. Here then was Endymion at last.

Clotilde MacPherson came up to her, touching her gently
on the shoulder, and Jo jumped, she had been so lost in her
reverie. David's mother's eyes went right through her, right
down to the marrow of her soul.

"That's back home," Duncan said, coming up to the two
women. "That's back home, before it was damaged in a raid.
David always loved to fish there—he did everything outdoors
there."

But Jo wasn't listening.

"My greatest fear now is forgetting," Jo said softly.

The old woman took Jo's hand in hers; her skin was soft and
smooth, like a baby's.

"Forgetting how he looked, how he sounded, the words he
said. Once I lose that—lose the memory, I mean—then I've
lost him forever."

Jo stood, rooted in place, until the boys' mother managed
to finally, gently pry her away, get her to sit down again, to
take some brandy.

Then the clock over the mantle was striking 11:30. "My
curfew, ma'am, I must get started back."

And the old woman insisted that Duncan escort her. Jo
smiled at her stubborn determination. Did their mother know
what wild places she had walked alone in? Jo tried to compare

London with North Africa or Sicily or Occupied France, to explain it to her. But the older woman would hear none of it, and Duncan was already putting on his hat, a silk scarf superfluous in the heat; she was being kissed by Kit and shaking hands with their uncle and when she came up to David's mother she had the picture of David in her hands and she gave it to her. Jo took it and she and Duncan started down the front steps. Then she turned and ran back to his family—David's family—hugging them each in turn, holding on to them, crying.

"Now I know why he loved you all. I would have loved you too."

DUNCAN GAVE HER his arm, and it had been so long since anyone had made the gesture that she had looked stupidly at him for a second before registering what it meant. "Oh, oh, yes, thank you." They walked down the street the way Jo had come earlier that day, stepping gingerly over sandbags, over holes in the road, under great elms, stately and dark in the night.

"Good evening, governor," someone said, and Duncan touched his free hand to the brim of his hat as they walked past. If David had made Jo feel like she was running barefoot across the moors, Duncan was the very soul of propriety, of refined manners—here was a man who would always know which fork to use, how to pronounce the names of difficult hors d'oeuvres. He was sophistication itself, and Jo found it hard to believe he was the son of a Scottish farmer. They stepped out from under some overhanging boughs Duncan held back for her, and she found herself eyeing him surreptitiously.

"Go ahead, look," he said, with a little laugh.

Jo was ashamed, but she couldn't resist. She was hungry for

David, starving for him. She looked at Duncan as if she were memorizing every inch of his face.

Duncan smiled and they walked on, Jo devouring his profile, his gestures in the light of the streetlamps, against the canopy of stars. He prattled on about London and his club and where you could get a fairly decent steak and the DeSoto he wanted to buy from America when they lifted the restrictions and started making civilian cars again. Jo looked at him, at his mouth that was David's, but the words were all wrong, and she wondered for a second if David would have been like this too in peacetime. Duncan seemed to read her thoughts and broke off in the middle of a sentence.

"You're comparing me to my brother—"

Jo started to protest.

"No, no, I don't mind. David was a wonderful person, but you're wondering—what? If this is what he'd be like?"

"Please, I'm sorry, I don't mean to do it—"

"Not to worry, sweetheart," and he smiled again, his eyebrows raised coyly. "I'll tell you honestly. No, my brother and I were quite different people."

Please stop using past tense. Please.

"He never seemed to develop a taste for the finer things in life—no, that's not quite fair. Well, David and I disagreed, let's say, about what the finer things in life really were."

They were at Jo's barracks now; the clock tower above the colossal building read five minutes to twelve.

"I had no desire to live out my life as a Highland herdsman. Can you even imagine?"

And Jo couldn't, looking at him now, the smooth lines of his tailored suit, the pearly white of his scarf, perfectly tied; she could not imagine him whistling for the sheep to come down, to be fed, to be sheared. *Singing and laughing in the sunlight.*

"The ironic thing is that David had the real refinement out of the two of us, as rough as he seemed on the outside. If I had one-tenth of that—"

He looked past her for a moment, frowning; then he shrugged and came back.

"He was a great one for poetry, he was. For singing, for talking about life, about what he felt in his soul—that's it, exactly. David was soulful—anyway, more soulful than I am, honey."

Jo knew that was why she loved David, loved him in the present tense. That was what she had recognized beneath his lice-ridden clothes, in the letters she wrote for him. Even in his feverish ramblings he had prayed, recited poetry; whether it made sense to her or not, he had done it, it had been a part of him, so deeply ingrained it would never leave him—not even if he died. No one could take that from him, not ever.

The hands of the old clock inched closer together—they were nearly vertical now.

"Thank you for walking me home."

And for talking about David—thank you for talking about David.

"Could I call on you tomorrow?"

Jo panicked.

"I can't, Duncan, it—it would be selfish—it wouldn't be fair. Looking at you, I see David."

He stepped closer to her, was facing her now; in the half-light he looked more like David than ever.

"Thank you," she said again, slowly mouthing the words. "Thank your mother again for me. For the picture." She was almost whispering.

His eyes were the same, his eyes and his mouth were the same; the pale skin under the dark head of hair. She felt herself slipping—she was mesmerized.

"Oh, I have something for you too. Something of David's."

The Milky Way spread out above them, a swath of pure light taking up the whole sky.

"This is from David."

And he kissed her, a simple kiss, the kiss of a man used to kissing every girl he walked home good-night. But then Jo kissed him back, and it was so violent, so desperate, he drew her close instinctively, and her hand was behind his head in an instant and it felt like David's, her fingers were in his hair—and she was back in the hospital tent and here right now and the truck was honking outside and the rain came down through the canvas and soaked them both where they stood beneath a sea of stars and he was David and she was his and she was cursing him and loving him and telling him all he had to do was live.

The clock struck twelve, and Jo stepped back, horrified, covering her mouth.

Duncan was apologizing: "I had no right, I'm sorry, I—I didn't understand—"

But she was running up the stairs, leaving no glass slipper behind, no prince to follow her. She was running and crying, and she pulled open the door and pushed past the matron without explanation just as the last chime sounded and the old spinster locked the door for the night.

14

∞

Kay Elliott

February 3, 1945, Santo Tomas Internment Camp,
Manila, Philippines

In the end, the cavalry came. MacArthur pushed through
Manila without securing the ground he covered, even bringing his injured along with him; time was of the essence for the
internees at Santo Tomas, and he knew time was running out.
The Forty-Fourth Tank Division, the First Cavalry rolled right
through the gates and played their searchlights over the com-
pound. A soldier walked in front and called out for survivors:
Are there any Americans here? Is anyone left? Then the prisoners
pounded on doors and called from windows: *You betcha we're*
here! We're in here! The Japanese commander had given the
order to kill them all—to light the barrels of gasoline stacked
in the stairwells and burn them alive—but the tanks had been
too fast, had come in time, and the doors were broken down
and then the courtyard was filled, and people were cheering,
were screaming, people were crying.

Kay heard some of it. There was motion and sound where
it had been still for so long; there were bright lights playing
on the ceiling where all had been blacked out before. She
was carried downstairs and laid down on the hard ground—

there were others, all around her. The new soldiers looked like supermen—they were so healthy, so filled out, they looked like gods. People were hugging each other and dancing and hugging each other again, but all this was happening off to one side. Kay had to turn her eyes as far as she could to see the celebration. She was a little distance away, lying with many others in a corner of the courtyard where the searchlights didn't play. Then she realized where she was. Nearby there were doctors and medics and internees already volunteering, already helping out only minutes after liberation—but she had triaged patients herself, she knew how it was divided: those likely to survive no matter what care they received, those likely to die no matter what care they received, those for whom immediate care might make a difference. And those beyond help. The morgue.

The bodies around her were still, too still. No one called out, no one complained, there wasn't even a whisper or a moan rising off of them. The soldiers were busy securing the buildings, going floor to floor; the Japanese had retreated to the educational building just behind Kay. They were holding the Americans trapped there hostage, Kay could hear the angry American and Japanese negotiators going at it, back and forth—*You damn well better give them up, you bastard . . . Not without safe passage to city limits . . . You can all go to hell . . . So can the hostages,* back and forth, back and forth. Kay had to make herself heard, make herself known, before they forgot all about her, before they buried her alive. She tried moving, but her legs wouldn't budge; her brain sent the message to lift her arm, but all that happened was her little pinky twitched twice.

"Where'd you put her, you blockheads?" came a voice. "She's not with the injured anywhere. Yes, I'm a nurse, I'll help you in one second, doc, but I have to find out where your men put my—oh shit," and then Sandy's voice broke off midsentence. "You two orderlies, come with me." Kay heard them give her flak about it, and then one of them yelped, "Hey, she slapped me," and then four strong hands were lifting Kay up, off the ground, out of her grave, and Kay managed to whisper, "Not. Dead. Yet."

THE C54E LANDED in Hawaii. The nurses wore new uniforms flown in from Australia, ten sizes too big; they had them pinned, had them rolled up to stay in place. Their caps were newly issued, snatched so quickly off the assembly line they didn't have insignia yet—no caduceus, no eagle, no stars. Photographers were there when they stepped off the plane, someone put leis over their heads and the girls knelt to kiss the ground. A man made a speech, and everyone cheered, and they were driven off to a base hospital for their physicals.

"Step on the scale, miss," the doctor said. He was big-boned and bulky and dressed all in white; he reminded her of Mr. McCann, the butcher back home when she'd been a kid.

He scribbled something on his clipboard, looking quickly up at Kay.

"How much do you weigh, miss? I mean, before the Japs took you captive?"

Kay thought back to her Army physical, when she had joined the Nursing Corps in New York. "We only take women in *perfect* health," the recruiter had emphasized, smiling. "You'll do nicely, miss."

"A hundred and twenty-five pounds, sir. Although I've lost a little since then."

The doctor looked at her again through his rimmed glasses. The lenses had fingerprints all over them. She wondered it

didn't bother him, wondered why he didn't clean them off.
He wrote something down, then held the chart to his chest,
arms crossed in front of him, looking at her strangely. Kay
wondered what was wrong. She was so much stronger now, so
much better than she had been in Manila, on the transport.
She could walk and talk again, she was healthy, she had eaten
every day for a week, and for a week before that she had been
able to keep down coffee. Well, after the first few days anyway.

"Sir?"

There was no mistaking it. The man's eyes had gone red,
they were shining and brimming behind his dirty glasses.
Then he came to attention and saluted her—saluted a woman,
a full rank beneath him—and everyone else in the clinic
stopped and stared.

"Seventy-four pounds, Lieutenant."

THE SUN POURED into the railway carriage, and Kay looked
out at the Pennsylvania scenery streaming past. She was
nearly home after all this time, after the thousands of days
and miles behind her. The conductor had called out—he had
really called out—*Mount Carmel, next stop, Mount Carmel*. Kay
looked at the fields already green with last year's winter wheat,
at the red buds ready to burst on the bare maple trees. It was
drafty in the passenger car reserved just for her, and Kay put
her hand up against the windowpane, feeling its smooth coolness; she had been hot for so long, it felt delicious. She never
wanted to be hot again. She looked out at the small farms, at
the mountains showing gray, showing blue in the distance. It
was March, and she was going home. A month ago she had
been in Santo Tomas, in hell, and here she was nearly back.

When they had arrived in California, the nurses had

been given six days off. Six days. After being in captivity for three years. The head nurse at their new barracks had told them, straight-faced, that they'd get six days' leave, and no one laughed because that would have been Sandy's job. Sandy would have laughed, and covered her red mouth, and said, "No, no, I'm sorry," and then burst out laughing again. Everyone knew it and no one said anything, because Sandy was dead, they had buried her back in Manila. Beautiful, faithful Sandy, who had been untouchable, who had been invincible, who had seen Kay through hell and survived the entire fucking war in the Pacific. But after she found Kay lying there in that graveyard, the Japanese had started shelling the camp, and a little while later they had found Sandy's body, crushed under the plaster and mortar of the hospital floor above her. She had been feeding a baby in the nursery. Its mother was dead, its father was dead. One minute Sandy had been cooing and cradling the child—and the next there was the telltale whistle, then the crash of glass and fire and stone. But she had gone down as she had lived, throwing her body over the tiny infant in that last second. They had heard the baby crying as they dug Sandy out. The back of her head was smashed in, and half her face was gone, but the baby was fine, the baby was crying for the other half of its bottle.

Kay thought of Sandy, who had saved her life a dozen times over; of everyone they were leaving behind them; of Aaron. She was returning home as Kay Elliott. No one knew she had married. She had loved Aaron and worshiped Aaron, and he was perfect. He would remain eternally perfect, more perfect than he ever could have been if he had lived. But the end had come too soon, before they were ready, before either of them could even write home about it, about them. The minister who had married them had died, and the witnesses (Sandy had been maid of honor) had died, and even the Army offices where marriage records were kept had gone up in smoke when the Japanese attacked. If she had had her baby—if the Japanese had not stolen even that from her—it might have been different. She would have found his parents, gone to California, seen the vineyard that he played in as a boy, that would have been his, and then his son's, one day. But Aaron was dead, and his son was dead, and she wanted to make no claim on his family. She knew Aaron would have wanted her to, but this was one thing she wasn't willing to do, even for him—she would not share him. No, Aaron had been perfect, their love had been perfect, and she was a nurse (she was so empty and dead inside, that's all she had left) and that was what she was and how she'd support herself, that's how she'd live. She would ask for nothing from his family. Nothing.

As they passed the crossings, people outside waved and cheered.

"Twenty-five thousand," Miss Billings, her chaperone for the trip, had said delightedly, popping her head into the carriage for a moment. "Twenty-five thousand people are lining up along the route, to cheer you on, honey. To welcome you home."

Home.

She had called home long-distance when she got to the States. It was late in Pennsylvania, nearly midnight, when the call went through. Kay had asked the Navy ensign to make the call, to break it to her parents gently, so they wouldn't hear Kay's voice right off and faint or have a heart attack. And then she was listening to her mother's voice—small and tinny across that great nation—and all her mother could do at first was cry and thank God and say Kay's name over and over again. But when Kay asked for her father, asked about her brother, the line went dead for a moment. Her mother's voice had trembled, and she was saying, *Dear, they died, they died years ago.* Her brother in Africa in '42, and her father in his bed a few months later. The black soot in his lungs from a lifetime of mining had finally claimed him, taking him back into the earth. Kay's heart had stopped, and she'd felt queer, gone numb all over. Someone she had thought was alive, someone she had loved in the present tense, in the here and now, had been dead and buried for years, the grass grown green, then brown, over his grave with the passing of spring and winter and another spring and winter again. Kay was going home. But not to the home she remembered.

The train pulled into the station. It didn't look like her hometown at all; she couldn't see the sidewalks or the streets because they were filled with people. She didn't recognize anyone—even the mayor was new. He was motioning to her to step forward onto the platform, he was yelling and giving her the key to the city, but she couldn't hear anything for the cheering, for the boys' choir singing along with the brass band right behind them. She couldn't hold all the flowers the little girls brought up to her. Boy Scouts kept parading around and around in the confetti that poured down from the second floor of the Feed 'n' Seed—teenage boys were tossing it out with pitchforks. She had a sash on now, over her dress uniform with its new Bronze Star, its oak leaf clusters, and then she was standing in the back of a convertible—they were going so slow, it was easy to stand up—inching their way through the crowd that kept crying and cheering and tossing streamers at her. If it had been summer, they would have torn up the flower beds and thrown those at her too.

They stopped at Saint Paul's, and everyone grew grave—except the little boys, who were turning somersaults in the rectory yard and wondering why no one stopped them. They went inside and knelt down and no one spoke and it was silent, and that was the best part, the part Kay would remember forever, all cool marble and tapered candles and the morning light coming in through the stained glass and it was Christ in the garden and He was in agony and she looked up and prayed, *I know now, now I know.*

When the car started up again, it could hardly move. They were almost at her house, and people had camped out, had lined the streets and yards the night before so they could see her, could be there when their war hero came home. And then, just as she had imagined it, just as she had dreamed it a thousand times before—in Manila and Corregidor and the jungle before that—she saw the roof of her house come into view as they rounded the corner. It looked the same, thank God, in a world gone mad everything here was the same—the birdbath in the yard, the ceramic lovers kissing under the willow tree, the vines creeping up the chimney painted white. The chimney pot was still cracked, it still needed to be replaced after all this time, and that in itself broke her heart. She was so happy, so very happy something small and meaningless like that could still exist, could still matter. Then she heard someone screaming, high and shrill over the roar of the crowd. The car had stopped—it couldn't go any farther. Kay jumped out, and people grabbed at her, thumped her on the back, but it didn't matter, she was running forward, pressing her way through the neighbors and strangers and families wishing they were welcoming home their own son, their own daughter. The voice kept screaming, and suddenly she realized it was her own.

"Mother! Mother!" she was yelling.

Her mother was on the front porch. Kay had known she would be there—not at the chaotic station, not in the silent church—she had dreamed she'd be there and now she was, standing on the weathered, paint-flecked porch, welcoming her daughter home. Her mother was wearing her best dress (at least, it had been her best dress four years ago) and some-one had curled her hair and put silly little bows in it and she had forgotten to take off her apron. She stood there with her arms outstretched, moving her mouth and saying words no one could hear, no one but God.

Mother, Mother.

And then Kay was in her arms, and they held on to each other and they were all alone in that sea of humanity, they were all the family they had, they were all they had left in the world.

Kay was home.

15

Jo McMahon

June 1945, St. Bees, Cumbria, England

J o stood in line at the front desk. The seaside hotel was bustling: bells were ringing, newspapers were being folded and
refolded, page boys trotted to keep up with overweight women
telling them, *Pick up this suitcase, no, that hat box, can't you just
carry them both, now there's a good boy.* The smell of sausages and
eggs came wafting in from dining room B. A radio was playing as mothers counted off the heads of their children before
heading down to the beach. The sun reflected on the water far
out at sea, and the air was clean and bright and hard. It was a
perfect day, and the proprietor wore the exhausted and peaceful expression of someone finally turning a profit.

"No, I'm sorry, sir," she was explaining, tucking a pencil
into her disheveled hair, then removing it to check off a room
on her list. "We are completely out of rooms with private
baths."

"But I must have a bath, I simply must."

The conversation went on, the lady proprietor not really
minding; this was a ritual she did every day. What did it
matter; the bills were getting paid, she was putting a little
aside even.

"But I must—"

"We have a very nice suite, one overlooking the garden."

"But the bath—"

"It shares a full bath with only two other rooms."

That would never do, it couldn't possibly do, and the conversation went around and around again. Of course he would take it in the end, he'd be a fool not to, even he had begun to realize that already. It was such a perfect day, he should be on the beach. Everyone should be on the beach.

"Well, if you're absolutely sure that's all you have—"

"The very best I have at this time, sir."

The great register swiveled around to accommodate him, to accept his reluctant signature.

"If anything else should become available—" he couldn't resist saying, a parting shot.

"Oh, certainly, sir. I will inform you at once."

The woman smiled again, a tired, good-natured smile. She was dimples all over—her cheeks, her chin, even her elbows. She was fat, to be sure, but proud to be fat after a time of such shortages. A little meat on your bones never hurt anyone, it certainly hadn't hurt her. She glanced up at the next person in line, a lady officer, and chuckled contentedly to herself. You could knock the girl over with a feather.

"Yes, miss, looking for a room? I have just one left, the very nicest—although I regret to say it doesn't come with its own bath."

Jo hesitated, and the woman went on by rote.

"Oh, I daresay you could look around town, you're welcome to, but I happen to know everyone's sold out, completely sold out—the weather's so fine, and it's not always that way here, miss, I can tell you. You're quite lucky, you know, coming here in the height of the season. Very lucky indeed, but I shouldn't like to do it myself, too risky, you know, the way rooms can sell out."

The lady officer still hadn't risen to the bait. The hotel had half a dozen rooms still vacant, but she couldn't possibly know that.

"You're American, aren't you?" the proprietor asked, looking at the Silver Star, the golden eagle.

"Yes, ma'am. I'm sure your hotel is very lovely—it looks lovely—but you see, I haven't come for a room."

The woman's face darkened. "Now, I hope you've not come soliciting, young woman," she said, her voice changing completely. "I've posted out front—out back too, as your kind insists on coming at all hours, and through the back doors no less—no, I would *not* like to take out a subscription or buy a bond or so much as a postage stamp from you to help the war effort. The war in Europe is *over* and—and—" For a second the woman stopped looking angry and just looked terribly sad instead. Jo looked at her face, and it was like watching a piece of paper suddenly crumple up.

"No, ma'am. I haven't come for that either."

The woman was truly confused. Jo's dress uniform was impeccable, her shoes polished, her luggage new. Here was no charity case—someone down on her luck, asking for a meal and a chance to sleep out in the kitchen.

"You're not in *trouble,* are you?" Her eyes grew wide and she nodded her head encouragingly.

Jo laughed. "No, ma'am. Not that kind."

"Well, what is it then?" the woman exploded, exasperated.

"Jasper, come here," she snapped. Jo thought she was calling for a dog, but a very small man with bad eyes turned around from where he had been sorting the mail a moment before.

"Yes, love?"

"Oh, there you are. What are you doing underfoot? No, never mind. See to the rest of these guests. This woman here—"

"How do you do, miss?" the man said, squinting.

"Good morning, sir."

"Never mind about that, just take care of the rest of these check-ins. This woman"—she motioned for Jo to step into an adjoining office with frosted-glass doors with cherries painted around the border and a crooked sign hanging off one of them reading PRIVATE—"seems to have a story to tell."

She smiled broadly, and all of a sudden she was a human being.

Jo sat in that office for half an hour. At first, the woman wouldn't hear of it: *It's ridiculous, you don't know what you're saying.* But Jo had stayed firm, repeated herself: she was done with nursing, done with the military. Her office in London had closed, its personnel were moving back to the States or to the Far East; they were gearing up for big things in the Pacific. She wasn't cleared for duty—she was a liability, really. They had said she could go home, get out, but she had stayed behind. She couldn't go home, not yet. And then, over biscuits and tea—*This is the good tea, don't worry, not the kind I serve my guests*—Jo had told her about David. About how he was still missing—how they had lost all trace of him—how he was from Scotland and St. Bees was halfway there, how this was the third place she had stopped at today on her way up from London. She needed to find work, to make a go of it—*I have to do something, ma'am.*

"But you're a *lady*," the woman had said, truly shocked.

Jo smiled. "I wasn't so much of a lady, not that kind anyway, before the war. Out of my uniform, you wouldn't know me from anyone."

"But what would you *do*? My husband and I run the desk ourselves."

"I kind of had laundry in mind, ma'am."

"Laundry?" the woman spluttered.

"I figured, a big place like this, in the summer, must make a powerful lot of laundry."

"God knows we do, and the silly little chits never can remember to iron things properly. But if you think I'd let a decorated American officer do laundry—"

"Please," and Jo grabbed on to the woman's flabby arm. "Please."

And she looked like her heart would break.

"I need to do something where I won't have any—any terrible responsibilities. Not have to interact much with people for a while—do something mechanical, mindless even—"

The woman noticed Jo's hands were trembling; she had forgotten to hide them.

"I need to not think. I mean, be kept so busy I can't think—not all of the time."

The woman looked at Jo like she was crazy; her mouth was open in shock or disgust or disbelief. Jo let go of the matron's arm and stood up, sighing.

"I'm sorry. I've taken up too much of your time already. You couldn't possibly understand. Can you tell me when the northbound train comes in?"

But the woman's face was all crumpled again, like it had been before, but worse.

"No," she said, blowing her nose loudly into an embroidered handkerchief, frayed around the edges. "No, I *can* understand. I'm sorry I snapped at you earlier, when I thought you were looking for donations. It's just—I feel I gave enough—my son, you see—" and she blew her nose again.

"I'm sorry," Jo said, tiredly, for the thousandth time, the ten-thousandth time.

"No, no, he's alive." The woman stood up, straightening out her skirt, brushing the crumbs off the lace on her blouse. "But his mind, miss. They say he's lucky to be alive, but his mind—it's not there. He just lies in bed—I have the neighbor sit with him while I'm working, I sit up with him at night, but he doesn't need it really, he doesn't even know I'm there. He just keeps looking up at the ceiling and counting. He hasn't stopped counting, miss, since he came back. They say, in time—" Her voice broke, and she lifted up her hands in a helpless gesture.

The woman gave a little snort and sniffed loudly again. She took a deep breath in and let it out all at once and wound the little watch she wore on a gold chain around her neck.

"He gave a lot, miss. You did too, I'm sure. You all did. And if all you're asking for is a little time, some space to heal, maybe forget—well, I'll be damned if I don't give it to you."

Jo's face lit up in surprise.

The woman was pumping Jo's hand up and down, up and down, and smiling.

"You're hired."

THE SUMMER SPED by, and it was hard to believe there had ever been a war—in St. Bees anyway. To Jo, the American, the place seemed timeless. Back home, the oldest church she'd ever stepped foot in was St. Peter's, in the city, built around the time of the Revolutionary War. But in St. Bees, any aspect of the village commanded a view of the Priory, tall and towering above it all, built over sacred ground—back in the eleven hundreds. Jo would sneak inside its silent nave, all rose-red and beautiful, a red-patterned carpet running down the aisle, ornate metalwork filling in the arches. It was ageless, it was solid, it would stand forever. The place was holy.

Of course, she didn't have much time for sightseeing, for exploring or holidaymaking. Her employer, Mrs. Greerson, was true to her word: there was plenty of laundry to keep both her mind and her hands busy. Jo washed and ironed, folded and starched, from morning till late afternoon. She took an inordinate pride, a misplaced pleasure, in her work, bringing to it an exactitude that was completely unnecessary. She measured out Farmer's soap as if it were cc's of plasma; she heated the iron till the spit on her finger sizzled when she touched it, gauging it carefully like she was sterilizing equipment.

On some level, Jo realized what she was doing and she told herself it was odd, but not unbalanced. She was trying to clean off the dirt, the grime, to wash the smell of blood out of her hair, her hands, her memory, replacing it with the powerful, stinging smell of bleach. Everything now was white, everything was clean. She had taken a mop and brush and disinfected the laundry room that first day as if they'd be using it for surgery later on. Mrs. Greerson had two enormous Bendix washers in the laundry room that overlooked the kitchen garden, and had even invested in their newest gimmick—something they called a drying machine. But it wasn't good enough for Jo. *No, I don't mind ironing, ma'am, just wait a minute, I'll have your sheets for you. They look so much nicer when they're fresh, when they're freshly cleaned and ironed.*

Jo had been given a little room of her own on the third floor. It certainly did not have its own bath, and no view to speak of, but it was hers and it was quiet and she kept it immaculately clean. She lined up her pins every night, each hairpin adjacent to but not actually touching its neighbor; she rinsed and dried out her washbasin, setting her pitcher of water for the next day right next to it, filled exactly to the three-quarter mark; she dried off her bar of soap with a towel after using it, then placed it, imprinted side up, on a little porcelain dish.

She was kind of okay. That's what she told herself. *Kind* of okay. She'd been better, of course, but she'd certainly been worse. She was hanging on. She didn't see Gianni anymore, didn't see any dead people at all usually. Practically speaking, that had to be a good thing. Sure, she was obsessing about silly little things—washing and rewashing towels that didn't come out right, for example. Or the way she'd hung up her uniform in the back of the tiny closet, for the last time, like she was burying the dead. She had bought herself six dresses—each exactly the same, plain dresses, gray pinstripe—and hung them up, two inches apart, not letting them touch at all. But that was just a little bit eccentric—unusual perhaps, but harmless—not that strange at all when you really stopped to think about it.

Jo tried not to think.

She hadn't been thinking when she walked into the laundry room that morning, hadn't been thinking of anything at all. It was early, too early—the dirty laundry wasn't even down, the maids hadn't gotten to it yet—and she looked at the sheets she had hung up the night before. They were clean, they were ironed, but they had needed to air, a little air never hurt anything. So she had hung them up, and now she looked at them in the gray light seeping in from the windows high above the enormous steel sinks.

The sheets were white, they were beautiful, they hung all around her in that spacious room like clouds, like billowing snow. She surveyed their barren perfection with something bordering on satisfaction as she sat down at the great oak table with a cup of coffee she had brewed herself; no one had been up yet in the kitchen. One second the sheets were pristine, flawless—and the next they were covered in blood, spattered with blood, and she held on to her cup with both hands and repeated, "It isn't real, it isn't real," like a child, like a little girl trying to wake up from a dream. "It isn't real," she said again, eyes shut tight, even though she could feel them, feel their fingers picking at her sleeve, tugging at her arm. "They're not there, they're dead," but she could hear them breathing, feel their hot breath on the back of her neck. She could smell them too, smell the blood and the rot rising off of them, and the smell of bleach was gone from the room, she couldn't find a trace of it, although a minute before it had been so strong it had stung her eyes when she came in. It smelled so bad, like the amputation dump in Sicily, like the tent where they had kept the dead and she'd gone corpse by corpse looking for one of the nurses, killed in her bunk when the shell dropped. The tent was so hot, it stunk, she couldn't find Ilsa, couldn't find all of her. Then the whispers started and she said, "Please, God, no," still holding on to her cup, but her head was down now, on the table. She couldn't listen, she couldn't let herself listen, because at first they'd make sense, they'd tell her things only she could understand. But then the voices would change, no longer be the voice of her brother or her mother or her friend, but become shrill and piercing, in a pitch she could no longer hear with her ears but only with her mind, cold and terrible. The words wouldn't be words, but they would always mean the same thing—despair and anguish and death. She cried out, as David had done, with some prayer from the past, something memorized in grade school when the words hadn't made any sense: "Soul of Christ, sanctify me, Body of Christ, save me." *Save me, oh Lord, from my madness, you saved the lunatics, save me, come to me and save me, Lord, for I have no one. Come to me.* It was a prayer and it was a command and she opened her eyes—not to her Savior but to Mrs. Greerson, shuffling into the room in her worn slippers, eyes bloodshot and puffy, half her hair pulled up messily into spit curls. She yawned.

"That big family in 12 wants some more beach towels." The woman itched furiously at her outer thigh, the thick fabric of her robe getting in the way.

Jo looked down at the table, her knuckles showing white where they still clasped the cup.

"I see you've got the sheets done," Mrs. Greerson remarked absently, turning to leave and yawning again. "Better get them out of here before the maids come down, you know how they bitch about their space."

"Yes, ma'am," and Jo took a gulp of cold coffee.

Thank you, Lord.

THE WAR ENDED. America dropped two bombs, and the war ended. Far away in St. Bees, there was no way to understand, no way to gauge, the destruction, the devastation: two cities leveled in a second, 160,000 dead, twice that number dead a month later from injury and radiation poisoning. It all seemed so simple, people said. *Why didn't the Americans do it earlier? It would have saved my Petie's . . . my Danny's . . . my Billy's . . . life.* The pubs were crowded. People danced in the streets. Atheists waited with everyone else in the line that wrapped around the Priory to take off their hats and thank God, thank God, it was over.

August ripened into thick, full summer and still there was no word about David. Jo walked the long way to Egremont on the old North Road to check the postal box she had taken there, but no message arrived. She could have taken a box in St. Bees, in the little village post office that also sold candy and postcards, but each time she walked home from Egremont holding letters from David's family, she was glad she hadn't, glad they didn't know how to find her. She had given them the mailing address in case they heard anything, had any news, but she hadn't been able to explain to them why she couldn't be a part of their lives without David. Duncan had apologized, back when she had still been in London; he had been careless, foolish, he hadn't known how much his brother had meant to her, he had been a cad. But his invitations to dinner, to plays, to punting and picnics had fallen on deaf ears. Jo would not fall in love with a facsimile of David, with someone who lacked his soul. She felt sorry for his sister Kit, sorry for his mother; their letters were clinging—they wanted her, wanted to take care of her. *Please stay with us, child, here in London with my brother, back home in Scotland when the repairs are done. We love you, we want you, we need you.* But Jo couldn't do it, couldn't stay with these kindhearted people who would mean no harm but would slowly bleed her to death, remembering. What did he do? What did he look like? Then what did he say? Over and over again until she would be just a conjurer at a séance, bringing David back for them, bringing back the dead.

Jo kept to the back of the hotel, never interacting with guests. All she knew of the vacationers were their preferences for extra towels, for fresh linen every day, whether they smoked or drank coffee in bed. The young girls working at the hotel were thrilled with peacetime, with the boys coming home, any boys coming home. They'd run into the laundry room and Jo was saying yes before they were done asking, *Can you cover for me? I'm dishes tonight . . . I'm pots . . . I'm pans . . . I'll cover for you sometime, miss, don't worry, thank you so much.* But they knew they'd never have to return the favor because the solemn laundress never went out, never socialized. *She doesn't wear a black armband, but I think she must have lost someone, don't you?* Then they'd giggle, laughing out loud as soon as they stepped onto the street, skipping the short way down to Paddy's where the sound of music and laughter already reached their ears. *Why shouldn't we have a little fun? It's been a long, long time.*

ONE DAY MRS. GREERSON stepped into the laundry room, looking more disheveled than usual. She surveyed Jo's modest, almost clinical appearance severely—hair pulled back, starched white apron over her monotonous gray dress.

"It's four o'clock, McMahon," she said sternly.

"Yes, ma'am, I just have these linens here to—"

"I said four o'clock and I meant four o'clock." Mrs. Greerson was scowling. "We had an agreement. Done by four."

"Yes, ma'am," Jo said reluctantly, putting down the tablecloths with difficultly, forcing herself to turn away from them.

"You're putting in ten-hour days as it is," her employer continued. "And we're not nearly so busy as when you first came here—by next month, the season will be over. You've kept up your side of the bargain—you've done your work and then some, I'll say. But I don't know that I have."

Jo looked up at the woman, anxiously.

"I wouldn't want you to think that. I've been very happy, ma'am, very thankful you've given me this position."

"Happy and grateful are not exactly the same thing." The woman frowned again. "What I mean is, yes, I was giving you a job, but I was supposed to—well, I got so busy with the hotel, and my boy—but what I *meant* to do was also give you a chance to rest."

"I'm getting plenty of sleep—"

"Well, maybe not 'rest' exactly. Oh, blast," and it was funny for Jo to see the English woman stamp her foot vexedly and curse. "I've grown to care for you, and—and when I say 'rest' I mean relax . . . heal maybe." Mrs. Greerson looked flustered, then embarrassed, then she thrust something into Jo's hands. "Here. And if you're not down there every afternoon until the summer's out— you're—you're fired." With that, she stomped clumsily from the room.

JO STARTED SWIMMING every afternoon, every evening, until the long warm summer days melted effortlessly into night. She wore the black Jantzen bathing suit Mrs. Greerson had given her—smooth and sleek and fitted with darts. She had learned to swim as a child because Sister had said they must, raised funds, and taken the poor city kids out to a camp, a convent or motherhouse somewhere in the country. With the same precision and authority with which she taught them spelling and grammar, she had taught them front crawl, backstroke, dead man's float.

Now Jo luxuriated in floating effortlessly, swimming a few strokes, and then turning lazily onto her back, like a drowsy seal. She hadn't been in the water since North Africa, since their amphibious landing, and that had been all shrapnel and fire and death. She floated peacefully now in the water, the strong rays of late summer baking her brown. When she could swim no longer, she picked her way across the pebbly beach until she found a particularly isolated spot. The beaches were nearly empty, the long line of coast curving smoothly from end to end with no one on it but the occasional cleric, the tired governess, the child too young for school or swimming who would run into the waves and scream and run back out and do it over and over again. Jo found a place to nestle in the sun, the heat baking the tiny stones beneath her. She curled up in the old blanket, in the thick towel she had brought from the laundry room and closed her eyes and felt the warmth against her eyelids.

It was over.

Not all her pain, not all the injury, but the war—it was over.

She let that reality sink in—sink in like the rays of the sun.

And I forgive myself.

The thought came to her out of nowhere, and it was so startling that it made her open her eyes and sit up. But she lay back down, forcing herself to relax, to ask herself what she was seeking, what she was granting herself forgiveness for.

For being alive.

For being alive when everyone else was dead, when 5 percent of the world was now dead—the strangers she had tried to save and the friends she had failed to save and her mother and her father and her brother and her—

She couldn't think of David as dead. In the dormitory back

in London, in her pristine room on the third floor, she could imagine it, imagine him dead and buried a thousand times over. But not here. Lying on the shore—or floating, surrounded by the undulating waters that seemed to cradle her and soothe her and buoy her up—she couldn't think him dead, not for a moment. She could imagine him at sea, far away. But it was as if they touched—across the vast ocean, she touching its edge here, he touching it half a world away—but touching nonetheless. Even after she had climbed the long way back to the hotel, there was something deep inside. It felt real and warm and alive inside her. He felt alive.

JO WALKED OUTSIDE with the plumber, past the kitchen garden with its herbs already starting to go to seed.

"Just where's it backed up, miss?"

The two of them looked for the drainage pipe that ran from the laundry, underground, through the garden.

"Here it is—it comes out here."

And they looked at the pipe, tilting their heads, poking at it with the toes of their shoes.

"Looks all right to me, miss. Water's coming out. How long you say it's been not draining proper?"

Just then there was a crack of thunder in the clear sky, the heat lightning exploding without rain, without light. A second later it was over, the birds flying across the lawn, perching in the old copper gutters, and twittering contentedly to themselves.

Jo and the plumber lay flat on their faces on the muddy ground, hands crossed protectively behind their heads. The man looked up sheepishly, grinning at Jo.

"Been in the war too, miss?"

* * *

JO SWAM OUT past the breakers. The waves weren't much—
she dove through them more for fun than necessity—then she
was past them, out in the swelling sea moving and breathing
like a living thing. She turned around and looked at the beach,
slender and curving in the sun, at the small village set behind
it, at the headland to her left, jutting out into the sea, its high
emerald cliffs dropping off into the surf below. Jo turned on
her back and squinted up into the sky—great cloud masses
played above her, leaving her in light, in shadow, in light again.
She was all alone in the glittering water, shining with sun—
little fish jumped up out of the water escaping some predator,
flashing silver, flashing white for a second before disappearing
again. She closed her eyes and time slipped past.

It was September. The days were getting shorter—she
could still swim, but only when the sun was out; when it set,
it was too cold to be wet and she would huddle on the beach.
All around her, life was returning to normal, to its set rou-
tine. Jo thought of June brides, already counting the days,
checking and rechecking their calendars; of reluctant students
sweltering in their school uniforms, starting a new term, looking longingly out of windows. Jo thought of the hotel, of its
dwindling guest list—of the letter she had received from Mrs.
MacPherson: their home in Scotland was repaired, they were
going back, back to the farm—so even David's family would
be leaving soon, would migrate North with the cooler weather,
would be gone.

She thought of her letters to Kay that had come back as
undeliverable and the other letters that had disappeared, never
coming back at all. She hoped that some of them had gotten
through somehow. She wondered where Kay was, and if Kay

was, and breathed a prayer she was safe, she was whole, she was found. Jo realized that even the pain of what they had gone through in New York was beginning to lessen. She never thought that it would, but it was. She had survived that, she had survived the war. Had one prepared her for the other? Had the horror of one hardened her against the violence that would be unleashed on her, on the whole world? But both were behind her now, she was healing from both. If that could happen—if that searing, burning rage inside her could diminish with each passing day, if being surrounded by a gentle sea, by an ageless strength, could ease that—if even *that* could heal, well then, given enough time, given enough peace, maybe anything could.

Jo opened her eyes for a second to gauge how far she had drifted. She was out a little bit—she judged how far she had gone by the buildings, by their rooftops; she counted the chimneys. She'd be fine, she'd start swimming back in a moment, there was plenty of time yet. Jo closed her eyes again, and the water filled her ears and covered her belly, and she felt surrounded by goodness and smoothness and warmth. The power of the ocean, of the silky water around her, filled her and she floated on it effortlessly. The nightmares were fewer, both waking and sleeping. It'd been a week—no, two weeks now that she had slept all night without dreaming, without waking at all. Her body relaxed and her mind relaxed, and she knew she was mending. She was almost well.

JO MARCHED ALONG the dreary road to Egremont in the drizzling rain. She pulled the borrowed rain jacket closer around her, turning up its collar. She glanced at her wristwatch, wiping the water from the dial. She'd make it to mass yet; she'd done it every Sunday this summer, but never in the rain—it was miserable in the rain. She looked back at the village far behind her—she could still see the Priory, standing tall and proud over St. Bees—and silently cursed King Henry. It seemed ridiculous, all these years later, that a monarch of old England should be inconveniencing her, a modern Yankee, like this, but there it was. She was Catholic, the Priory was Church of England. So she walked the long way to Egremont, to the mission there—where they congregated in the old dance hall, using the grand piano as an altar—just because of an argument four hundred years old. Jo's foot stepped into a puddle, and she cursed him again. Even the king himself, she reasoned, on his better days must have admitted, on some level, that what he wanted was human—a male heir, a better lover—understandably human even, but not divine. Not divinely appointed. Not worth all the bother and bloodshed and division; not worth the long walk to Egremont. Christianity should reunite. God would be pleased. It would help conserve her shoe leather too.

A noisy delivery truck came along the road and pulled up beside her.

"Mademoiselle," the man inside called out to her; it was Luc, the French baker in town, and his wife, Ellie. They had escaped with their children before the war, ending up in provincial St. Bees of all places, where they stuck out as foreigners even before you factored in their faith. "We take you along the path to mass *Catholique*. We cannot accept you in the"—here he lost his train of thought in English and gesticulated wildly to himself, his wife, the tiny cab—"but if you return to the rear, you permit to ride with our children."

"Thank you," Jo called, smiling. "I will return to the rear."

She hopped onto the flat bed of the truck, sitting alongside six children who dangled their tiny legs over the tailgate with her.

"Bonjour," they said politely, their eyes big, the girls' blond curls dripping in the wet.

"Bonjour."

Jo thought of when she had first gotten to France, how she and everyone in her medical corps had put on armbands with American flags on them and worn them all the time; how they had not wanted to be mistaken for British officers. The FFI were not above taking potshots at the English, at their enemy from another war, from countless other wars. The Channel wasn't big enough to separate England and France—it never had been.

After mass ("We say to you she is sorry, but the family does not return to Sint Beez at this time"), Jo started back on foot; the rain had let up, puddles dotting the long road back.

"Oh, miss, miss." The postmaster trotted out after her as she passed his house; his dinner napkin was still tucked into his collar, spread over his enormous belly. Jo turned curiously. The post office was not open on Sundays; this couldn't be official business.

"Miss, I saw you out the window and just had to mention it. A man stopped in this week, asking for you."

Jo stiffened. "A man?"

"Yes." The postmaster was clearly delighted. He gossiped like an old lady and knew everything that happened in town. "Came in right after you had left on Tuesday, couldn't have been more than a quarter-hour. Told me your name, described you perfectly, said his family was looking for you, trying to trace your whereabouts."

"Did he leave his name?"

"Yes, he did . . . now let me see . . . what was it? Something with a 'Mac' in it . . . MacDonald? No, no, MacPherson," he said decisively. "It was MacPherson."

"Duncan?"

"Yes, that's it, I'm sure of it. Said he wanted to reach you. Wanted to know what day, what time, you usually checked your box. An—an admirer of yours, miss?"

"What did you tell him?"

The man looked taken aback, fluttering his hands in front of him. "What do you take me for, miss? I didn't know him from Adam. Told him where to get off, I did. I said I didn't know anything about you other than you pay your rent on time and are entitled to your privacy, same as anyone else. He asked where you were staying, if you were here in town . . ." The man left that dangling, like a question, waiting. "I never see you, miss, other than when you come in for your mail. *Do* you live in town? Or do you come over from some neighboring parts perhaps?"

His wife was in the doorway now, calling him to come back to his supper, to stop standing there in the street in his shirt-fronts. He gestured impatiently in her general direction.

"If he stops back, you can tell him I've left. I was staying in the country with some friends, but I've left—gone home. Tell him he knows where to reach me."

"Oh, he does—a great friend of yours then?" he asked hopefully.

"Just someone I know. Thank you for telling me. Enjoy the rest of your dinner."

All the long trudge home, Jo scowled. Duncan had no right. She had made it clear she was not interested in him, in his attentions; she hadn't answered his letters, even her correspondence with his mother had been terse, to the point. She was not pursuing them, and the thought that he would track her down like a maid absconding with the silverware irked her to no end. Luckily, the postmaster had had little to tell him—she could only imagine his running after her like that was the result of Duncan offering some sort of remuneration. Duncan was clever, no doubt. But two could play at this game. She'd just be more cautious—maybe send Luc's son over with his bicycle to get her mail for her; he'd do that for a bob. And even if Duncan had tracked her that far, she hoped the false lead she had left would only strengthen his assumption that she was a guest somewhere, in a home or hotel surely, but certainly not the hired help. No, he was too proud himself to ever look for her there.

Jo reached the crossing that forked either down toward St. Bees or out onto the headland itself. Her stomach tugged at her to return—Sunday brunch would be ending, the piles of hot ham and sausage and scrambled eggs the guests left untouched on the sideboards would come back to the kitchen. Even with rationing, the relative plenty of peacetime still amazed Jo. That she could eat until she was filled, until she was stuffed and sleepy, was still new to her. Mrs. Greerson was not stingy with her guests, nor with her domestic staff. Jo had filled out, grown strong; she was no longer the skeleton that had waited in line to ask for a job. Her skin was tan, her cheeks were rosy; she had plenty. She had enough to make it out to the headland without breakfast.

It was green almost instantly. She left the road, and then it was green beneath her, green in front and all around her. The clouds had cleared out at sea, and the water beneath them shone ever brighter, ever stronger, as the front moved in toward shore. St. Bees was nestled below her, to her left, like tiny toy homes set up for play. The wind off the sea was bracing and drowned out all other sound. She was out to the end of the headland before she thought it possible. She didn't go all the way to the edge, to the cliffs themselves, but stopped a little way in, surrounded by a sea of green.

Jo lay down in the sun that was now directly over her, ignoring the grass stains, the damp on her dress; lay down and splayed her arms like a snow angel, grabbing on to great tufts of slippery grass, twisting it around and around her fingers like it was hair. She was all alone. Then she closed her eyes and felt the great solidity of the earth, rising up into her, and she was safe, she was well, she was well enough to ask:

Did David ever love me?

It had been too terrible a question even to acknowledge before, but now . . . now she could. She was centered, she was nearly whole.

They had known each other for such a short time, they had been thrown together. She felt her heart tugging, felt her love for him raging there, bottled up—but what had he felt? Was it gratitude? Or just proximity? Was it anything?

Did he love me? Did he ever really love me?

The world beneath her was solid, was silent for a moment longer. Then one of Kit's letters—the letter that had come Tuesday, the one she had picked up just before Duncan had traced her that far—came floating back into Jo's consciousness. And then she knew that David had loved her once, that there had been a time when he had truly loved her.

Dear Miss McMahon,
I hope to see you again, you were so sweet, although a little sad, which is, I guess, what happens in war. Your uniform was

*awfully nice. We have not heard anything about David, but
I said a novena to save him, so don't worry about him anymore.*

*I snuck into Mother's room and copied out his last letter
home. He wrote to us twice after he went back to fighting. A
lot of it is about us and the farm and him worrying about it
since it got hit in a raid. But there is a part about you, and I
know it's wicked that I copied it down (don't tell Mother), but
I think it's dramatic and love is wonderful, don't you think?
and if I were you I'd want to hear it, so here goes. There are a
lot of boring parts, and then he says,*

*"You can tell Bumpy I fell in love, which he'll laugh at
since he falls in love every week and says I'm such a clod I
never could. But she is an angel and I love her and, of course,
you know from my last letter (when all I could do was write
about her) that it is Josephine McMahon, the nurse who saved
my life. And when I say she saved my life it's not just because
she nursed me through the typhus (although she did, she did
that, God bless her), but because she saved the rest of my life
too, the life that I thought I could be happy with on my own,
just farming the land and entering the fair and each year
being just like another. But now I see how foolish I was—
that the poetry and songs I liked so much never got into me,
into my heart—and it's probably too late, I mean, to love her
like I ought because I want to—"*

*and then there's this big part where the censors blacked it
out, I don't know what he was going to say, but then it starts
up again, halfway down the page,*

*"—and I would marry her, more than anything else in
the world. But the world has turned evil. There's something
evil just in front of me, that much I know. The people are
running from it, it's so black and terrible they can't even talk*

*about it. I can't tell you where I am, the censors would catch
on, but I'm at mass today, at some convent or monastery,
I won't tell you which order—and there are a lot of little
children here, wee children, Mum, no different from us when
we were young.*

"*And they're putting them in uniforms, like for school, and
cutting their hair and changing their looks with glasses and
such; these children are sad, their parents must be gone. And
they have names like Ephraim and Sarah, but they're changing
that too, to Peter and Bridget, and asking them over and over
again until they remember. The children are crying, they are
teaching them prayers, simple prayers any Christian would
know, but they don't know them and they're telling them they
have to memorize them, in case they're stopped and asked. Why
they're hiding, what they're running away from, they won't tell
me, no one here will say. But whatever it is, that's where we're
heading next, Mum. So pray for us. And pray for them.*"

*(That last part wasn't about you, but I got so caught up
copying it and anyway it sounded exciting—I should like to
go about in disguise and wear glasses and cut my hair, but
Mother won't let me—Kit)*

Jo sighed and she thought of the children, losing their families, their identities, being smuggled farther back, back to
France, back to England, to strangers who would hide them,
who would take them in for a day, for a week; children crying
in the night until they forgot their own names. She thought of
David, marching blindly into that blackness, into that darkness and night where all would be death, all would be want,
cold and ruthless and real.

She was pulling so hard on the grass that it came out all

at once in her hand. She let go of the tuft, the blades blowing
away in the wind; she breathed deeply, praying for the lost—all
the lost—for the children, and for David and herself. She joined
her hands over her belly and the sun beat down. She could feel
her nose starting to burn. The world was evil, the world was
cruel, but the mountain rising beneath her comforted her; it
was solid, it was firm. It said there is yet hope. Hope and peace
and love.

So David had truly loved her once.

But did he love her still? If you died, what happened to
your love? What would happen to the love that was bursting
inside of her, looking for an outlet, for some way to break free?
For the thousandth time, she asked herself, *Is David alive or
dead?* And then, from the depths of the earth, from the depths
of her soul, she heard his voice, calm and clear. It wasn't her
imagination—it wasn't her at all. It was David, her David, and
her body thrilled at his voice, at his words; they were touching
her, caressing her, from wherever he was.

"Do you think a little thing like death could ever separate
those who love?"

All at once, it wasn't her loving a ghost, loving a memory; it
wasn't a one-sided love at all, but now he was loving her back,
she could feel his love. Whether they were parted by distance
or time or by death itself it didn't matter—she knew that now.
His love was reaching her, and she was sure (she knew) he was
feeling hers. She had him at last, after all this time. The sheer
relief of it all, of being able—fully and without fear—to love
another and be loved back, without reservation, without threat
of ever being parted again, overwhelmed her. She lay alone on
that vast expanse of green glowing in the sun like a jewel, and
her heart filled, burst with joy, filled up again. Death could not

defeat her, could not destroy her or her ability to love. She had that. She was that.

Jo was free.

SHE WAS IN her room. Her plan had been to lie down, just for a minute; she had taken out her hairpins, started to line them up. She looked around her room, contrasting it with other places she had lived, other places she had called home—a squalid tenement, an Army base, a silt-covered tent in a field. Jo looked again, and now she knew this room for what it was. Cold. Antiseptic. A tomb. She looked at the hairpins, each exactly alike, each equidistant from each other—and she scattered them, sending them flying around the room, falling down cracks, under radiators, behind furniture. She dumped the water pitcher onto the floor, then smashed it against the wall; she ground the ceramic bits into powder under her heel. She threw the bar of soap out the window, as far as it would go—she lost it in the afternoon light. This was not what she wanted, this was not real, this was not her anymore.

She didn't remember throwing herself onto her bed, but she woke up suddenly and the sun was much lower in the sky. She must have been asleep for hours. Someone had been shaking her, shaking her shoulder, Jo could still feel the imprint of the fingers on her arm. It had been Queenie. But she hadn't been bloody and she hadn't been angry; it hadn't been a nightmare, but Queenie the way she remembered her, the way she loved her. Queenie had been shaking her and shaking her like she was late for her shift, like she had to get out of her bunk and the moment before she opened her eyes, Jo had heard her voice, heard what she said.

"Wake up, honey."

* * *

JO NEEDED TO clear her head. It was too late in the day, but she put on her swimsuit anyway and walked through the laundry room, past the piles of laundry that now meant nothing to her. Who cares if they're ever washed, ever dried. She picked her way over the dry, prickly grass near the garden, down the rocky slope through the hedges, until she reached the beach, more deserted than ever with evening coming on so fast. She heard laughter and, slipping behind the cover of a shed used for shovels and weathered umbrellas, she saw a teenage couple as they embraced, kissed, laughed again. The girl squealed as she escaped from the boy's arms, running a little way up the beach. She let herself be caught, pretending to twist her ankle. She kissed him, laughed at him again, at herself, at life, at the unpredictability, the inevitability of love. The two ran off together.

Jo dove into the waves, and it didn't matter if she was crying, if she was wracked with sobs—the ocean took it all, took the tears and the pain and the sorrow, and absorbed it into itself, freeing her, making her whole again. She couldn't swim long—the water was icy—but she walked the length of the beach until the wind whipped her dry, her hair long and loose without its pins. She turned to face the sea. The sun was directly in front of her, setting into the west, sinking into the Atlantic, into America on the other side of the ocean. She couldn't let the sun set, couldn't let it go down, without deciding once and for all whether she would continue living as she had been or not.

She knew what she wanted; she had seen the lovers, she knew she wanted that—not a cold, clinical nothingness that did nothing to protect her, that walled up her heart alive. She

wanted a way to find it, to make it real. She took the chain off
her neck (where it always was, she never took it off), slipped
David's ring off the golden loop, and held it in her hand. The
chain slithered into the water and was gone, but she held on
to the ring, pressing it, crushing it in her clenched fist until
it hurt, until her eyes stung from the pain. She had to decide.

Fling it into the sea and let him go.

Or hold on to it forever.

Those were her choices, and the sun was going down. She
had to decide, she could not live another day, another night,
without choosing. She was a tempest inside, she was bursting
at the seams, she could not contain her love for David any
longer. But she could not have him and she could not let him
go and the sun was lower now, much lower. Something surged
up within her—she wanted to be that girl laughing, turning
her ankle in the sand, laughing and kissing and hiding behind
the shed; she wanted love, physical love, not just a spiritual
connection, a hope, a dream coming up from the sea, from a
cold mountain. She opened her palm and looked at the ring—
the only thing she had of David's, the only thing he had had
to give her—

Keep it without promising anything. Keep it so I can know it goes
with you—that my love goes with you—so I can hope, one day—

But what if one day never came? Without him, what did
life hold for her? She was no modern woman, she had no am-
bition outside of a home—children and David and a home—
where he could make love to her and recite his poetry and
sing her songs when the Morning Star came out. She held the
ring in her hand, but lightly now, as if gauging its weight. She
would have to leave this place soon, and it would be either
with or without David, his ghost, his love. She could choose to

be haunted, or she could throw this ring and the waves would swallow it up and he would leave her forever.

The words of her prayer came back to her: *Separated from you let me never be.*

The sun was still up; it was suspended in space. The world must have stopped turning, waiting for her. Her hair streamed back from her face in the wind. The wind filled her ears, made a wild sound like a canvas tent, stakes pulled up, blown out and flapping violently. Above it she heard something, faint and far away, someone calling for her, and she thought it was David. She turned her head and then she saw the man coming, still far off down the beach.

She wanted to run away. Damn him, damn Duncan, so smug, so obsessed with himself that one woman denying him had made him into a megalomaniac, tracking her down, following her like this. For a second more she wanted to run, then her anger took over and she started walking toward him deliberately, both fists clenched now; she would tell him, tell him to his face, what she thought of him, of his arrogance.

And as he started toward her, she could see he carried a stick and was limping slightly.

Duncan didn't have a limp.

THEY CAME UP to each other. The sun was still up, they were bathed in it, his tousled hair, his weather-beaten face was aglow. She was just a few paces away now, slender yet strong, basking in the warm, pink light. Her hand hurt—she remembered that, her hand hurting and hurting, clenched around something hard—but she couldn't look down at it; she was staring at him, staring at a dream. They looked so different from the last time they had seen each other—cold and wet and miserable. They were healthy now, they were whole—the limp wasn't much, he had thrown away the cane as soon as they got close. He was looking at her now—she was gorgeous, she was more beautiful than he had imagined her, she was a goddess come down to him.

"David," Jo whispered, and the wind carried away her voice, carried away the word so that just her lips moved; they parted for an instant and were still.

They held on to each other, clung to each other as the sun set, as the water swallowed up the last glowing ember of the sun, holding on to each other as if he'd vanish, as if she'd disappear with the last of the light. They opened their eyes, looking about them, and the beach was silvery gray, the light had gone, the water was dark and choppy—but they still had each other, they were home, it was real.

David was crying now, and kissing her all over, and holding her so close she couldn't breathe. His eyes glanced heavenward for a moment, as if his joy were too much, as if he would burst; then he laughed through his tears, still struggling to speak, to get even one word out.

"Aye."

16

Kay Elliott

January 1947, Fitzsimons Army Medical Center,
Aurora, Colorado

Kay looked out the second-story window at the snow below. An enlisted man shoveled furiously as two officers came down the narrow walkway, then leaned back on his shovel, cupping his hands to light a cigarette as soon as they passed. Kay smiled.

The snow swirled outside the window, traveling upward in glittering vortices that caught the light before smashing against the glass. Kay couldn't get enough of it, of the cold and the snow; she never wanted to be hot again. She looked around the waiting room, at its cheap furnishings, its vinyl upholstery, the galvanized steel—you could hose the place down when you were done with it, it'd be none the worse.

She felt in her pocket. It had arrived in the mail today, and she still couldn't believe it. Without looking, without having to look, she felt again the worn scrap of paper—the IOU she had signed back in Manila, in prison camp. Someone had saved it and found her, and incredibly, a clerk in accounts receivable on the twentieth floor of some corporation in New York was now calling in the debt. It didn't seem possible, but there it was—the IOU was in her pocket. Well, she'd pay them back their $60, every cent of it. It had saved her life. But still, she just couldn't believe it.

Kay glanced at the clock on the wall—her appointment had been for ten o'clock, and it was nearly eleven now. She shifted in her chair. She thought of the other office much like this one, back in the Pacific, where the nurses had had to sign that oath of secrecy. They had sworn never to reveal or to discuss their imprisonment, their wartime service; if they did, they would lose their pension and military benefits.

"Do you understand, miss?" the clerk had repeated. "This is a very crucial point."

Kay must have seemed groggy, swaying back and forth on her feet.

"Is she even listening? Now, miss, I need you to sign this." Kay had reached for the pen—and missed. "But before you do, I need to be quite clear. You cannot repeat anything that you saw, before or after Santo Tomas. *Nothing* you saw, understand?"

"Nothing I saw."

"You can repeat none of it—even to family members—in any format, oral, written, or recorded."

"Yes."

"You understand?"

"Yes."

"By signing this form, you acknowledge that I have explained the penalties for breaking any of the clauses, and you agree to not divulge any information—"

"Yes, yes."

"—for sixty years."

"*Sixty* years?"

"Yes . . . until the year 2005."

Fuzzy-headed as she was, Kay had laughed a little at that, at the thought that any of them would still be alive by then. Or maybe they would—maybe science would defeat old age, maybe they'd all be driving around in flying saucers and taking holidays on the moon. She signed the form.

Maybe it was best not to remember. Kay tried not to remember. She had stayed with her mother all that spring, trying not to remember, but you cannot unlearn, overnight, the very skills that kept you alive. So Kay was forever hiding things— her hat, her gloves, her handbag. She couldn't leave anything out in the open—even in her home, even in her own room, she would stuff things under rugs, under pillows, tape them to the underside of drawers. Kay remembered the first time they had had steak—thick, juicy steak—and Kay had eaten half of one and carefully wrapped up the other half, asking her mother to keep it for her, to save it for tomorrow, for the next day.

"Land's sake, child, save it? We have more, we have plenty. You only had a bite." And then her mother had been crying at the table, not understanding, thinking that Kay didn't want it, that she didn't like her mother's cooking anymore.

Kay had tried not to remember, tried to be normal again, to fit back into society—but every time someone offered her a cigarette at a party, she thought of the homemade dobies they had smoked in camp; or of how the civilian internees had burned the Japanese lieutenant with their cigarettes as he writhed on the ground after the Americans shot him, the grenade he was about to use on them rolling harmlessly from his hand, an American private picking it up and putting it in his helmet before walking quickly out of camp.

She had tried to be normal, but small things, unexpected

things, tripped her up. There were mosquitoes down by the church carnival, and Kay couldn't ignore them like everyone else did. She couldn't let them land on her skin, couldn't convince herself that they didn't carry malaria, that she didn't need quinine, didn't need it to turn her skin yellow.

Mount Carmel had changed. No, Mount Carmel had stayed the same and Kay Elliott had changed. She was not the same girl who had gone off to the big city to join the Army, to be a nurse. When she finally heard how the United States took back Malinta Tunnel—how the Japanese had detonated explosives, had caved in the laterals around themselves rather than surrender—she couldn't join in everyone else's excitement and celebrate that American victory as she ought. She shuddered violently instead. She knew what it was like down there—she had been trapped down there for so long. *What a terrible way to die.*

Kay had re-upped just when everyone else was leaving the Army. Her friends, the nurses from her class were all leaving but it was the only place she fit in anymore. Brooke Army Medical Center at Fort Sam Houston; St. Elizabeths in D.C.; Letterman General in San Francisco; Walter Reed in Maryland. Anywhere she could find training, she did. This was all she had. This was all that was left of her.

But it wasn't this way for everyone. The Army was a strange sort of a home, Kay knew that—a home without a fixed house, a commanding officer for a father, a head nurse for a mother, and no children—never any children. Kay's very soul felt barren—she had lost that part of herself—but she knew it wasn't this way for everyone. It wasn't this way for Jo. Kay had gotten the letter, taken leave already (she had it coming, she'd never used up a single day, she could take a week, take two).

She was taking time off in between this and her next assignment, between this institution and the next, one hospital, one single bed looking very much like the last. Jo had written that she'd found that man, or he'd found her, but somehow they were together again, they had been married. Kay had missed the wedding last year. It had been during her clinical rotations for anesthesia; she couldn't miss a day of rounds, let alone the week it would have taken her to get to Scotland and back. But she wouldn't miss this now—the christening of Jo's first baby. Jo had given her plenty of warning so she could make it, writing to her in her sixth month; she hadn't even had her baby yet, but sometime this month it would come, early next month at the latest. She'd have her husband telegram Kay as soon as the baby arrived, they'd hold the ceremony when she got there. If it was a boy, they were going to name him Johnny. If it was a girl, Regina. And Kay was to be the godmother.

We'll be together again, after all this time. We will be strong again together—just as we had to learn to be strong apart.

A secretary stepped out, catching Kay's eye.

"Miss Elliott, you will be seen now."

The secretary was buzzing her in; the door unlocked and Kay had to push it open, entering the inner office, stuffy and noisy with air heat.

"Good morning, miss, sorry to have kept you waiting, my first appointment took a little longer than I had expected."

Kay saluted, then shook hands with the man who would decide her fate. She sat down.

"Not at all, sir."

He rambled on about a friend of his in the Pacific. He had known someone at Santo Tomas. Did she know a Karl Thompson? No? Maybe it was Thomas. No, maybe it was Thomas

Carlson, that was more like it. Or something like that. Kay nodded, or shook her head, or raised her eyebrows at the right time. The man liked to pontificate. She cleared her throat but the man took no notice, so Kay nodded encouragingly and he kept on talking.

Finally he began to run down, like a clock. He shifted through some papers in front of him.

"—busy, miss, I can see you've been very, very busy. Twenty-six weeks psychiatric nursing at Brooke—good Lord, in the heat, in Texas no less—fifty-six weeks anesthesiology here at Fitzsimons; you've gone above and beyond Army requirements . . . Presidential Citation, Bronze Star," he mumbled, flipping over the pages of her file. "See you were promoted one grade, miss. Looks like I'll actually have to call you 'Lieutenant' when we get rid of relative rank in the spring," and he laughed conspiratorially, as if it were a joke, a game they would all start playing. "And you'll be eligible for a base pay raise to, let's see, my, my—$166 per month. Don't know if I make that, miss," and he laughed again, showing his tobacco-stained teeth. "As well as a 5 percent bonus for staying in as long as you have, plus food, plus housing allowances . . ." The man reached the last page, turning it over to make sure there was no more.

"And just what can I help you with today, miss?"

"I hear there's a VA hospital opening up in Mount Alto. In D.C."

"Yes, miss."

"I'd like to serve there. I need your recommendation before I can."

He looked at her, expressionless.

"I feel I've helped a lot of these boys get this far, I don't want to leave them now, sir."

The man bit his lower lip, as if trying to keep himself from saying something. The wind rattled at the windows, making a low whistling sound that rose and fell. Finally, the man spoke.

"Miss, I'll be frank with you. No one is denying the good work you gals did during the war. But the war is over. This is a man's world, a man's Army. You've applied for the GI Bill, and in doing so, I don't know if you realize, you would be taking funds away from real veterans, you know, men who really fought in the war. That is what it was intended for."

"Sir, I am a veteran."

"Excuse me, miss," the man said, raising his voice, "but no woman won the Combat Infantry Badge, and *that's* what makes a veteran in my book."

The man was clearly flustered. He took a sip of water, without offering Kay a drink, and when he spoke again his voice had a forced calmness about it.

"C'mon, miss. You've done all you could do, done yourself proud even. Don't you think it's time you went back to— pardon me—but back to being a lady? You know, marriage and a family and all that?"

Kay thought of Aaron, of her baby for a moment, but only for a moment.

"Sir, this war took away everything. My youth, the only man I will ever love—"

The man snorted loudly. "Now, come now, miss," he pooh-poohed.

"—the one thing that kept me going all those years was my determination, not just to survive, but to do my duty as an Army nurse. If I could do something—something meaning-less maybe, to you—to help those around me, I did it. And I want to keep on doing it now."

Kay sat up straighter in her chair.

"I'm a military nurse, sir." She grimaced slightly. "This time, I know what I'm in for. I'm good at this, this is where I can do the most good."

The man had put down her file, the pen he had been playing with; he was looking at her now.

"This is my fight now. Marriage, children, whatever you called it, 'being a lady'—once, maybe, that might have been for me. But I'm a lifer. This *is* my life, and with my experience, I could teach others what I learned the hard way. You say this is a man's world, sir, and I am not so naive as to disagree with you. But"—here Kay leaned forward, staring the man straight in the eye—"if the world of men ever tears itself apart again, it will take an army of nurses to put it back together."

The room was quiet. Even the wind, the snow, had stopped.

The man regarded Kay silently for another moment; then he slowly shook his head.

"If I can't persuade you otherwise, miss?" and he let his voice go up at the end, raising his eyebrows hopefully. "No?"

He looked at the last page of Kay's file. Then he picked up his pen. "Well, then," he sighed. "In light of your record, Miss Elliott, I will recommend you for transfer to the new veterans' hospital."

The man gave her a cheerless smile as he handed her the form, shrugging his shoulders as he turned back to his paperwork. She left his office, passing the secretary scowling at her typewriter. Kay's heels clicked loudly on the waxed linoleum. She walked down the long, antiseptic corridor that smelled like every other corridor of that hospital, of every hospital she had or would ever work in. Long, fluorescent bulbs buzzed overhead, one flickering spastically as it gave off its sickly light.

She paused in front of a stainless steel door, the one that led to the patient floors, to the hospital wards. Kay looked down at the floor without seeing it, pausing for a moment, remembering the past. She exhaled sharply, tugging down the front of her jacket resolutely; then she pulled open the door and stepped into her future.

Acknowledgments

Having an author in the family is a lot like having chicken pox. Like chicken pox, a sudden attack of writing can strike at any time without warning, is often uncomfortable, and always inconvenient. My family has stood by patiently during lengthy interviews, listening to me tell the same stories over and over again (*oops, I'm sorry, it wasn't on, could you just say that again into the microphone?*). Very often, when I should have been grading their math samples or conjugating Italian *verbi* with them, I was, instead, researching obscure German medical terms, drawing elaborate plot diagrams, or sketching out a realistic world for Jo and Kay to inhabit. I think it is a testimony to the mutual respect and support inherently found within our family that—much like the times I supported them in their respective desires to become a champion bowler, learn to unicycle, run the mile in five and a half minutes, or sleep on the top bunk at summer camp—when I decided to write a meticulously researched historical fiction novel, everybody hitched their wagons to that star right along with me, no questions asked. While today many people are immunized against the *varicella zoster* virus and will never get to go through that itchy rite of passage, there are currently no vaccines available to guard us against lady novelists. That being the case, first and foremost, my thanks must go to my family. I love them more than life itself.

Next, I owe an enormous debt of gratitude to the historians and veterans of World War II who gave me the factual data and feedback that allowed me to create an authentic work of fiction. World War II reenactors—especially those in the medical tents—helped bring history to life for me. Once they knew what I was about, they let me photograph and handle original equipment and supplies. (I have held in my own hands Queenie's quarter-grain syrette, Jo's cardboard box of penicillin.) Evelyn M. Monahan and Rosemary Neidel-Greenlee's *All This Hell* (University Press of Kentucky, 2000) was an invaluable resource documenting the fate of imprisoned military nurses in the Pacific. Their excellent counterpart, *And If I Perish* (Anchor Books, 2003), took that level of factual research and detail and applied it to nurses serving in the European theater of war. Both books gave me a firm grasp of the topic, spurred me on to further research, and sparked my desire to meet real veterans from that era. I would like to thank two in particular here. Evangeline R. Coeyman (Second Lieutenant, 59th Field Hospital 90th Infantry Division), nearly ninety years young when I met her and sharp as a tack, sat with me in an old field hospital and showed me the ropes, teaching me everything from the evacuation chain to where the X-ray machine used to stand in the tent, to how the nurses washed their hands before surgery. More than just imparting this firsthand medical knowledge however, she also exuded a pride in and enthusiasm for her work and her country that was contagious, and had not diminished in three-quarters of a century. To me, she will always remain a hero.

Another veteran I would like to thank personally is Eugene

Chovanes (Staff Sergeant, 1123rd Engineering Combat Group). One of the few Battle of the Bulge veterans alive today, Gene literally swept me off my feet, remaining my all-time favorite swing dance partner. I treasure our conversations about the war and about his life. I will never forget the late nights we spent in his stately old home (where he still lives with his lovely war bride, Claire), the grandfather clock chiming out midnight, one in the morning as he compared my book to his recollection of the war, this world to the one he knew. He read my entire manuscript before its publication, verifying for me as few people living today could have done, *yes, this is exactly right, how are you doing this? How could you* know? *Not just the dates and places, but the nuance, the feel of the thing, this is just what it felt like, just how it was.* I knew at the time how invaluable that experience was—and how irreplaceable our friendship would become. Today, our lives intersect like two circles in a Venn diagram, just barely overlapping—he a teenage boy at the time of the Ardennes Offensive, I a grown woman in the twenty-first century. But our friendship is no less sweet because it is fated to be short. It is a joy and a blessing.

The business of publishing books is just that—a business—and I would be remiss indeed if I did not thank the people who saw promise in my work and helped promote it in a highly competitive field. I thank my aunt, Dr. Eloise Messineo, who first brought my manuscript to the attention of Diane Volk, philanthropist, activist, and supporter of the arts. Diane is my very own Lady Catherine de Bourgh (of *Pride and Prejudice* fame)—if Lady Catherine had been nice, that is. Much like Mr. Collins, I claim Diane as my "patroness," and owe nearly all my success to her. Diane handed my manuscript to Greer Hendricks (late of Simon & Schuster, now a talented author herself), who, in turn, introduced me to my literary agent (Gráinne Fox, Fletcher & Co), who sold my book to Rachel Kahan at William Morrow (a HarperCollins imprint). I will forever remain indebted to Rachel for taking a chance on a debut novelist, and for doing it with so much enthusiasm. She is an incredibly gifted editor, and I look forward to a long and mutually rewarding relationship with her. I would also like to thank my literary attorney, Kim Schefler, for her unfailing guidance and advice.

How does one become a writer? Well, usually there are the teachers and mentors who first recognize and then nurture a latent talent, and my story is no exception. First among these, I must thank my parents, Salvatore and Maria (Chiaramonte) Messineo, who provided a safe and extraordinary environment for me to spread my wings in and try out my creativity. In the '70s, my parents ran their own Dharma Initiative–style school, and I enjoyed every minute of it. While I freely admit now that most of my formative years were spent feeding gerbils, riding tricycles, and operating an enormous movie-reel projector, what I gained from that experimental schooling experience proved invaluable later in life. *The innate belief that I could do absolutely anything.* Learn a foreign language? Birth four babies (without pain medication)? Write a novel in my spare time? I never once wondered if I could do these things—doubt never entered my mind. If anything, I've been slightly bemused all my life that the rest of the world didn't just jump in and try crazy things along with me. I mean, if you cannot fail, what can you possibly stand to lose? So, for that punch-drunk take on life I thank them, with all my heart.

I would like to thank Carroll McGuire, who, when I was an impressionable college kid, told me I'd be a writer one day. Not just that I *could* write, but that I would *be* a writer. To me, the distinction between the two was enormous, and I took every word he said as gospel truth. Did he have incredible foresight, or did it just become a self-fulfilling prophecy on my part? Either way, he was a most welcome prophet in my life—a man who literally changed the course of my future—and I am forever indebted to him for that.

I would also like to thank two of my college professors (both of DeSales University), Dr. Stephen Myers and Dr. Joseph Colosi. Dr. Myers, a journalist at heart, pushed me to become a better writer, challenging (and rewarding) me by the caliber of his classes. Dr. Colosi, while not a humanities professor himself, nonetheless taught me the true meaning of Humanity, capital *H,* and no story of my personal search for meaning and its expression would be complete without reference to him. Stepping backward in time, I must thank my two high school English teachers—Sharon (Wright) Winter, who introduced me to some of my greatest literary loves, and Sister Jonathan Moyles, SCC, to whom this book is dedicated.

More than anyone else, Sister Jonathan held my fate in her hands, and this book most certainly would not have come about without the positive impact she made on my life. When I first appeared in Sister Jonathan's Sophomore Honors English class (I was fifteen years old and had never spent a day in a school desk), she asked us to write an essay on a book we had read. Creative to a fault, I handed in a free verse on spiders. Not one to be trifled with, Sister called me up to her desk after class. I can still see myself standing there—gauche, inexperienced, wearing my school uniform sideways because I still hadn't figured out anything in this weird world of "real school." Sister reiterated that she had requested an essay, not a poem. And then I asked her, "What's an essay, Sister?" Here, dear reader, is where everything hinges, where my academic life could have been spent from that point on in remedial classrooms, or catapulted (as it eventually was) to a full college scholarship. *"What's an essay, Sister?"* Either I was the rudest, cheekiest kid to ever walk into her classroom—or, incredibly, here was a fifteen-year-old female student with little or no conventional schooling *who had no idea what an essay was.* "It's an introductory paragraph, main body where you flesh it out, recap it in a closing paragraph. You've got until tomorrow, Teresa, or you're out of here." The next morning, she read my essay (on Arthur Miller's *The Crucible*) aloud in class. I can still feel my cheeks burn, as I was certain this humiliation heralded the end of my brief career as an honor student. When she was done, the other students asked who had written the essay, and Sister joked that she, herself, had penned it. "No, I'm just kidding," she said at last. "It's that new girl, in the back of class." She handed back our papers and, amazingly, there was a 98 on mine with "Super!" inscribed in red ink in the top right-hand corner. From that moment on, I went from one academic success to the next, never looking back. Twenty years later, when I told this story to Sister Jonathan herself, expressing my gratitude for the second chance she gave me, she commuted my grade and gave me the extra two points. This book is for her.

Finally, I thank the nurses of the Second World War. Without them and without their valor, this book would not exist—and, perhaps, neither would our country. For too long, their story has remained untold. For too long, there has been a collective consciousness that American nurses didn't do all that much during World War II. It has been an honor to help set that record straight. These women volunteered to go to a war most men were drafted into. They signed up willingly, believing in the ideals of democracy and freedom and independence—in everything that made their country great. And when those ideals began to fade in the horror of war—when these women were nearly crushed by hard labor, by isolation, by imprisonment or starvation or the loss of everything they held dear—they kept to their posts for no other reason than that they were women, they were humans and—for as long as they could endure—they would continue to bring humanity to a world gone mad.

I love these women. I love their story. I am proud—and humbled—to offer you a glimpse of their world.

About the Author

Teresa Messineo is an outspoken woman whose passionate social interest and positions have been featured in documentaries, magazines, and medical journals. Teresa was alternatively schooled until her freshman year, after which she transferred to a conventional high school. An honor student there, she earned a full scholarship to DeSales University, where she ultimately won the Ross Baker Award for Excellence in Writing, that university's highest honor for writers. She graduated with a BA in English and minors in biology and theology, and earned her ICCE and LIBSS while teaching at Pennsylvania's premier birthing center. Teresa is highly motivated about social justice and sticking up for the underdog. She volunteers at a food bank, is a "volunteer actor" at her local hospital during disaster drills, and hopes, one day, to also give of her time and talents as a medical missionary. She is the mother of four children, whom she has exclusively home-schooled (her eldest son earned a scholarship to her own alma mater). With her children, she performs in their own Celtic band, as well as in a traditional Philippine dance troupe. Teresa's other interests include swing dancing, travel, foreign language, poetry, philosophical debate, and personal fitness—she swims in her YMCA's 100 Mile Club, participates in several obstacle mud runs each year, and 2016 marked her first triathlon competition. A voracious reader and lifetime learner, Teresa lives by the motto "We learn from our mistakes."